"Good night, Ellen."

"I was told Two's Company escorts didn't kiss their dates," she called out to Seth's retreating figure.

He paused on the step. "They don't. I was off duty. Anyway, I didn't kiss you because I was your escort, Ellen. I kissed you because I like you."

She didn't know what to say. Her heart was beating in her throat, her skin tingling as if she were fifteen and had just been kissed for the first time.

"My phone number's on the back of one of those," he told her, pointing to the stack of cartoons he'd given her. "If your ex sticks around and you need me to put in another appearance, give me a call. I'd be delighted to do it—free of charge...."

ABOUT THE AUTHOR

Award-winning author Pamela Bauer has gained many fans around the world for her heartwarming stories. She particularly enjoys writing novels that center on family; when she's writing about her main characters and their romance, she finds that other characters, other relationships, just naturally enter the story. Pamela often takes a lighthearted approach as she explores the relationships between friends, within families—and, of course, between lovers.

Pamela lives in Minnesota (where *I Do, I Do* is set) with her husband, Gerr, and their children, Amy and Aaron.

She loves to hear from her readers. You can write to her at: P.O. Box 47888, Plymouth, MN 55447.

Books by Pamela Bauer

HARLEQUIN SUPERROMANCE

PAMELA BAUER

I DO, I DO

Harlequin Books

TORONTO • NEW YORK • LONDON
AMSTERDAM • PARIS • SYDNEY • HAMBURG
STOCKHOLM • ATHENS • TOKYO • MILAN
MADRID • WARSAW • BUDAPEST • AUCKLAND

ISBN 0-373-70605-7

I DO, I DO

For my brother and sister-in-law, Cliff and Deb Ronning
Happy Seventeenth Anniversary!

CHAPTER ONE

"I CAN'T BELIEVE I let you talk me into signing up for another session of this . . . this . . . torture," Ellen Richards stammered, gulping in deep breaths of air as she leaned against a bank of lockers.

"You told me you liked step aerobics," Jeannie Adler reminded her, resting her foot against a bench so that she could tie her athletic shoe.

"I lied," Ellen confessed. "I need to go home."

"Not until we've been to the Nautilus room," Jeannie stated firmly. When Ellen groaned in protest, Jeannie grabbed her sister by the arm and gently pushed her in the direction of the weight room. "Come on, you can do it."

"I don't think I can," Ellen answered weakly, dragging her weary limbs down the corridor. "I'm tired and I hurt. And remember how much trouble I had the last time we were here?"

"No pain, no gain." There was little sympathy in her sister's voice. "And don't forget—you have a good reason for doing this."

"So you keep telling me." Ellen sighed. "I don't know, Jean. I'm not sure Kenneth is worth all of this."

Jeannie stopped abruptly and turned to face Ellen. "You're not doing this *for* Kenneth, you're doing it *to* him. The better you look when he sees you, the more he's going to regret walking out on you."

Ellen knew what her sister said was true. As much as she hated the workouts, they were necessary. If Kenneth was bringing his child bride to the wedding, she needed to get her thirty-nine-year-old body to look the very best it possibly could. She shuddered at the thought of seeing her ex-husband again. "Gawd, I wish he wasn't coming to the wedding."

"But he is coming, which is why we're going to lift those weights," Jeannie coaxed, inching her forward.

"All right, all right," Ellen reluctantly conceded. "But only if there's not a lot of people around."

"Fine. We won't stay if there's a crowd," Jeannie said placatingly.

To Ellen's relief, the weight room was empty except for a couple of scrawny-looking teenagers doing chest presses. Neither one paid much attention to Ellen and Jeannie as they tried out the various pieces of equipment.

After much groaning and moaning, Ellen said in a low voice, "I'm on the lowest setting and I can't move any of these things. I told you I'm too tired for this."

"Maybe you should try that thing they're using," Jeannie suggested, nodding toward the teenagers.

"I don't want to try anything else," Ellen protested in a cranky tone. "I don't have the strength to lift or push or pull."

"If those skinny little boys can do it, you should be able to." She looked again toward the teenagers and nodded. "Look, they're leaving. Why don't you give it a try? You certainly have as much muscle as they do."

Ellen watched the pair exit the room. They did look rather wimpy. She should be able to successfully use such a simple-looking apparatus. She carefully climbed off the leg extension she had been straddling.

"If you wait a couple of minutes, I'll help you with the weights," Jeannie called out to her. "Just let me use the rest room first."

"Yeah, sure," Ellen called out dryly, wondering how difficult it could be for someone five foot five and 120 pounds to press what those puny-looking boys had pressed.

Without waiting for Jeannie, Ellen stretched out on the padded bench of the chest press and wrapped her hands around the steel bar. With a supreme effort, she pushed straight up, but the weights refused to budge. She groaned and repeated her effort, but with no success. She couldn't even do what those scrawny little boys had done! She squeezed her eyes shut and began to giggle.

Hearing the door open, Ellen called out, half laughing, "Oh my gawd. This is disgusting. I'm worse than a kid. Maybe you should come over here and make this thing lighter," she said, her forearm draped across her eyes.

There was a brief silence, then Ellen heard, "I'm afraid ten pounds is as low as it goes."

The voice was not familiar, and it was deep. Ellen's arm dropped and her eyes shot open. Standing beside her was a man. An extremely good-looking man with twinkling blue eyes, a broad grin and a well-defined physique that said he knew how to use every piece of equipment in the room.

Ellen could feel the color spread from the roots of her damp hair to the tip of her curled toes. Where was Jeannie? She lifted her head to take an inventory of the room, but her sister was nowhere in sight.

"The problem is, you're trying to push the bar straight up," the handsome stranger said, his eyes still twinkling. "You need to swing your arms up in an arc so that your hands meet in the middle. Would you like me to show you how?"

"Uh . . . no, that's all right. I was leaving, anyway," she stammered, slithering off the padded bench like a caterpillar inching its way along a twig.

"Are you sure?" he asked when she wobbled slightly, a protective arm coming toward her.

"Uh-huh," Ellen murmured, noticing that although his mustache was coffee brown, the hair at his temples was mixed with gray. She lowered her eyes, searching for a name tag. There was none. This was even worse than she first thought. He wasn't an employee, but a guest—a guest who was very close to her own age.

Seth Holloway stood with his hands on his hips, amused by the scene he was witnessing. He had encountered many women in his regular visits to the gym, but never had he had the opportunity to rescue any of them from the chest press. It was obvious that she was inexperienced, and judging by her figure, it was probably better that she hadn't asked him for a demonstration. Even if she were to use the correct approach, it wouldn't be easy for her to do reclining chest presses— not with such a large bosom.

As she awkwardly rose to her feet, he noticed that although she was definitely not accustomed to weight training, she had a body that was far from being out of shape. Not that it interested him. He had always preferred trim, petite figures like Laura's. He liked his women small and dark-haired, not big-bosomed and blond.

So why did the sight of her cause such a strong physical reaction in him? And why was he having such trouble keeping his eyes off her shapely figure?

Ellen was wondering the same thing. She wished he would quit looking at her as if she were a species of animal he had never seen before. Refusing to look in his direction, she crept toward the exit.

Once she was out of the Nautilus room, she practically ran to the women's locker room.

"Hey! Where are you going?" Jeannie called as her sister went hurrying past.

Ellen didn't stop until she reached her locker. "How could you do that to me?" she demanded irrationally, her cheeks still flushed with embarrassment.

"Do what?" Jeannie asked, perplexed. She walked over to Ellen's locker.

"Leave me alone in there." She gestured in the direction of the weight room. As she caught a glimpse of her reflection in the locker room's full-length mirror, she groaned. "Just look. I've got sweat all over me!"

"You should have. You've been working out. Do you want to shower?"

"Not unless they've added partitions and shower curtains since the last time we were here," she grumbled.

"We're on the economy plan," her sister reminded her.

"So what does that mean? We aren't entitled to privacy?" she asked irritably, wishing that for just once in her life she could afford to do something that didn't have the words "budget" or "economy" in its description.

"Not everyone is as modest as you are," Jeannie chided her as the sound of running water echoed through the locker room.

"If they're drooping in all the wrong places, they are. Adults on the slippery slope of middle age do not undress in front of other people," Ellen said, then sashayed over to a changing stall and yanked the curtain shut.

"We're not middle-aged," Jeannie protested.

"We're getting close," she retorted. "It won't be long and we'll be saying we're forty-something instead of thirty-something."

"Nowadays women are in their prime during their forties. Just look at Cher and Meryl Streep and Goldie Hawn."

"Yeah, right," Ellen retorted sarcastically. "Unfortunately, prime for most of us means little pleats in the skin over our knees and elbows that could be mistaken for albino prunes."

As she slipped out of her exercise leotard and into her shorts and T-shirt, she critically assessed her figure in the mirror. Kenneth had always said she had two blessings—big boobs and a good memory. He was right about her memory, but wrong about her chest.

She would never look skinny or even slender. But that was okay. She knew what clothing styles flattered her figure and she knew which ones to avoid. And if it wasn't for Kenneth, she wouldn't even have been dwelling on her appearance the way she had for the past six weeks. She shook her shoulder-length hair free of the cotton ponytail holder and cringed at the sight of smudged makeup on her cheeks.

When she threw back the curtain of the changing stall, Jeannie was waiting for her. "You still haven't told me why you bolted from the weight room."

Ellen picked up her gym bag and started toward the door. "Someone came in and I decided it was time for me to leave."

Jeannie had retrieved her gym bag, too, and eyed her sister suspiciously as they walked. "You know, you've been awfully edgy lately," she observed.

"You'd be edgy, too, if your nineteen-year-old was planning a wedding you couldn't afford," Ellen answered grimly.

"I thought you said Roger's parents were helping with the expenses." They had reached the corridor where several vending machines were located, and Jeannie stopped in front of one that dispensed beverages.

"They are, but I can't let them pay for everything," Ellen answered, setting her bag down to dig in her purse for some change. "Besides, the more Mr. Townsend contributes, the more Mrs. Townsend puts in her two cents' worth. First it was the flowers, then it was the menu. I swear she has her hand in practically every single detail."

"What's she up to now?" Jeannie bent over to get the can of soda that had landed with a thud in the dispenser slot.

"She thinks I need an escort," Ellen said as she deposited three coins into the machine.

"You're the mother of the bride, not a bridesmaid," Jeannie stated huffily.

Ellen twisted the cap off a bottle of cranberry juice and took a swallow. "Tell that to Dolores Townsend.

If I don't bring my own guest, she'll assign one of the ushers to take care of me.''

"Take care of you?" Jeannie repeated distastefully. "Ellen, you don't need to be taken care of by anyone. The past three years have proven that.''

"True, but as much as I hate to admit it, I am going to feel like a fifth wheel if I'm alone at the wedding. After all, Mrs. Townsend will have Mr. Townsend, Kenneth will have Tina and I'll have some usher who's probably young enough to be my son,'' she said soberly.

"So ask someone to be your guest.''

Ellen thought for a moment before saying, "I suppose I could ask Ned.''

Jeannie rolled her eyes. "Oh, puh-leez," she drawled. "You can't take someone like Ned Pickett to the wedding!''

"Why not?" she demanded, as they headed for the exit. "He's a fine man. He's decent and kind and hardworking.''

"And boring. Oh, and you might as well throw in rigid and stodgy," she said dryly.

"He's a little set in his ways."

Jeannie chuckled sardonically. "That's an understatement. If I didn't know better, I'd say he was trying to impersonate a senior citizen.''

Ellen didn't dare confess that when she had first met Ned she *had* thought he was a senior citizen. However, Ned had been good to her and she felt compelled to defend the man she had dated occasionally during the past year. "He's steady and reliable and honest.''

They had reached the entrance and Jeannie stopped to hold the door open for her sister. "Ellen, the guy

wears clip-on ties. And I bet you any money he goes to bed in flannel p.j.'s with little ducks on them.''

"I wouldn't know," she said primly as she walked past her sister.

"Surprise, surprise," Jeannie drawled sarcastically as she followed her outside.

Ellen blushed.

"Look, I think Ned's a great guy...if you're going to an IRS audit," she said as she followed her sister to the parking lot. "But if you're going to your daughter's wedding and you're about to see your ex-husband for the first time since you divorced, you want the man at your side to be charming, witty and sexy...someone who'll make Kenneth look like a cream puff."

Immediately, the image of the muscular man she had seen in the weight room popped into Ellen's mind. "And where do you suggest I find someone like that in three weeks time? I mean, the men haven't exactly been beating down my door lately, have they?"

"I'd offer to fix you up with one of the guys from work, but I know how you feel about my matchmaking attempts," Jeannie retorted. "Besides, you're looking for the perfect man and he doesn't exist."

Ellen took another sip of her juice, then said, "You've fixed me up on exactly two blind dates. One guy was a street corner David Letterman who had a fake car phone and the other was a weekend jock who spent the entire evening sucking down beer and discussing golf's greatest moments."

"They were nice guys," Jeannie protested indignantly.

"Nice and boring."

Jeannie gave her a sideways glance. "If you don't want me fixing you up with someone I guess you'll have to follow Mrs. Townsend's game plan."

"Or ask Ned," Ellen said in resignation.

Jeannie was quiet for several seconds, then said, "You could always hire an escort."

"Do what?" Ellen's mouth dropped open.

"Hire an escort," Jeannie repeated. "That way you could pick out some gorgeous-looking guy to flaunt before Kenneth and his child bride."

"You can't be serious?" Ellen stared at her sister in disbelief. When Jeannie didn't say anything but gave her a look Ellen recognized as her contemplative stare, she said, "Oh my gawd, you aren't joking, are you? Jeannie, I can't hire someone to be my date!"

"Why not? Men do it all the time. They pay for the privilege of being seen with a beautiful woman. Why can't women do the same thing?" she asked with her usual pragmatism.

"Because number one, I don't have the money and number two, I don't want to," Ellen protested. "It doesn't seem right."

"What's wrong with it?" Jeannie stood before her, pleading her case, while Ellen dug in her purse for her car keys. "You've contracted for someone to arrange the flowers, to chauffeur the wedding party, to serve the food, to play the music...why not to act as your escort?"

"Because I've never had to pay for a date and I don't intend to start now." Ellen unlocked her car door and flung her gym bag inside.

"Then don't think of it as a date. Think of it as hiring a professional who's going to create the right effect for the wedding,'' Jeannie suggested, resting her arm on the top of Ellen's open door.

Ellen thought about it for a moment, then shook her head. ''No, I can't do it,'' she said, then climbed into her battered and bruised Ford Escort.

''The alternative is to go alone... be the only unattached member of the wedding party and get stuck with some usher who would rather be with his twenty-year-old girlfriend but is obligated to take care of you.''

Ellen frowned. ''I'd better ask Ned.''

''You can't,'' Jeannie said impatiently. ''If you invite him to your daughter's wedding, he's going to think you have special feelings for him. Look at it this way. At least if you use an escort service, when the wedding's over, the date will be gone and there'll be no misunderstanding because each of you will have known from the start what your intentions were.''

Ellen knew Jeannie had a point. She had purposely avoided introducing Ned to Rebecca because she hadn't wanted to give him the impression there was anything more to their relationship than friendship.

''Okay, maybe I can't use Ned, but I'm not going to use an escort service. If anyone found out I was paying for a man—'' She broke off with a look of distaste on her face.

''No one's going to find out.''

''I know they're not because I'm not doing it,'' she said stubbornly.

''Aw, come on,'' Jeannie cajoled. ''Don't you want to see the look on Kenneth's face when you waltz in with someone who looks like he just stepped off the pages of *GQ*?''

''What makes you think the guys at the escort services look that great?''

"I happen to know someone who used one."

"Who?"

"Linnea Cunningham. And it was for the same purpose. She was tired of going to weddings alone. There's nothing worse than being an extra person when the dancing starts."

Ellen agreed and found herself asking, "How did it work out?"

"She said it was great. She went to a place where lots of corporate types go. It was all very professional. She said it was more like hiring a bodyguard than an escort. It was all very legit."

"I didn't think there were legitimate escort services," Ellen commented.

"Well, there are, and this is one of them. Linnea said the woman who started the company was intent on providing people with safe escorts for special functions. That was her whole reason for starting the business. They tell you right up front that you shouldn't expect to find romance, just a safe and presentable date for the evening. Apparently, the escorts are screened pretty carefully. Do you want me to get the name of the place for you?"

Ellen didn't answer right away.

"Think of how good it would feel to have an attentive, good-looking man on your arm when you see Kenneth again," Jeannie said in a tantalizing voice.

Ellen had to admit it was a tempting thought. Ever since her divorce, her number-one fantasy had been that when she did finally see her ex-husband again she would be fifteen pounds thinner, not have a single gray hair on her head and be on the arm of a good-looking younger man who would gaze at her with adoration.

She had highlighted the few strands of gray that had recently begun to pepper her dishwater blond hair so that instead of gray it looked sun-streaked. And even though she hadn't returned to the weight she had been when they were first married, she didn't look all that bad with the additional pounds. Now the question was, did she really want to use a gorgeous young man to live out the rest of her fantasy?

She almost said yes. For one brief moment she let her imagination run wild. She saw herself dancing with a Kevin Costner clone while stuffy old Kenneth, who never wanted to get up off his chair, sat with his bimbo wife, watching. She saw her Kevin Costner clone holding doors open for her and pulling out her chair while stuffy old Kenneth let the bimbo follow him around like a puppy dog.

"So are you going to do it?" Jeannie asked eagerly, interrupting her daydream.

"I can't. I have to take care of Mom."

"I'll take Mom in my car."

"I...I..." she stuttered before finally saying, "No. It wouldn't work."

"El...len," Jeannie drawled in disappointment.

"I don't need to hire a man to face Kenneth or Roger's mother. I'll be the mother of the bride, period." She jammed her key into the ignition and started the engine.

"Okay, fine. If that's the way you want it, but don't come crying to me when you're all alone at the reception," Jeannie said before getting into her own car. "You could have had a man."

As hard as she tried, Ellen found it impossible to put Jeannie's suggestion out of her mind. The more she thought about being an unattached woman at the

wedding, the more uneasy she became. She didn't want
to ask Ned to be her guest, yet the thought of hiring a
man for the night was equally unappealing.

Then Rebecca came home for the weekend, and Ellen's uneasiness grew as the subject of the wedding was
discussed over breakfast.

Rebecca sat across from her with a stack of invoices
and a look on her face that warned Ellen the subject
matter was not going to be pleasant.

"Mom, there's something we need to talk about,"
Rebecca said quietly.

Ellen groaned. "This has to do with money, doesn't
it," she said grimly, getting up to refill their coffee
cups.

When she sat back down again, Rebecca looked her
squarely in the face and said, "We underestimated the
catering expenses."

Ellen heaved a long sigh. "I'll call the loan company on Monday."

"That's not necessary."

"Why not? Have you decided to postpone the wedding?" she asked hopefully.

Immediately, Rebecca became defensive. "Mother,
please don't start in again. I know all of your objections to this marriage. Just because you got married
when you were nineteen and it didn't work out doesn't
mean that Roger and I are going to have problems."

Ellen reached across the table to cover Rebecca's
hand with hers. "I'm sorry. I didn't mean to be face-
tious. I just don't want to see you make a mistake."

"Marrying Roger is no mistake."

There was such conviction in her daughter's voice
that Ellen couldn't contradict her. Not that it would
have done any good, for Rebecca was in the throes of

passionate first love and wasn't about to let anyone or anything shatter her dreams.

"Let's not argue," Ellen pleaded gently. "I seldom have you home for a weekend, and it won't be long before you won't be back at all." Her voice broke at the thought.

"Oh, Mom. It's not like I'm moving out of the country. I'll only be a few minutes away. I spent this whole last year away at college and you survived."

Having a daughter in college and having a daughter married were not exactly the same circumstances, but Ellen decided to let it slide. She simply forced a smile and said, "So are there any more underestimated expenses I should know about?"

"I'm sure there will be, but, Mom, that's what I'm trying to tell you. You don't need to worry about the money." With her honey blond hair pulled back from her face and secured with a barrette, Rebecca looked a lot like her father. So much so that Ellen felt a shiver of apprehension. Had Rebecca inherited more than just looks from him?

She frowned as she said, "You didn't run up your credit card balance, did you?"

"No!" she replied indignantly. "What I'm trying to tell you is that I asked Dad if he would help out."

Ellen sank back in her chair. "Oh, Rebecca! You didn't!"

"Yes, I did. Mom, he is my father."

A fact he had conveniently forgotten for the past three years, but Ellen didn't point that out. She could feel her blood pressure rising, and she took a long, deep cleansing breath, folding her hands in front of her before she spoke.

"I don't think your father's in a position to help out financially," she said tightly.

"He can afford it, Mom."

Ellen was unsuccessful in her attempt to hide her sarcastic chuckle.

"He can," Rebecca insisted. "He's doing really well with his new business. You should see the beautiful home he has in Colorado."

"You've been there?" She knew that Kenneth had been back to Minneapolis twice in the three years since their divorce, but she thought those visits were the only times that Rebecca had seen him. "No, but he sent me pictures. It's huge and he drives a Ferrari and has a couple of horses," Rebecca stated with more than a hint of awe in her voice.

"He's probably in debt up to his ears." Ellen didn't want to be catty, but she found she couldn't help it.

"Maybe we shouldn't talk about him if you're going to get upset," Rebecca said stiffly.

"I am not upset," she denied, ignoring the flutter of anxiety thoughts of her ex-husband always created. "I simply stated I didn't think your father had the means to give you money for the wedding."

"Well, he does," Rebecca returned. "Dad is doing very well with his new company, so well he was named one of the top ten entrepreneurs in Colorado."

Ellen could only stare in disbelief. This couldn't be the same man who for seventeen years had forced her to live from payday to payday, often going without essentials in order that he could invest in some opportunity that was too good to pass by. Not one of the harebrained schemes Kenneth had put money into when she had been married to him had paid off. Could it be that now he had hit it big and some young bimbo was reaping the benefits?

Ellen was speechless. Was there no justice? Instead of voicing her feelings, she decided to keep silent. Swallowing back her pride, she said, "Well, if that's the case and he wants to help pay for the wedding, I think we should graciously accept his offer."

Rebecca smiled. "That will make things a lot easier."

For one of us anyway, Ellen said silently. She took a sip of her coffee. "Is there anything you need help with this weekend?"

"Most of the stuff's been taken care of. Roger's mother's been a big help," Rebecca told her, and Ellen had to bite back the nasty comment that sat waiting to spring forth from her lips.

"How nice," she said, tempering her sarcasm.

Rebecca was too engrossed with her box of alphabetically arranged response cards to notice. "I think our major task for this weekend will be to call those people who haven't sent in their RSVP cards. Roger's mother said I should give the caterer a definite number by next Thursday."

Ellen was reaching the point that if she heard "Roger's mother" one more time she might throw something. She decided to approach the subject carefully. "About Roger's mother, dear."

"What about her?" Rebecca's innocent face stared at her in an inquisitive manner.

"She called me last week to talk about the wedding. She wanted to know if I was bringing a guest."

"Are you?"

"I wasn't planning on it," Ellen admitted honestly.

"Good, because if Dad comes alone, I want the two of you to walk together."

"Becca, your father and I are divorced," Ellen reminded her.

"You're still my parents."

"But I thought you said he's bringing Tina," Ellen said, suddenly feeling uneasy with the direction the conversation was taking.

"He might be coming alone."

That piqued Ellen's curiosity. "Why would he do that?"

"Maybe out of consideration for your feelings."

"Consideration for my feelings? Does he think it's going to upset me to meet his wife?"

"Is it?"

"No!" It was a lie and Ellen knew it, but she wouldn't admit to her daughter just how upsetting the thought of meeting her replacement was. "Maybe I'd better bring a date to the wedding."

"Can you get one?" Rebecca asked with a lift of her brows.

The question struck a nerve in Ellen. "Maybe if I go down to a homeless shelter I could find some poor old guy who'd do anything for a free meal," she said irritably.

Rebecca reached out to touch her mother's arm. "Mom, I'm sorry. I didn't mean that the way it sounded. It's just that you've never mentioned any guy's name to me, so I just assumed you weren't dating anyone."

Without thinking of the consequences, Ellen said, "As a matter of fact, there is someone I've been seeing recently."

"There is? Why didn't you tell me?"

"Well, because he's just a friend. It's nothing serious. We've had a few dates. That's all." It wasn't exactly the truth, but it wasn't exactly a lie, either. Ellen had been seeing Ned Pickett on a somewhat regular basis.

Rebecca looked astounded. "When did all this happen?"

"Shortly after you left for college."

Rebecca stared at her mother in disbelief. "And you didn't tell me?"

"There really wasn't much to tell."

"I can't believe you're saying that. You start dating and you don't even tell me." She slowly shook her head in reproach.

"Does it bother you that I'm dating?" Ellen asked, suddenly aware that her daughter might resent the fact that she was romantically involved with a man.

"No." The reply came too quickly and too abruptly for Ellen's peace of mind. After a brief silence, Rebecca asked, "What's his name and what's he like?"

Now that she had opened the can, Ellen wasn't feeling good about what was coming out. "He's just a nice man I've been seeing. There's really not much to tell."

Rebecca eyed her suspiciously. "Are you going to bring him to the wedding?"

Ellen couldn't tell from the expression on her daughter's face whether the idea was appealing or appalling. "Let me think about it, okay?" she pleaded, wishing more than ever that she hadn't brought up the subject.

"All right, Mom." She leaned back and chewed on the eraser of her pencil, still looking at her mother.

"Are you sure it doesn't bother you that I'm dating?" Ellen asked for the second time.

Rebecca shrugged. "Not really, but I think Dad's going to be a bit surprised if you show up with a man."

"Why do you say that?" Ellen's stomach lurched. "Becca! You haven't been discussing my personal life with him, have you?"

"Of course not, Mom, but it's no big secret that there aren't any men hanging around, is it?" She quickly corrected herself. "I guess I should say there weren't any men hanging around."

This time there was no question as to how her daughter felt. It was obvious to Ellen that the idea of her mother dating bothered Rebecca. Before she could find out the reasons, the phone rang. Rebecca jumped up to answer it. Ellen, thinking it was probably Roger, busied herself with clearing the table.

She was carrying a handful of dishes when she noticed Rebecca was extending the receiver in her direction. "It's a man."

Several pieces of silverware slid off the plates Ellen was carrying, falling onto the linoleum with a clang. Why did Ned choose now of all times to call? Rebecca looked on curiously as her flustered mother bent to pick up the errant forks.

Ellen was relieved to hear her insurance agent's voice on the other end of the line. She looked pointedly at her daughter and said, "Oh, hi, Bob. I wanted to talk to you about dropping the collision premium from my insurance."

Rebecca only shrugged.

Later that afternoon, long after Roger had picked up Rebecca and taken her sailing, Ellen sat thinking about the wedding. There was one image that kept popping up in her mind—that of Kenneth smirking as she walked into church alone.

Over the past three years she had gotten quite used to being alone. Why should she now be experiencing such anxiety over not having someone to stand beside her at her daughter's wedding?

Just the fact that it did matter made her all the more annoyed. It was Kenneth's fault. If it wasn't for the fact that he was bringing his twenty-four-year-old wife she wouldn't even have been considering something so preposterous as hiring a date.

But even after three years of living apart from him she was still doing things she didn't want to do because of him. Would that never change?

Jeannie had once accused her of having a divorce hangover. At the time she had dismissed the accusation, thinking it was just another trendy term from the latest self-help book her sister was reading. Now she wasn't so sure. Maybe she did have a divorce hangover. If that was the case, how was she ever going to get rid of it after three years of living with it?

She reached for the phone and dialed her sister's number. When she heard the familiar voice, she said, "Hi. It's me. Find out the name of that escort service Linnea Cunningham used, will you?"

CHAPTER TWO

WHEN SETH HOLLOWAY stepped into the professional building, he automatically checked the directory of tenants. Sandwiched between Tunney Real Estate and Tyler Transportation Systems was the name Two's Company. Suite 517.

A burning sensation in his chest brought a grimace to his face. Something from lunch wasn't agreeing with him. He reached for the bottle of antacid tablets he had grown accustomed to carrying around in his pocket. By the time he arrived at his destination, he had devoured four—two orange and two cherry.

That was all life seemed to be lately—a steady stream of stress that wreaked havoc with his stomach, added gray hairs to his head and made him wish he could hop a slow boat to the Bahamas. Being a parent in the nineties was enough of a challenge without the added pressure of being the single father of three teenagers who were of the opinion that they didn't need parenting.

Which was why he found himself at Two's Company in the middle of the day. He paused with his hand on the doorknob to peer through a narrow panel of glass that allowed him a glimpse of the suite's interior.

A black leather sofa, glass-topped metal tables and a magazine rack filled with an assortment of popular periodicals gave the room the appearance of a doctor's office. On the walls were photographs—not of men and women, but of scenic views of the Twin Cities of Minneapolis and Saint Paul.

Behind a curved white desk sat a young woman, her dark brown hair tossed back over her shoulders, a telephone wedged between her ear and her shoulder while she stuffed flyers into envelopes. When Seth opened the door, she automatically looked up.

Her fingers stopped moving, and her eyes widened as Seth stepped inside the office. She stammered as she finished her phone conversation, her eyes never straying from his face.

"Dad! What are you doing here?" she squeaked. "I thought you had an appointment with Gwendolyn Whitney."

"The lunch hour is over," he pointed out. "Where's your grandmother?"

"She's not back from lunch yet."

"And you're in charge?"

"I am old enough to handle things," she said with a lift of her chin. "How come you're not at the paper?"

"Because I think it's time you and I had a little talk. I received a call today from someone who claimed to be the landlord of a house near the university. He said you had filled out a rental application." As hard as he tried, Seth couldn't keep the disapproval from his voice.

"I was going to tell you..." Kelly Holloway began, only to be interrupted by her father.

"When? After you had moved all your things out of the house? Good grief, Kelly. Moving into an apartment is not a decision you make without talking to your parents," he admonished her, raking a hand through his dark hair.

"I was going to tell you about it, but I knew you would get upset and you are!"

"Justifiably so. How did you expect me to react?"

"You didn't yell at the landlord on the phone, did you?"

"What if I did?"

She threw her hands up in frustration. "Oh, this is so embarrassing. I can imagine what all my friends are going to think when they hear my father messed up our deal."

"There is no deal without parental signatures, and this parent would like to talk to the other parents involved before signing on any dotted line."

"Oh, Dad, you wouldn't! I'm a college sophomore, not a kindergartner!" Kelly insisted, lifting her chin stubbornly.

"Well, for someone who claims to be so mature and so smart, you picked an awfully bad neighborhood to move into."

"There's nothing wrong with that area. It's all college students. Heck, it's probably safer living there than it is having to commute and park in some of those lots that are blocks away from the campus," she argued.

"Trust me, Kelly, it is not safe for any eighteen-year-old to live in an apartment alone no matter where it is," he said with a lift of one eyebrow.

"I'm almost nineteen, and I'm not going to be living alone," she protested, getting to her feet and coming around to his side of the desk. "Dad, please don't do this to me. If you make a fuss, you're going to ruin everything."

Again he raked a hand through his hair. "And what is it that I'm ruining?"

"My chance to live on campus. None of my friends' fathers are putting up a fuss."

"Well, maybe they should be," he retorted, his voice growing hoarse as he tried to control his emotions.

"Dad, it's a nice house and there's a good security system. Will you at least come take a look at it?"

Seth could feel a flush creeping up over his face and he loosened his tie. "How many roommates are you going to have?" he asked irritably.

"There's six of us altogether." Kelly looked at her father curiously. "Dad, are you feeling all right? Your face looks kind of blotchy."

Seth dismissed her concern with a wave of his hand. "It's just a little indigestion from the lunch I had. Of course it doesn't help that I found out my daughter's planning on moving out of my house and in with five other young women who have little or no experience of being on their own."

"Actually, two of my roommates are guys."

Seth shook his head. "You mean guys as in men?" he demanded, struggling to rid himself of the feeling that everything was closing in on him.

"It's not what you think," Kelly tried to explain, but Seth was vigorously shaking his head.

"No. No way," he stated firmly. "You're not sharing a house with any boys. It's hard enough explaining to people that my daughter works part-time at an escort service." When Kelly rolled her eyes, he added, "Of *course* I know it's not what people think." He sighed. "I just wish you weren't in such a rush to grow up...."

"Before you say no, won't you at least look at the place?" she pleaded.

He dropped an arm around her shoulder and gave her a paternal squeeze. "Do you think your mother would have wanted you living away from home while you're in college?"

She ducked out of his grasp. "Don't bring Mom into this," she told him in a defiant tone.

Seth faced her with an equally determined stance. "I don't want you moving out and that's that."

"But what about what I want?" She broke down in tears.

Seth hated to see any of his children cry and he reacted in his usual manner. He wrapped his arms around her, his anger dissolving.

Although Kelly's temperament was very similar to her father's, she couldn't let go of her anger quite as easily as he did. Annoyed with him, she tried to shove him away.

To anyone who didn't know better, it could have been a woman fighting off the unwelcome advances of a man. Which was exactly what Ellen thought when she stopped outside the door of Two's Company and peered through the narrow strip of glass. She saw an older man forcing his arms around a young woman.

Ellen hadn't wanted to come to the escort service in the first place and now that she was here and could see what kind of activity was going on in its waiting room, she knew she had made a mistake. The sight of such a big man grabbing such an innocent-looking young girl stirred a whole host of emotions inside her that she couldn't ignore.

Without giving it a second thought, she thrust open the door and commanded, "Get away from her!"

When the man turned around at the sound of her voice, Ellen wanted to bolt for the door. There was something disturbingly familiar about him, and it was only as his eyes met hers that she knew why. He was the man who had witnessed her humiliating experience at the gym.

Only this time there was no amusement in his eyes. No white teeth showing beneath his mustache.

He glared at her. "I don't know who you are, but this doesn't concern you."

"Will you please let go of me?" the young woman pleaded with him.

Seth wasn't about to loosen his grip on his daughter. He couldn't. Not while his chest felt so tight and he was having such difficulty breathing. Something strange was happening to his body, something he had no control over.

To the two women in the room, he appeared only to be very upset, his face red, his breathing erratic. When he didn't move away from Kelly, Ellen spoke again, this time in a much more threatening tone of voice.

"It's obvious she doesn't want you near her, so I suggest you get away or I'm going to call the police."

"Please, it's not what you think." Kelly was about to explain the situation when suddenly Seth started wheezing. Her expression changed to one of concern. "Oh my gosh! What's wrong?"

"I...can't...breathe," Seth managed to rasp between gulps of air.

"We've got to do something," Kelly cried out to Ellen. "I think he's choking."

It only took a second for Ellen to take charge. She reached Seth's side just as he was doubling over onto the sofa. "He needs a doctor," she announced. "Call 911."

Kelly couldn't move. She simply looked on in horror as her father clutched his chest and struggled for air. "Oh my gosh! Is he having a heart attack?"

Ellen didn't waste any time pushing Kelly aside to get to the phone. She punched in the three digits and gave the necessary information, while a bewildered Kelly stared at her father in disbelief.

"They're on their way," Ellen told her, then eased Seth's jacket from his shoulders.

"Are you a nurse?" Kelly asked shakily.

Ellen shook her head. "A medical secretary."

"What's happening to him?" She watched as Ellen loosened the buttons on her father's shirt. "Are you sure he's not having a heart attack?"

Ellen looked up at Kelly. "You have to try to be calm. He's going to be fine once the paramedics get here," she said in a reassuring, motherly tone.

"How can I stay calm? It looks as though he's choking to death!" Kelly reached for one of Seth's hands and murmured, "Dad, are you okay? Dad, talk to me." She turned back to Ellen. "What are we going to do? He's blue around the lips!"

"Dad?" Ellen repeated. "He's your father?"

Kelly didn't answer, but went on speaking to Seth, tears trickling down her face. "Dad, I'm sorry. I shouldn't have gotten you so upset." She looked at Ellen and said, "This is all my fault. I made him angry."

"You didn't cause this," Ellen spoke calmly. "He's having an allergic reaction. That's why he has all those red splotches on his face—they're hives."

"But he doesn't have any allergies."

"He does now."

In between the wheezing Seth tried to tell them what he had eaten for lunch, but his words were inaudible.

Again, Kelly's eyes filled with tears. "Don't try to talk, Dad. The ambulance is on its way."

Within minutes the paramedics arrived and quickly took over, administering epinephrine to Seth before strapping him onto a stretcher and taking him to the hospital. When it was all over, Ellen felt a strange mixture of relief and curiosity.

During the paramedic's questioning she had learned the man's name was Seth Holloway and that he was forty-three years old. What she didn't know was what his connection was to the escort service.

It was obvious his daughter was the receptionist. When another employee of the dating service returned from her lunch in the midst of the excitement, Kelly quickly explained the situation, then followed the paramedics as they wheeled her father out of the office. With the exception of an effusive "Thank you," she left without saying another word to Ellen.

Not that Ellen minded. The entire experience had only left her feeling unsettled and more uncertain than ever about the wisdom of using the escort service. She wondered if she wouldn't be wise to forget she had ever heard of Two's Company.

However, long after she returned to work that afternoon, she kept seeing Seth Holloway's face. There had been something in those vivid blue eyes that had first glared at her with hostility, then pleaded for her to help him.

Ellen wondered what it was that had caused the anaphylactic reaction. Why had he and his daughter argued? What would he have said to Ellen had he not collapsed? Had he recognized her from the health club?

Unable to stop thinking about him, she finally called the hospital. As she expected, he had been treated and released. There was no reason for her to worry about him.

However, throughout the remainder of the evening she found her thoughts filled with Seth Holloway. She kept remembering the grin that had been on his face when she had asked for lighter weights at the gym. Then she recalled the panic that had been on his face when he couldn't catch his breath.

As she ate dinner alone that evening, she realized it was only natural that she would be preoccupied with thoughts of him. After all, she had been with him in a potentially life-threatening situation. In a few days she would forget all about him.

She hoped.

"YOU ATE SNAILS? No wonder you almost croaked. They're disgusting," fourteen-year-old Brian Holloway told his father as he plopped down beside him on the couch.

"You can bet I won't be eating them again," Seth said without looking up from the yellow legal pad in his hands.

He had come home from the hospital and deposited his weakened body in its favorite spot on the sofa, the place where the cushions sagged just enough so that he could wedge his shoulder into the corner and prop his knee against the arm.

"Are you going to use that in the strip?" Brian gestured to the sketch his father was working on.

"I'm not sure there's a place for killer snails in *Holloway's House*," Seth answered evasively, as he always did whenever anyone asked about one of his cartoons.

Holloway's House was something he had started shortly after his wife, Laura, had died. A complete departure from the editorial cartoons he drew for the newspaper, it depicted the day-to-day traumas of a single father and his teenage children. It was autobiographical, and except for his family, no one knew the strip existed.

Brian leaned closer to his father and studied the snails in the cartoon. "You gave them feminine characteristics, Dad."

Seth looked up innocently. "I did?"

"It's probably because Gwendolyn Whitney's responsible for his near brush with death," Kelly said, carrying a serving tray into the room.

"It's not Ms. Whitney's fault that your father's allergic to escargots," Bernice Benson pointed out, following on Kelly's heels with a hot cup of tea for her son.

"You ate snails just to please a girl?" Brian puckered his face in disbelief.

"She was petite and a brunette. Dad's a sucker for that combination," Kelly said, setting a club sandwich in front of him. "She probably could have gotten him to eat anchovies."

"I hate anchovies," Seth reminded her. "And tea." He gave his mother a look of censure as she set the steaming cup next to his sandwich.

"There's nothing like hot tea when you've had an upset," Bernice crowed maternally.

Seth gave her a sour look. "The reason I ordered escargots is because I like them," he snapped a bit impatiently. "Unfortunately, they don't like me."

"Didn't you have them that time you took us to that fancy French restaurant?" Brian wanted to know.

"Yup, he did," Kelly answered for him.

"So how come you didn't choke then?"

"Because you don't always have a reaction the first time you eat something." Again Kelly answered for her father. "The doctor said allergic reactions usually occur after the second or third time—it's something to do with antigens or antibodies or whatever." She shrugged and dismissed the medical explanation with a wave of her hand.

"What's important is that now your father knows he shouldn't eat them again," Bernice stated matter-of-factly. "At least his allergic reaction happened when there was someone around to help him."

"It's a good thing Kelly was there, eh, Dad?" Brian said with a grin.

"Good thing," Seth mumbled, sounding more disgruntled than grateful.

"I for one am glad she was there," Bernice declared emotionally. "Who knows what would have happened if I had been the one working the front desk. The good Lord knows I've never been very good in emergency situations."

"Me neither," Kelly admitted, giving her grandmother a reassuring pat on her hand. "Fortunately, this really sweet woman showed up at a crucial moment."

I DO, I DO   39

"Really sweet woman?" Seth mimicked in disbelief. "Are you talking about the Florence Nightingale in the nurse's uniform?"

Kelly nodded. "Uh-huh. I wish I would have thanked her properly. Everything happened so fast I didn't get a chance to talk to her once the paramedics arrived."

"She thought I was assaulting you," Seth reminded her between bites of his club sandwich. "If I hadn't been choking to death she probably would have Maced me."

"Well, you were acting rather weird, Dad." Seeing her father scowl, she quickly added, "Because of the antigens, I'm sure."

Seth took a sip of the tea and grimaced. "Did you get her name?"

"I thought she said it was Elaine or something with an E. I'll look it up in the appointment book when I go to work tomorrow."

"Don't worry about it. I'll call her and thank her personally," Bernice said, patting her son on the shoulder.

"She was a customer?" Seth's brow wrinkled.

Kelly gave her father a bemused look. "Why else would she have been at Two's Company?"

Seth didn't want to admit that he had concocted several reasons for his Florence Nightingale to have been at the escort service. She could have been a messenger. Or maybe just someone passing by who happened to glance in and see an emergency situation.

Seth shrugged. "I suppose it doesn't matter."

"Of course it matters!" Bernice exclaimed. "The last thing we need is to be driving customers away." She looked at her watch, then said to Seth, "You should be resting, and I have to stop by the office and make sure Wendy locked up."

"You go ahead, Ma. I'll be fine," Seth assured her, accepting her motherly inspection without any protest.

She had no more than stepped out the door when Kelly announced, "I've got to go, too. I'm meeting a couple of friends at the campus library."

Seth thought she had on an awful lot of makeup for someone who was going to the library to study. "What about our discussion we didn't get to finish?"

"We'll talk tomorrow, all right?" She bent down and brushed a kiss across his cheek. "You rest."

She had barely stepped around the corner when Brian jumped to his feet and said, "I'm outta here, too, Dad. I'm going to shoot some hoops with the guys."

"Where's Matt?" Seth asked, wondering why he hadn't seen his seventeen-year-old son since he'd come home.

Brian shrugged. "Hanging out somewhere, I guess."

"He might be over at Gleason's working on his car," Kelly called out from the kitchen.

"So I guess that means I'm on my own tonight," Seth commented to an empty room.

Kelly must have heard him, for she poked her head back around the corner. "You're going to be all right by yourself, aren't you, Dad?"

Seth almost said no. On any other night he would have welcomed the peace and quiet of being alone in the house. But not tonight. Tonight he wanted all three of his children at home where he knew they would be safe and sound. It was a sentimentality he could only attribute to his body chemistry being out of whack.

"Dad, are you going to be okay?" Kelly repeated when he didn't answer her.

Seth fought back the overprotective impulse and forced a grin to his face. "I'll be fine. You go on to the library. Just make sure that you're careful. A young woman on her own—"

"Is a target for carjackers and muggers," Kelly finished for him. "I know, Dad. I'll use campus security, okay?"

Seth nodded and pretended it didn't matter that she was leaving, but deep in his heart he couldn't help but worry. It came with the territory of being a parent.

He finished the remainder of his sandwich, then slouched back into the corner of the couch and reached for the yellow legal pad. This time, however, he didn't sketch killer snails or any of the characters in *Holloway's House.*

He drew a nurse. A very shapely nurse with an oxygen mask in one hand and a barbell in the other.

THE FOLLOWING EVENING Ellen sat at her kitchen table staring at the application for Two's Company. Ever since dinner, she had been sitting there with her pencil poised, studying the questions, searching for one that would be easy to answer.

The problem was, she didn't want to answer any of them. Not the one about her age, not the one about her occupation and not the one about her personal preferences.

She simply couldn't pick out a date as if she were ordering a dress from a catalog. "What kind of man do you find attractive? Do you prefer tall or short? What about the color of the eyes?'' she read aloud.

Immediately Seth Holloway's image popped into her head. He wasn't much taller than she—probably around five ten. His eyes had been the bluest shade of blue she had ever seen, and they had looked at her in such a way that she still felt a little tingly sensation every time she thought of him.

And he had smelled good, too. Like the forest right after a rain.

Come to think of it, for a man who had been choking to death, he was quite attractive. She chuckled. What would Two's Company think if she put down she preferred men who were green at the gills and had bulging eyes?

When Bernice Benson had called to apologize for any inconvenience she might have experienced, Ellen had learned that Seth Holloway was, indeed, one of Two's Company's escorts. He was a man for hire. Should she request him?

It was a tempting thought. He would make the perfect escort for the wedding. That touch of gray in his hair, the well-defined muscles, the heart-stopping baby blues . . .

Another tingly sensation spread through her at the memory. She had never cared for men with mustaches, so why had she found him so attractive?

It didn't matter. She wasn't going to request his services. How could she, after he had seen her wimping out in the health club and she had seen him choking to death?

Knowing she would probably regret it, she indicated her preference for a man under thirty years of age with blond hair and no mustache on the Two's Company questionnaire.

"There. That ought to be safe," she said to herself and called to set up her interview at Two's Company.

CHAPTER THREE

SETH COULD HARDLY BELIEVE his luck when he awoke on Friday morning. It was hot, sunny and dry. After a cold, wet spring that had included several weeks of monsoon-type weather, summer had finally arrived in the Midwest and he was ready to enjoy it.

By noon he had finished his cartoons for the weekend papers, made reservations for a campsite in Jay Cooke State Park and was home scrounging around in the garage for the tent he and Laura had pitched on dozens of occasions. Nostalgia hurried his movements as he searched for the gas lantern and stove, then went into the kitchen.

"Dad, what is going on?" Kelly asked when she found him rummaging through the cupboards.

"We're going camping," Seth said with a childlike grin.

"We?" Kelly repeated, her eyebrows lifting.

"You, me, your brothers. I checked the weather channel and it's going to be a perfect weekend." He set several cans of beans beside the camp stove.

Kelly eyed them distastefully. "I'm not going. I hate camping."

"I beg your pardon?" He must have misunderstood her. He thought she said she hated camping.

"I don't want to go camping, Dad. I hate sleeping on the ground."

Dumbfounded, Seth stared at her. "You used to beg your mother and me to take you up to Jay Cooke State Park."

"That was when I was a kid and I enjoyed eating dinner out of a can and washing up with cold water," she said dryly.

"There are hot showers at the campgrounds."

"Yeah, and a couple of hundred people standing in line to use them and lots of creepy crawly things slithering across the floor." She shivered at the thought. "No, thank you. I'll pass."

Seth couldn't hide his disappointment. "I thought you'd want to come with us."

She gave him a quick hug. "It's better if you just take Matt and Brian. It's really a guy thing, anyway."

"A guy thing," Seth mumbled under his breath while Kelly turned her attention to the contents of the refrigerator. He wanted to ask her why her mother never had thought it was a "guy thing" but let it go. "I suppose I should call Grandma and see if she can stay here with you."

That brought Kelly's head out of the refrigerator in a hurry. "I don't need Grandma to come stay with me," she informed him, a bottle of mineral water in one hand and a container of yogurt in the other. "I'm almost nineteen."

Seth rubbed a hand around the back of his neck and sighed. "I'd feel better if you weren't home alone."

"Why is Kelly going to be home alone?" Matt wanted to know, entering the kitchen on the tail end of their conversation.

"Because I'm taking you and Brian camping this weekend. I thought we'd go up to Jay Cooke...climb some rocks, hike in the woods, maybe toss around a Frisbee.''

''You want to go camping today?'' He looked at Seth as if he had just asked him to carry the tent on his back and run alongside the car.

''Yup. The weather's going to be great. I've got a campsite reserved, and the Explorer's packed. All we have to do is get some chow loaded and we're off.'' He grinned in anticipation.

''We haven't been camping since Mom died,'' Matt said quietly.

''I know. There never seems to be any time,'' Seth acknowledged, not wanting to admit the true reason he had avoided taking them. Until now, he hadn't wanted to do anything that would remind him of Laura. It was only this morning when he awoke and smelled the fresh summer air that he had felt it was time to start doing some of the things she had enjoyed.

Matt shoved his hands into his jeans pockets. ''Dad, I can't go. I have to work at the Pizza Palace tomorrow.''

Seth's brow furrowed. He had totally forgotten about his son's summer job. ''Can't you trade hours with someone?''

''No one wants to work on Saturday, Dad.'' His tone of voice made Seth feel as if he were partially brain dead to even ask such a question.

''Why don't I give your boss a call and see what I can do?'' He walked over to the wall phone, but to Matt's relief, it rang before his father reached it.

It was a familiar voice that sounded in Seth's ears. ''Oh, good. You haven't left yet.''

"No, Ma, we haven't left," he repeated, looking pointedly at Matt. "We've encountered a few obstacles."

"Thank heavens!" Bernice Benson sighed. "Something's come up and I'm going to need you to work this weekend."

"Work? Oh, Ma, no way!" he protested, sounding more like one of his teenagers than an adult. "This is the first time the sun's been out on a weekend in six months."

Kelly and Matt rolled their eyes at the exaggeration.

"I wouldn't ask you if it weren't an emergency," Bernice said apologetically.

"What kind of emergency?" A scowl marred his handsome face, put there not only by his mother's request but by the gleam of delight he saw in his children's eyes at the thought that the camping trip might be off.

"Clarence Grissell had a motorcycle accident. Broke his left leg, cut up his arm. Fortunately he was wearing his helmet."

"He's going to be all right, then?"

"Eventually, but he's not going to be able to work for quite some time."

"And you've got clients booked for him this weekend," Seth said on an understanding sigh. "Ma, I'm not working this weekend. I told you that last week when you wanted to pair me off with that Carter woman."

"I wouldn't be asking you if it wasn't an emergency. Clarence only had one booking. The same woman for both Friday and Saturday."

"Are you sure you can't find someone else to take it?"

"There is no one else, Seth. You know how busy we are in June."

"Then you'll have to call the woman and tell her what's happened."

"How can I? It's her daughter's wedding. The poor thing has enough on her mind without losing her escort for the occasion."

Seth glanced outside to where his forest green Explorer sat on the driveway. He could see the flaps of the blue canvas tent sticking up in the back window. Then he looked at the propane camp stove sitting on the kitchen table. He was going to give up blue skies and rippling rivers to escort some middle-aged mama to her daughter's wedding.

"When I agreed to help you out, you told me this wouldn't get to be a regular thing," he reminded her.

"I know, dear, and I'm sorry. Truly, I am. I wouldn't ask you if I had any other option."

"Ma, my weekends are important to me. It's the only time I get to spend with the kids."

"Your children don't want to go camping, Seth."

"The boys do," he corrected her, not wanting to admit that she might be right.

"There'll be other weekends. Seth, the woman has contracted with Two's Company for an escort. We won't be in business for long if word gets out we renege on our agreements," his mother said, putting just enough apprehension in her voice to provoke his sympathy.

Not that she needed it. Seth knew how important the business was to his mother. Until she had started Two's Company, she had been like a lost soul, unsure of what she was going to do with the rest of her life. Initially, Seth had been against the idea of her running a professional escort service—and hiring his daughter over the summer to fill in for a receptionist on maternity leave. But Bernice had impressed him with her dogged determination to provide single women with safe escorts. She screened her employees vigorously, and made equally sure that her clients had no false expectations about the services for hire. Consequently, Seth had decided that as long as she was happy and the business went smoothly, he would support her endeavors.

He had even gone so far as to offer his own services until she could afford to hire more escorts—and as long as the assignments didn't interfere with his full-time work. It was a good arrangement for him. He didn't want a complicated involvement with a woman—he hadn't since Laura had died—and at least Two's Company got him out of the house every now and then. Lately, however, the forced gaiety had started to get to him. And he suspected the business was doing well enough that Bernice could afford to hire at least one more escort. Still, tonight was an emergency....

"All right, Ma, I'll do it," he told her now in a resigned tone. "What's this woman's name?"

"Ellen Richards. If you come by the office on your way to pick her up, I'll fill you in on all the details."

"What time?" he asked impatiently.

"She needs you by six, so stop by Two's Company around five. Oh, and wear your gray suit."

"Anything else?" he fairly barked.

"There is one minor complication."

"What's that?"

"She specifically requested someone under thirty and blond, like Clarence."

Seth sighed. This was even worse than he first suspected. A middle-aged mama who wanted to date younger men. "I hope she's not going to be one of the difficult ones."

"Actually, she's rather sweet."

Seth uttered a sound of disbelief. "Is there anything else I should know?"

"Well..." she trailed off.

"Ma, what is it?"

"She's the woman who saved your life when you were choking."

Seth groaned. "This is not going to be easy, Ma."

"What could be so difficult?"

"I'm sure she doesn't want to go out with me any more than I want to go out with her."

"And why wouldn't you want to go out with her?"

"Ma, I told you what happened. She thought I was accosting my own daughter."

"She knows now that you weren't. I would think you'd appreciate the fact that she wanted to come to Kelly's aid."

Seth could only groan. "Ma, you're going to owe me big time for this one."

"I think you're going to be pleasantly surprised. She's a lovely woman. Now go and have fun!" And with that she hung up, leaving Seth to wonder how she always managed to talk him into doing things he didn't want to do.

JUST A FEW MINUTES before six that evening Ellen sat in front of her dressing-table mirror dabbing at her eyes with a tissue that had been dipped in cold cream. No matter how hard she tried, she couldn't steady her hand enough to apply the liquid eyeliner. Her latest effort had made her look like a child who had been playing with her mother's cosmetics.

To make matters worse, her eyes were becoming red from repeatedly rubbing off her aborted attempts. She debated whether she should forget about applying eye makeup at all. The state her nerves were in, she was only going to make a mess.

She wasn't sure what was making her more nervous—the thought of seeing Kenneth again or the prospect of spending an evening with a hired escort. Both were equally unappealing and had been wreaking havoc with her insides all day long. She wished that she had called and canceled the escort. It was bad enough that she had the heebie-jeebies over seeing Kenneth again. She didn't need the added stress of having to pretend a total stranger was an intimate friend.

Feeling panicked, she reached for the phone and dialed the number for Two's Company's. When she heard a recorded message, she hung up. What good would it do to cancel now? Clarence Grissell was probably already in the neighborhood.

The thought brought another wave of nausea to her. She took a sip of Coke to settle her stomach, then finished applying her makeup the best she could. Just as her hand followed the contours of her lips with a tube of Rio Red, the doorbell rang.

Ellen froze. Clarence wasn't just in her neighborhood. He was at her door. Waiting. She didn't want to let him in.

Briefly she contemplated not answering the door. Maybe she should pretend she wasn't at home. She had already paid for his services. What did it matter whether she used them or not?

The doorbell rang a second time. And then a third. Still she didn't move. It wasn't until the fourth ring, which was rather prolonged and steady, that Ellen was jolted into action. She hurried down the stairs to the front door and looked through the peephole at the man on the front steps.

He had his back to her, his hands in his pockets. Ellen's heart raced even faster. His hair was darker than it had looked in the picture, and either he wasn't six foot two or else she had grown. She took several deep breaths to steady herself, then pulled on the knob.

At the sound of the door opening, he turned around, and Ellen's eyes widened. What was Seth Holloway doing on her front porch?

"Oh, you are home. I was just about to leave." He looked as surprised to see Ellen as she was to see him.

"I was upstairs...I...I didn't hear the bell right away," she stammered, her mouth as dry as cotton. "Can I help you?"

"I'm looking for Ellen Richards."

"I'm Ellen Richards."

There was the slightest lift of his eyebrows, then he produced a business card from his breast pocket and handed it to her. "I'm Seth Holloway from Two's Company."

"I know. I was there in the office when you..." She trailed off when she realized that he recognized her, too.

"Nearly choked to death," he finished for her. "I know. I never got a chance to thank you for your help." He smiled then. A warm, sincere grin that made his mustache twitch.

"I really didn't do much. The paramedics are the ones who saved your life," she explained, trying not to notice just how attractive he was.

"I'm not sure they would have been called had you not been there," he admitted with a wry grin.

"Oh, I'm sure someone would have called them."

He shrugged. "Maybe."

Neither one said anything for several moments and silence stretched awkwardly between them. Finally Ellen said, "It really wasn't necessary for you to come all this way to thank me."

"I didn't."

When she gave him a puzzled look he added, "Come all this way to say thanks. I'm your escort for this evening."

Uneasiness slithered through her. "I don't understand. Where's Clarence?"

"No one called you?"

She shook her head. "Isn't he coming?"

"He's in the hospital. He had a motorcycle accident this morning."

"So you're taking his place?"

He smiled again, and once more Ellen experienced a tiny shiver of pleasure. "With your approval, of course."

Ellen didn't approve. Not at all. How could she? He was all wrong for the part.

When she didn't answer right away he asked, "Are you having second thoughts about using the service, Ellen?"

To her dismay, she blushed. "It's just that Clarence was familiar with the circumstances."

"So am I. Bernice filled me in on the details," he said reassuringly.

Ellen could feel her skin warming to an embarrassing pink. Just how many details did he know?

"That may be, but the problem is I've told everyone my date's name is Clarence."

"That's not a problem. I can be a Clarence."

"You don't look like a Clarence," she found herself saying aloud and he smiled. A devastatingly attractive smile that did funny things to Ellen's equilibrium.

"What I mean is it probably wouldn't be comfortable for you to assume a different identity."

"Is that what's really worrying you, Ellen?"

Blue eyes pierced hers and she felt tongue-tied. Memories of her humiliating experience at the health club caused her cheeks to warm. There was no way she could be in his presence for the next two days without feeling like an idiot.

"I'm just not sure this is going to work out," Ellen said as delicately as she could.

His answer was to give her another of his wonderful smiles. "I think it would, but if you want to cancel the agreement, I understand."

It was the last thing she had expected him to say. Shouldn't he be persuading her to use Two's Company's services?

Concerned about the fee she had already paid, she asked, "Is it okay if I cancel on such short notice?"

"I don't see why not."

Ellen could hardly believe what she was hearing. Here was the opportunity she had been seeking, the way out of a situation she should have never gotten herself into.

"What about the contract I signed?"

"We can void it."

No one could accuse Two's Company of pressuring their clients into doing anything they didn't want to do, Ellen thought to herself. On the contrary, Seth appeared to be eager for her to cancel the agreement. Could it be that he didn't want to go out with her any more than she wanted to go out with him?

"It's up to you, Ellen. What do you say?"

She was about to accept his offer when a red convertible pulled up into her driveway. Sitting behind the steering wheel was Rebecca, with Roger across from her on the passenger side. Because the top was down, Ellen could see a third person sitting in the back seat. It was a man wearing a cowboy hat and as the car drew nearer, she realized it was Kenneth.

"What is he doing here?" The words escaped before she could stifle them, causing Seth to regard her curiously.

As soon as the car came to a stop, Rebecca jumped out. "Mom! Look what Dad gave us for a wedding present!" she exclaimed, running toward the house. "Isn't it gorgeous?"

Ellen stepped out onto the porch, wondering what she should do with Seth. She would have liked to shove him behind the bushes lining the front walk, but it was too late. Rebecca had already seen him. As soon as her daughter reached the front porch she extended her hand to him.

"Hi, I'm Rebecca. You must be Clarence, the mystery man."

Ellen nearly fell off the step. "Rebecca!"

"I guess I was supposed to say I'm glad we finally get to meet," Rebecca amended with a less than sincere smile.

Seth looked to Ellen for direction as to what he should say. When she gave him a helpless lift of her brow, he simply took the hand Rebecca offered and said, "Why don't you call me Seth? I never did care for Clarence." He gave Ellen a sideways glance.

"Then Seth it is," Rebecca answered coolly. "I didn't expect to see you until later this evening. Only family is going to be at the wedding rehearsal."

The situation had gone from bad to worse and Ellen needed to do something quickly. "Seth, could you excuse us for a few minutes?" she asked, nudging her daughter toward the door.

"No problem. I'll just go check out the new car," he said amiably.

"I won't be but a minute," Ellen said apologetically.

He flashed her a reassuring grin and gave her a pat on the arm. "No problem."

Ellen pulled Rebecca inside. "If you didn't want me to invite a guest, why didn't you just say so instead of being rude to him?"

"I'm sorry if you thought I was rude. I didn't mean to be. It's just that I didn't expect to find him here. You told me he was meeting you at the restaurant so he wouldn't feel out of place at the rehearsal." There was censure in her tone and Ellen didn't like it one bit.

"He stopped by to talk to me," she said defensively. "Why are you so upset?"

"Because I thought you were going to be home alone. That's why I brought Dad along."

Ellen moaned. "Oh, Becca. Why are you so bent on putting your father and me together?"

"I'm not!" she denied. "I just thought it would be easier for both of you if you could meet and talk a little before everything got started."

"If I had wanted to talk to your father, I would have called him. I really wish you hadn't done this."

"How was I supposed to know he was going to be here?" She motioned toward the outside.

"If you had called me I would have told you."

"Can't you ask him to leave?"

"No, I am not going to ask him to leave!" Ellen replied indignantly, forgetting that only a few minutes ago she was going to do just that.

"Well, don't you think it's a little awkward for Dad?"

"Why should it be awkward for your father? He has a wife," she retorted. "Where is she, anyway?"

"She's back at the hotel getting her nails done. That's why this is the perfect opportunity for you and Dad to talk without anyone else around."

"No," Ellen said firmly.

"Mother!"

"No."

"What am I supposed to do with Dad?"

"Take him back to the hotel." Suddenly aware of the hostility between them, Ellen reached for her daughter's hands. "Let's not start off your celebration by arguing. Your intentions were good, and I appreciate your sensitivity to the situation, but it's best if you let your father and me work this out by ourselves."

Rebecca's eyes misted over. "I was just trying to help."

Ellen pulled her into her arms. "I know, sweetie. You want everything to be perfect for your wedding.

But you have to trust me and your father. We're not going to do anything to jeopardize your big day.''

Ellen had to keep that thought in mind as she walked outside and saw her ex-husband leaning up against the rear fender of the shiny new red Mustang. He didn't look at all as she had expected he would, and she had to stifle the urge to giggle.

It was obvious he had left his Midwestern life-style behind him. Gone were the oxford shirts and dress pants that had been his wardrobe standards while they were married. In their place was Western wear—a suit, a bolo tie and cowboy boots. And around both wrists and on his fingers was gold. Lots of gold.

The receding hairline he had always camouflaged by combing a swatch of his blond hair forward was covered by a black cowboy hat. His skin was a golden brown, but whether it was from being outdoors or in a tanning salon was anyone's guess.

Ellen walked toward him until she was close enough to smell his after-shave. It was the same brand he had always used. The one that used to make her swoon when she was seventeen. Fortunately, she wasn't seventeen anymore.

For weeks she had been rehearsing what she would say when the time came for the two of them to meet again. He was nothing to her anymore and she had vowed she would not let his presence affect her in any way, yet when he spoke to her, her mouth became dry, her skin clammy.

"How have you been, Elle?" he asked.

No one but Kenneth had ever called her Elle. A rush of memories came flooding back and not all of them were bad.

"I'm okay," she said shakily, hating the fact that he still had the power to throw her off balance.

"You're looking good," he said with a bit of a drawl. "Actually, you're looking great."

For just one moment his words made her feel a little light-headed. Then she came to her senses. Flattery from Kenneth was about as genuine as a compliment from a used-car salesman.

"Thank you," she said stiffly, annoyed by the look of interest on her daughter's face.

"It's hard to believe our little girl is big enough to be getting married, isn't it?" Kenneth pulled Rebecca into the crook of his arm, smiling at her with paternal pride.

Rebecca groaned. "Don't tell me you think I'm too young to be getting married, too."

"Every father thinks his daughter's too young, but I was your age once, and I know that sometimes there's nothing that can stand in the way of love." He stared pointedly at Ellen.

A sentimental feeling washed over Ellen, and she deliberately looked away as Rebecca hugged her father and said, "Thanks, Daddy."

"I think you and Roger are going to be very happy together. That's why I bought you the car," Kenneth explained. "Newlyweds have enough troubles without having to worry about financing a new car."

Ellen wanted to ask him who had financed the Mustang and if the newlyweds needed to worry about it being repossessed but wisely kept silent. Instead she found the social grace to say, "It's a very generous and thoughtful gift."

Her reward was a smile of gratitude from her daughter and a gleam of admiration in her ex-husband's eyes. She appreciated the former but was uncomfortable with the latter. She deliberately looked away and noticed Seth patiently listening to Roger explain all the options on the new car.

"I'm sorry. I haven't made introductions," she apologized, moving toward the Two's Company escort nervously.

"It's all right," Roger assured her. "We've already introduced ourselves."

It was obvious from the way Roger was speaking to Seth that he had taken an instant liking to the man. Kenneth, on the other hand, wasn't as impressed. There was a suspicious glint in his eyes as he glanced from Ellen to Seth. Ellen felt as though she were in the middle of a boxing ring with Kenneth and Rebecca in one corner and Seth and Roger in the other.

If Seth had any inkling about their hostile feelings, he didn't show it. He was a pro in the art of conversation, she could see, smoothly answering questions and listening attentively. No wonder he was a professional escort. The man had buckets of charm.

After what seemed to Ellen like an eternity of small talk, Roger slid his cuff back from his wrist to look at his watch. "I think we ought to leave. We're due at the church in less than an hour, and we still need to pick up Tina."

"Dad, maybe you should go in the house and give her a call," Rebecca said, fluttering about nervously. "I want to make sure she's ready."

"Is the phone still in the same place?" He looked at Ellen.

"No, I've changed a lot of things. Becca, why don't you show him inside?" Ellen suggested, not wanting to be alone in the house with her ex.

Ellen was grateful that Roger had taken an instant liking to Seth, for he was able to keep up the conversation while Rebecca and her father were inside.

"Say, listen, Seth," he said to the escort. "There's no need for you to meet us later at Kincaid's. Why not come with Ellen to the rehearsal?"

Again, Seth looked to Ellen for a hint of what he should say. And once more, she could only give him a confused look.

"I don't want to get in the way," he said.

"You're not going to get in the way."

"Get in the way of what?" Rebecca demanded when she returned.

"I thought Seth should come to the church so your mother wouldn't have to drive alone," he explained to his bride-to-be.

"Mom can ride with us. There's no need for Seth to sit through the rehearsal," Rebecca told him. "Actually it would work out better that way because Tina's not going to be at the church, either."

Kenneth had opened the car door and was gesturing for Ellen to get inside.

"No, I think Roger's right," Ellen said shakily, taking a step backward. "Seth can come to the rehearsal with me."

"It'll probably be boring for him," Rebecca warned.

Seth shrugged. "I'll do whatever Ellen wants," he said, which only made Rebecca's mouth tighten and Kenneth's eyes narrow.

"Then it's all set," Roger said cheerfully, jiggling his keys in his palm. "We'll see the two of you at the church." He shook Seth's hand, then gave Ellen a peck on the cheek. "I like your friend," he whispered in her ear.

It was with a sigh of relief that Ellen watched the three of them climb back into the convertible. It wasn't until the car had rolled out of the driveway and was out of sight that she was able to breathe normally. Then she heard Seth's voice.

"I take it this means I'm not fired."

CHAPTER FOUR

"I GUESS you'd better come inside," Ellen grudgingly conceded.

Seth knew from the look on her face that this was not going to be an easy assignment. It was one thing to escort a woman who wanted your company, quite another to be with one who looked at you as if you had crawled out from under the nearest rock.

"Can I get you something to drink?" she asked as she showed him into the small but cozy living room.

"I'll have whatever you're having."

She disappeared for a few minutes, then returned with two glasses. She handed one to him, saying, "Iced tea."

Served him right. He should have asked her for a beer. He would have, but she didn't look like the kind of woman to have a Pig's Eye Pilsner in the refrigerator.

Because his throat was dry, he took a sip of the tea. To his surprise, it wasn't bad. It had a raspberry flavor and left a pleasant taste in his mouth.

She motioned for him to take a seat on the faded camelback sofa. Seth had an idea that the lace doilies on the armrests hid worn patches; the springs sagged as he sat down.

"You have a nice place," he said in his polite escort voice, trying to keep his eyes on her face and not on the shapely bosom that had drawn his attention the moment she had opened the door to him.

"Thank you." She put two coasters on the pecan coffee table, then sat down across from him.

Some devilish impulse made him ask her, "Been to the health club lately?"

She turned a deep red and he immediately felt remorse. He wondered what she would say if he told her that he had made a couple of extra visits to the health club recently, hoping he would see her again.

"We should probably get right down to business since there isn't much time before we have to leave," she stated in a businesslike voice.

"That's fine with me. What's on your mind?"

She folded and unfolded her hands in her lap, then picked up the glass of iced tea. "This is the first time I've ever used an escort service." She blushed when he arched one eyebrow, then shifted uncomfortably. "This wasn't my idea."

"It wasn't?"

She shook her head. "My sister, Jeannie, talked me into it."

Normally he would have made some charming remark to put his date at ease, but she was looking at him with such obvious dislike that all thoughts of charm flew out the door. The woman was acting as though he had blackmailed her into using the service. Ever since he had told her he was replacing Clarence, she had looked at him as if he were too old, too short and the biggest disappointment of her life. He didn't need this, not tonight when he could have been sleeping in the north woods.

Forgetting that it was his job to be charming, he asked, "Do you usually allow people to talk you into doing things you don't want to do?"

"Right now I'm wishing I hadn't." She set her glass down with a thud.

"That makes two of us." The thud of his glass matched hers. "I'll save you the trouble of asking me to leave." He rose to go, but she stopped him.

"Wait! You can't go!"

"I can't?"

"No! I paid for you!"

"Correction. You didn't pay for me, you paid for an escort. I'm not that person and I've changed my mind about filling in for him."

"So you're just going to leave me with no one?" she asked, her voice rising in panic.

His mother would kill him, but he was in no mood to be dangled about like some puppet on a string. "I'll see that your money's refunded in full."

"I don't need my money refunded. I need for you to be my date." She followed him as he made his way to the front door. "You just told my daughter and her fiancé that you're going to be at their wedding rehearsal and the dinner that follows. What do I tell them when you don't show?"

"Make up a story. I'm ill or there's been a death in my family. You ought to be able to think up something . . . after all, you fabricated a boyfriend." It was below the belt, but he didn't care. She had been making him squirm ever since she had opened the door to him.

"For your information, I have been dating a very nice man."

"Then why isn't he escorting you to your daughter's wedding?"

"That's none of your business."

Indignation put a glow in her cheeks and a sparkle in her eyes that had Seth looking at her in a whole new light. Maybe there was fire behind that icy reserve, after all. He found himself softening toward her.

"I'm sorry. I shouldn't have said that, but I'm not used to women not wanting to go out with me," he confessed candidly.

What he meant to sound sincere must have sounded conceited to her ears, for sarcasm edged her words. "Well, you'll have to forgive me if I don't get in line for the privilege, but I thought I was hiring a professional, not an ego."

He grimaced. "All I meant was that the women I usually meet through Two's Company are looking for escorts, not sending them away."

"I'm not sending you away. You're leaving," she reminded him. "I haven't said I want to cancel the arrangement I've made."

He rubbed a hand across the back of his neck. He knew she was right. He was letting his own emotions get in the way of business and it had to stop. Why should it matter to him if this woman was disappointed in him as an escort? This was business, not pleasure.

Again he apologized. "I'm sorry. I think the change in plans has caught both of us off guard. You weren't expecting me and I wasn't planning on working this weekend. How about if I go outside and we start over?"

"That won't be necessary."

"You want me to leave?"

She shook her head. "I meant it's not necessary for you to go outside. We can just start over."

"I think it's better if I go out." Without another word, he opened the door and left. A few seconds later, he rang the bell.

When she answered, he said, "Hi. You must be Ellen. I'm Seth Holloway from Two's Company." There was a warm smile on his face.

She greeted him with equal warmth. "Come in. I've been expecting you."

She ushered him in and asked him if he wanted something to drink. He glanced at the two glasses sitting on the coffee table and said, "Iced tea would be nice."

She gave him a nervous smile and gestured for him to sit down.

"There are a few things we should discuss before we leave," she announced, folding her hands in her lap as she once more took the chair across from him.

"I'm listening."

"First of all, as you know from reading the file, my daughter is getting married tomorrow. Because I'm single and I didn't want there to be an odd number in the wedding party, I thought it best if I hired an escort."

"I understand," Seth told her.

"Not wanting to complicate things," she continued, "I allowed my family to believe that I had invited an old friend to the wedding."

"I see," he said evenly, thinking of how different she was from Laura. Besides the obvious physical differences, there was an elegance about her. It was there in the way she crossed her feet at the ankles, and sat ever so straight on the chair. Laura had never lost her schoolgirl look, not even when she was thirty-nine and the mother of three teenagers.

"So it's important that you give everyone the impression that we've been friends for a while," Ellen continued, shifting uncomfortably under his steady gaze.

"That won't be a problem," he answered smoothly, deliberately looking her in the eye. "As long as you fill me in on what I should know about our friendship, I won't slip up."

Her hand trembled as she reached for her glass. "There really isn't much to know. Supposedly, we've known each other for about nine months."

"How did we meet?"

"We were introduced by a mutual friend."

"And my occupation?"

"You're an accountant."

"An accountant?" Instinctively, he grimaced. Couldn't she have picked something a little less boring?

"Is that a problem?"

"No, that's fine," he answered, not wanting to tell her that in the two years since Laura had died, he hadn't yet managed to balance his checkbook. "Where do I live?"

"Anywhere you want, I guess. I don't think I've mentioned that detail to anyone."

"What about family? Do I have any?"

"None that I've mentioned. Fortunately, my daughter's been so caught up in planning this wedding she hasn't asked a lot of questions about you."

"Well, if anything does come up, we'll figure out a way to pass the information back and forth." He took a sip of the iced tea, then asked, "What should I know about you?"

She shifted uneasily. "I'm a medical secretary at the Parkers Lake Health Clinic. I have one daughter, a sister, a mother and one grandfather. There was quite a bit of personal information in my file."

Did he sense a criticism on her part or was he simply overreacting? "That's true, but you should probably fill me in on the dynamics behind the scene I just witnessed outside. Is there something I should know about you and Kenneth?"

She stiffened. "There's nothing to know. We're divorced."

At whose instigation? Seth wondered. Her ex was bringing his wife to the wedding and she was bringing a paid escort. It didn't take an Einstein to figure it out.

"Are things always that tense when you two are together?"

She gripped the arm of the chair and tried to keep her voice calm and confident. "It's only natural that everyone's a little nervous. My daughter is getting married tomorrow."

"Which doesn't make you very happy, does it?" he observed.

"I think she's too young, but as you can see, she isn't listening to her mother's advice."

"Teenagers seldom do." He took another sip of the tea, then said, "So tonight it's a rehearsal at the church, then dinner with the future in-laws?"

Ellen nodded. "The dinner's being paid for by the groom's parents, so there won't be any need for you to worry about money..." She broke off, looking very uneasy with the topic.

"Two's Company's escorts have expense accounts, should the need arise," he stated smoothly.

"Well, it shouldn't," she assured him. "You're my guest for the weekend."

"I understand," he said. "What time would you like me to pick you up tomorrow?"

"I thought I'd meet you at the church since I have to be there early."

"No problem."

She glanced nervously at her watch. "We should probably get going."

She paled slightly, and Seth could see that despite her efforts to pretend otherwise, she was a ball of nerves. Was he the cause or was she simply suffering from pre-wedding jitters as she wanted him to believe was the case?

"One other thing," he interjected. "What should I call you? I noticed your ex referred to you as Elle."

"I prefer Ellen," she said stiltedly, giving him one more reason to believe that there was more going on between Ellen Richards and her ex-husband than she wanted him to know.

He crooked his arm for her and said, "May I have the pleasure of your company, Ellen?"

For a moment he thought she wasn't going to put her arm through his, but then she accepted. "Thank you, Seth" was all she said, and then she allowed him to escort her to his car.

OVER AND OVER Ellen asked herself what she was do-ing with Seth that evening. Ever since she had opened her front door to him her life had resembled some-thing out of *The Twilight Zone*. Seeing Kenneth in Western wear, arguing with Rebecca over a man she didn't even know, and pleading with Seth to be her date when she wanted nothing better than to cancel the whole deal—all of it was too weird for words.

Now she was sitting in Kincaid's Steak House with a professional escort at her side, trying to make polite conversation with the woman who had stolen her husband from her. Actually, Ellen was grateful that Seth was sitting beside her. With bossy Mrs. Townsend on one side and Kenneth and his wife across the table, she needed to know that there was one person who was concerned about her, even if it was a bought-and-paid-for concern.

Any fear she had that someone would discover Seth was a paid escort was put to rest by Seth himself, who easily blended into the group gathered for dinner. He was completely charming, yet still managed to give the impression that he was a regular guy. Ellen found herself admiring the way he put people at ease.

Several times during dinner when he reached for the condiments, his suit coat stretched across his taut muscles, causing Ellen to remember what he had looked like in the gym. Often she caught him looking at her out of the corner of his eye and she wondered if he was remembering how disgustingly wimpy she had looked that day. She hoped not.

If he was uncomfortable in his role as her escort, he hid it well. No one would have suspected that he was at the restaurant under duress. Only Ellen knew that his charismatic behavior was all an act.

He was, as Two's Company had promised, the perfect escort, and she could find no fault with his service. He behaved impeccably all evening. At the rehearsal he had stayed in the shadows while the members of the wedding party walked through the ceremony that would take place tomorrow. At the restaurant he had even allowed Mrs. Townsend to choose his entrée for him. Now he was listening with interest while Kenneth spouted *Wall Street Journal* quotations and recounted tales of his stock market killings.

All of which caused Ellen to ask herself, Was he dumb enough to believe Kenneth's bogus financial adventures? And did he really like swordfish steak?

She found out the answer to both questions on the way home. As Seth maneuvered his Explorer through the freeway traffic, Ellen couldn't resist asking him if he had enjoyed his dinner.

"The swordfish was excellent. I usually have steak when I'm at Kincaid's, but I see I'll have to try the seafood more often." He stopped at the base of an exit ramp, waiting for a red light to change to green. "Were you satisfied with the way things went this evening?"

"Kincaid's is always marvelous."

"I wasn't talking about Kincaid's, Ellen. I meant the service I provided."

She was glad it was dark, for she was certain her cheeks colored. "Yes. Everything was fine."

"Good."

He didn't probe any further but returned his attention to the road. As the silence stretched between them, Ellen grew restless. They had just spent several hours pretending to be close friends, and now he was acting as though he was the taxi driver and she the fare.

To break the uncomfortable silence she asked, "What about you? Did you have a good time?"

"I wasn't the one who was supposed to be entertained," he replied, evading the question.

Entertained. Ellen thought about the doors that had been held open, the attentive smiles and the solicitous care she had received. It was all entertainment she had paid for. Even though she knew it was irrational, she felt disappointed.

"You're very good at your job. Everyone at that table thought you were sincerely interested in what was being said." She couldn't keep the disapproval from her voice.

"I was interested."

Her silence said she didn't believe him.

He shot her a sideways glance. "I like people, Ellen. That's why I do this kind of work."

"You mean you like women," she corrected.

"Women are people."

"Well, it's nice that you find your work so interesting."

"Oh, I do," he said, his voice as smooth as silk.

There was another uncomfortable silence, then she asked, "What was it that caused your anaphylactic reaction that day at Two's Company?"

"Escargots. I had them for lunch."

"Does your daughter work at Two's Company, too?"

"On a part-time basis."

"Is she a student?"

"Uh-huh."

"At the U?"

"Yup."

Ellen would have had to have been obtuse not to realize he didn't want to talk about his daughter. She wondered if the disagreement she had interrupted at Two's Company had become a full-blown tear in their relationship. She also wondered if Seth approved of his daughter's working at the escort service. She immediately dismissed the thought. After all, he was an employee there himself. The place was squeaky clean, and grandmotherly Bernice Benson seemed the ideal employer.

"How old is your daughter?"

"Eighteen."

"Oh, she's only a year younger than my daughter. When's her birthday?" When he didn't answer the question, she asked, "If you'd rather not talk to me, just say so."

"I enjoy talking to you, Ellen. It's just that I make it a policy not to discuss my personal life when I'm working," he told her.

"I'm sorry," she said quietly, feeling like yesterday's biggest jerk. "I didn't mean to pry."

Again, Seth felt remorse. She was too nice to treat as if she were some pathetic middle-aged woman looking for the company of a younger man. Yet he couldn't forget that she had specifically requested someone young like Clarence.

"You weren't prying," he assured her, his voice softening. "And to be perfectly honest with you, Ellen, I did enjoy myself this evening. I even learned a few things."

"I hope you're not talking about the financial advice Kenneth was freely dispensing."

"And if I was?"

"Then you ought to know that he hasn't had much success when it comes to making a profit on anything." As hard as she tried, she couldn't keep the derision from her voice.

"One wouldn't know that from the way he was talking this evening," Seth commented, finding it rather interesting that she found it necessary to warn him about something he found obvious.

"Well, I thought you should know that he isn't exactly an authority when it comes to investments."

"You don't think so?"

"No, I don't." She stiffened her spine as she answered, and Seth couldn't help but admire her concern for a stranger like himself.

"Would you rather I didn't talk to the guy tomorrow?"

"I don't care if you talk to him."

"Are you sure?"

"Of course."

"Good, because personally I wasn't crazy about the guy, but I thought it might look a little odd if I didn't act interested in what he was saying. After all, I was only doing my job."

Ellen wondered how he would have behaved if he hadn't been working that evening, if he had been a real date. Would he have spent more time talking to her? She quickly shoved that thought aside.

It was no use thinking about Seth Holloway in personal terms. He was her hired escort. Period. Just because he had a smile that could charm the socks off stuffy Mrs. Townsend and blue eyes that could make her forget what she was going to say didn't mean she should regard him as anything but a business acquaintance.

Yet when he dropped her at her doorstep and wished her a good-night, she couldn't help but feel a little sad that there was nothing personal in his goodbye. No touch on the shoulder, no gentle squeeze of her hand, no kiss. As he drove away, she couldn't help but wonder what it would be like to be the object of Seth Holloway's affection.

SETH AWOKE Saturday morning to find sunlight peeking through the window blinds. He spread two of the slats with his fingers, squinted, then groaned. He could just imagine what it was like up along the North Shore. Birds would be chirping, and the air would be fresh with the scent of pine.

He tossed the sheet aside and was about to head for the shower when the phone rang. Did he dare hope that Ellen Richards had had a change of heart and he wouldn't have to spend a gorgeous afternoon inside some church?

"Good morning. How did it go last night?" his mother asked.

Seth yawned as he said, "It was fine, Ma. I hope you're calling to tell me she canceled today's job."

"Why would she cancel?" she asked suspiciously. "Seth, you were nice to her, weren't you?"

He didn't answer her question. "How come you didn't tell her I was substituting for Clarence?"

"I tried to contact her, but her line was busy. Did she complain about the switch?"

"She wasn't exactly thrilled to see me. It was awkward, considering everything that happened that day I nearly choked to death."

"Well, if she hasn't called to cancel she must have been pleased with the way things went last night. Is there anything you need for your assignment today, dear?" she asked sweetly.

"I need a replacement."

His mother clicked her tongue. "Oh Seth, it can't be that bad. I've met the woman. She's lovely."

"She's a client. She only hired someone to make her ex-husband jealous."

"Her personal reasons for using us are really none of our concern," she reminded him in an admonishing tone.

"Well, I don't like being used as bait."

"Bait?" Bernice sighed. "You never used to fuss over your assignments. You just went and did what you were told. I don't know what is happening to you."

Seth didn't know, either. Once he had gotten over the shock of finding out what his mother wanted to do for the rest of her life—and once he'd been convinced that her clients would be respectable—he hadn't minded being a part-time escort. But lately... "Maybe I'm getting too old for this business," he said, rolling his shoulder muscles.

"Old? You're just entering your prime. It's men your age who are in demand."

"I'd rather be out of demand," he said dryly.

"You will be if you talk to your dates the way you talk to your mother," she said tightly.

"I'm sorry, Ma. It's all this sunshine after so much rain. I don't know how to act."

"Well, take a shower and liven up a bit. Otherwise the poor woman's going to wish she'd never seen our door."

"Anything else, Ma?"

"Be nice to her, Seth."

ELLEN STARTED THE DAY with a glass of Alka Seltzer. By the time her sister called, she had added a dose of Pepto Bismol and was digging through her medicine chest for pain relievers.

"Becca says you're not feeling well." Jeannie's voice was filled with concern. "Are you going to be okay?"

"I don't know. I might have to sit in the back of the church," Ellen answered, one hand on her stomach, the other clinging to the receiver.

"Good grief, what's wrong?"

"You mean besides the fact that my head feels like it wants to split open, my stomach is gurgling like a waterfall and my nerves feel like someone sprayed them with starch?"

"Do you want me to bring you something?"

"I've already devoured half the medicine chest."

"Ellen! No wonder you're ill. You need something natural."

Ellen groaned. "Oh, please don't lecture me on the importance of using natural remedies. Not today."

"All right, all right. I didn't call you to sell you on the benefits of natural foods. I've been dying to hear how it went with Clarence last night."

"Oh, don't ask," she said discouragingly.

"Why? Did he come on his motorcycle or something?"

"He didn't come out all."

"But Becca just told me she met him."

"It was another guy. Apparently Clarence had an accident, so they sent someone else in his place," she said, deliberately keeping her voice low.

"What does he look like? Is he even close to a ten?"

"I'm sure you'll think he is."

"But you don't?"

"Look, I'd rather not talk about this right now. I'm already running late and Becca could come waltzing in any moment."

As if on cue, her daughter poked her head around the doorjamb, motioning for her mother to look at the time. Ellen nodded, then said to Jeannie, "Becca's worried that we're getting behind on our schedule. I'll tell you about it after we get to the church."

Jeannie had no choice but to agree. Advising Ellen not to take any more over-the-counter medicines, she promised to bring her cache of natural remedies to the church.

As Ellen forced her limbs out of the bed, she said a little prayer. "Oh, please, God. Let this day go smoothly. And please don't let anyone find out who Seth Holloway really is."

CHAPTER FIVE

"Do you know how lucky you are?" Jeannie asked her sister as they stood on the sidewalk outside the church, watching the bride and groom drive off in the red convertible decorated with shaving cream. "That man is perfect."

"Rebecca's too young to be married," Ellen said with a sniffle.

"I wasn't talking about Roger," Jeannie said. "I was taking about your date. You know, the man who's getting the car for you?"

"Oh, him," Ellen said, looking out toward the parking lot where Seth had gone to retrieve his Explorer.

"You must be one sick lady if you don't think that he's a ten. Good grief, the guy could be in movies."

Ellen didn't disagree. How could she when every time she saw him she felt like a schoolgirl on a blind date with the class heartthrob? "Two's Company wouldn't be in business for long if they sent out men who looked like dirt bags."

"You're probably right. I wonder if it's too late to hire someone for this evening," she mused.

"You want to hire a date?"

"I don't like being a single woman at a party any more than you do."

"Have you forgotten about Mom? You said you would take her in your car."

"She could probably catch a ride with Uncle Albert," Jeannie answered absently, eyeing Seth with interest.

"You're not going to dump Mom on Uncle Albert."

"No, I'm not going to dump Mom on Uncle Albert," she repeated a bit impatiently. "But you can't blame me if I'm a little envious that your dance partner is wearing pants and mine is wearing a dress."

Ellen put a hand on her hip. "In case you've forgotten, I would have been perfectly content to take Mom with me, but you were the one who insisted I have a date."

"And it's a good thing I did. Everyone thinks you've traded in an old broken-down cowboy for a man with brains and brawn. What happened to Kenneth, anyway? He and his rhinestone cowgirl don't make nearly as handsome a couple as you and Seth do."

"Seth and I are not a couple."

"I know, but the nice thing is everyone else thinks you are."

"That's what bothers me. I feel dishonest," Ellen said, her forehead wrinkling.

"You, big sister, need to relax. The ceremony's over. It was beautiful. Everyone's happy. It's time to enjoy yourself with your handsome date."

The Explorer rolled up to the curb and Seth hopped out. He flashed Ellen a warm, dazzling smile that made her already queasy stomach a little more unsettled. "Are you ready to leave?"

"Yes. I just want to check the dressing room to make sure no one left anything," she answered, annoyed that

Jeannie was ogling the man as if he were a hunk of chocolate.

"Jeannie, do you want to come with me?" she asked when her sister was in no hurry to offer her assistance.

"No, you go on. I have to find Mom."

Ellen was reluctant to leave her sister alone with Seth. She told herself it was because she was worried someone would overhear them talking and learn that he was a hired escort. The truth was she had noticed her sister eyeing Seth throughout the ceremony, and her interest in him stirred an unexpected emotion in Ellen—jealousy.

Before she left she pulled Jeannie aside and said in a near whisper, "Be careful what you say. There are still people around who might overhear."

Jeannie gave her a look of exasperation. "Will you relax? I'm not going to spoil it for you."

Ellen wished she could feel as confident about that as Jeannie did. She hurried to the church's dressing room and checked the closets and vanity tops. All she came up with was an empty film canister and some hair spray.

When she got back to the car, Jeannie was gone. Seth was leaning up against the door. He smiled a rather lazy, slanted smile that made Ellen's heart skip a beat. In order to get her heartbeat back to normal she needed to remind herself that he was a pro at such gestures. Despite all the smiles and affectionate glances he tossed in her direction, he didn't want to be with her. She sensed it, and it annoyed her.

When she slid into the leather interior, he asked, "Do we have to go right to the reception?"

Ellen cast him a suspicious glance. "We're supposed to go for cocktails at the Townsends' home until the reception begins."

"Are the bride and groom going to be there?"

"No, they're driving around the city with the rest of the wedding party, letting everyone know they're married," she replied.

"Then is it okay if we pass on the Townsends?"

"I can imagine what Mrs. Townsend would think if I didn't show up."

"Are you sure it's Mrs. Townsend you're concerned about?" He slammed her door and walked around to the driver's side of the car.

"What's that supposed to mean?" she asked him when he had slid behind the steering wheel.

"I'm wondering if you're not worried about what your ex might think."

Ellen shivered uncomfortably. "Just what did my sister tell you?"

"She only confirmed what I had suspected ever since I saw you and the Colorado Kid together last night."

Heat spread slowly through her body at the thought that he knew she had hired him to make Kenneth jealous. What must he be thinking of her? That she was a pathetic ex-wife bent on revenge?

"His name is Kenneth and I would appreciate you keeping your thoughts to yourself," she said stiffly. "Now, are you going to take me to the Townsends?"

"If that's where you want to go, then that's where we'll go," he assured her, although his tone was one of resignation, which only annoyed Ellen.

She had paid for his services and paid well. The least he could do was feign an interest in her.

"If you had wanted a break, you should have ne-
gotiated one," she told him in no uncertain terms.
"I'm sorry if my daughter's wedding isn't as exciting
as most of your assignments."

"I'm not looking for excitement, and I didn't say I
wanted a break." His voice softened. "You look tired
and I thought you might like to go someplace where it's
quiet. You know, unwind for a bit before the excitement resumes."

There was no smile on his face, just a sincere concern in his blue eyes that made Ellen feet a bit foolish.
"I'm sorry. I didn't mean to snap at you. You're right.
I am tired," she said, squeezing her hands together in
her lap. "Being the mother of the bride is more stress-
ful than I realized."

Then to her horror she began to cry. Not misty-eyed
tearing, but body-racking sobs. Without saying a word,
Seth started the engine and pulled the car out onto a
side street while she huddled next to the door.

Where he was taking her, Ellen didn't know, nor did
she care. She was too busy trying to stop the flood of
tears that was threatening to destroy her makeup.

After only a few minutes, he pulled into a small
opening in a copse of trees. Scattered beams of sunlight broke through the heavy foliage and Ellen saw a
small pond surrounded by tall grass. Wildflowers grew
in abundance with only a small path of cultivated lawn
leading to a secluded park bench.

"Where are we?" Ellen asked.

"On the south side of 394. Cedar Lake is only a
couple of blocks away," he told her. He reached over
into the glove compartment and pulled out a package
of sunflower seeds. "You'll like it here. It's a good
place to come when you feel like life is crowding you."

When he came around to her side of the car, Ellen hesitated only a moment before placing her hand in his. Her heels sank into the lush green grass as he led her over to the park bench beside the pond.

"It's hard to believe this is in the middle of the city," she remarked, appreciating the tranquillity of the setting.

"Not many people know it's back here." He brushed off the seat of the park bench with his hand before she sat down. "Occasionally you'll find a few nature lovers tossing bread crumbs to the ducks or watching the birds, but most of the times I've been here it's been quiet."

"I'm surprised no one's discovered it."

"It's not easy to find. I call it Lost Lake. I only stumbled upon it because I was trying to find Cedar Lake so my kids could go swimming."

"How many children do you have?" she asked, then immediately retracted the question. "Oh, I'm sorry. That was personal. You don't have to answer."

Normally he would have let it go, but he found he wanted to talk to her about his family and to find out more about hers. "I have three teenagers."

"You do? I would have never guessed," she said, slowly shaking her head.

"No?"

She shook her head.

Seth suspected that what she was really thinking was that she hadn't expected to find a father of three working for an escort service. Her attitude didn't surprise him. Most women hiring an escort didn't want him to be Father Goose. Consequently, he had developed his own code of conduct, which included never revealing much of his private life when he was working.

"You've met Kelly and then there's Matt, who's seventeen, and Brian is fourteen," he told her, his eyes on the pond.

"Is Kelly still living at home?"

"For the time being," he said uneasily. "She wants to move into an apartment or a house near the campus, but I'm not so sure it's such a good idea."

"Is that what you were arguing about at Two's Company that day I walked in?"

"Yes." He studied her face for a moment, then said, "You were quick to come to the defense of someone you didn't even know."

"I couldn't stand by and watch anyone get hurt and not do something," she told him. "Although now as I think back I realize I probably overreacted because I was expecting the worst at an escort service."

"You thought I was some old lecherous guy looking to make time with a sweet young thing, eh?" His lips curved in a knowing smile.

"My mistake," she said apologetically.

"I'd rather have someone making such a mistake when my daughter's welfare is concerned," he told her.

They sat in silence for several minutes, with the only sounds coming from the flock of ducks that were splashing about on the glasslike surface of the water. Finally, Ellen said, "This is nice."

"Are you feeling better?"

"Yes, thank you. I'm sorry about breaking down like that in the car."

"There's no need to apologize," Seth reassured her. "Watching your only daughter get married must be an emotional experience."

She nodded. "It is. The only reason I was able to keep from crying during the ceremony was that I knew the wedding was being videotaped. The last thing Rebecca and Roger needed was to have my sobbing drown out their vows." She smiled weakly.

Seth reached into his suit coat for a package of sunflower seeds. He ripped open the package with his teeth, then began tossing the seeds to the ducks. The way the birds scrambled for the bits of food brought a smile to Ellen's face, and he gestured for her to join him.

As she reached for a handful of seeds he said, "Make sure you toss them far enough away. If they discover we're sitting with a whole bag of them between us they'll be in our laps," he warned.

They sat side by side, quietly tossing sunflower seeds to the ducks. Seth could see by the way her shoulders had relaxed that she was no longer as tense as she had been at the church.

"Now isn't this better than standing around listening to Dolores Townsend explain the way things ought to be?" he asked, noticing how smooth her skin was in the sunlight.

"Uh-huh, but I can't help but feel a little guilty. I should be there."

"From what I saw of Dolores last night, I'd say she will manage just fine without you," he observed wryly.

"You're probably right, but I should still be there."

"Do you want to go?"

"It isn't a question of what I want."

"Ah," he drawled in understanding. "You feel it's your duty."

"I am the mother of the bride," she reminded him.

"No one would have guessed. You look more like her sister." As soon as Seth had uttered the words, he wished he could take them back. She was looking at him as if he had just used the oldest line in the book. The women he dated usually accepted compliments graciously, but not Ellen.

"I wasn't paid to say that," he told her, annoyed by the look of suspicion on her face. "You really do look too young to have a married daughter."

"That's because my daughter is younger than most brides. She's only nineteen," she answered with a sigh.

Which meant Ellen could be anywhere from her midthirties to midfifties, Seth thought. Of course he had read her file and knew that she was thirty-nine. The same age Laura had been when she died.

"You're really troubled by this marriage, aren't you?"

"Would you want Kelly getting married next year?"

"Good heavens, no," he was quick to reply. "She's still a kid."

"That's the way I see Rebecca, too. I'm not sure she's ready to tackle the problems that come with marriage."

"What makes you think there will be problems?"

"Every marriage has problems," she stated firmly. When he didn't comment on her statement, she shot a sideways glance at him and added, "Maybe I'm just being cynical because my own marriage failed."

He wanted to ask her why she and the Colorado Kid had divorced, but from the sad look in her eyes he had a feeling he wouldn't like what he heard. He hadn't been at all impressed with Kenneth Richards, and it bothered him to think that Ellen was still hung up on the man.

"Part of being a parent is not wanting our kids to make the same mistakes we did," Seth said soothingly. "It seems to me you just want what is best for your daughter."

She shrugged, obviously not convinced. "I don't know. Sometimes I wonder if I'm simply not being selfish. Maybe I just don't want to be alone." As if suddenly realizing what she had said, she looked away in embarrassment. "I'm sorry. I don't know why I'm telling you this."

The sun had shifted so that now there was a single shaft beaming down between them. It highlighted her hair so that it looked more blond than brown. Wearing a pink chiffon dress, she looked almost ethereal as she sat statue straight in the sunshine.

Seth wanted to reach out and touch her. Instead, he leaned toward her, sliding his arm up behind her on the back of the bench and softly called to her. "Ellen?"

When she turned to look at him, he had the sudden urge to kiss her. The thought startled him: never as an escort for Two's Company had he initiated any physical contact with his date. He hadn't wanted to, until now.

But Ellen looked so vulnerable and so fragile that all he could think about was wrapping his arms around her and kissing her until there was no sadness in her eyes. Before he had the chance, however, she jumped to her feet.

"We'd better go. The reception will be starting soon."

Seth watched her scurry toward the car, a bit stunned by the feelings of desire she had aroused in him. Why had he felt that sudden burst of longing? Even if Ellen weren't a client, she wasn't his type, yet his body had reacted as if she were. Telling himself he had responded to her vulnerability, not her sexiness, he shoved the sunflower seeds back into his pocket and headed for the car.

When he opened his door, she was powdering her cheeks. Before he started the engine, he turned to her and said, "I only brought you here because I thought you could use a little peace and quiet."

"So you said" was her ambiguous reply.

Again there was that suspicious look in her eyes. Did she think he didn't have an honest thought? Seth backed the car out of the narrow parking lot, wondering why he should care what she thought. She was just another assignment, and after today he would never see her again. Somehow, the thought didn't give him any pleasure.

ELLEN WAS BOTH relieved and dismayed that she had missed cocktails at the Townsends'. Even though her sojourn at the park had been a much-needed and welcome interlude, her social conscience would not allow her to totally dismiss her guilt, no matter how bossy and unreasonable Mrs. Townsend could be.

To her surprise, the older woman accepted Seth's apology with a gracious smile. Actually, it shouldn't have come as a surprise at all to Ellen. The more she saw of Seth's charm, the more she understood why he was a professional escort. The man had a grin that could make a nun bat her eyes provocatively.

As the evening progressed, Ellen forgot that he was a hired escort. The more they talked, the more she discovered how many interests they had in common. Throughout the evening he was attentive to her every need, and when it was obvious that everyone had accepted him as her date, she was finally able to relax and enjoy herself. That was until a petite redhead in a tight black dress with cutout shoulders appeared on the scene.

"Oh, my goodness! If it isn't Seth Holloway!" she exclaimed in a voice Ellen thought had come out of a megaphone. "What are you doing at Roger's wedding?"

"Liza? I don't believe this!" Seth's grin and welcoming hug triggered a warning bell in Ellen's brain.

When he said, "I didn't think I'd ever see you again," the warning bell became a full-scale alarm. Could this shapely predator have first-hand experience of Seth's escort services? The hair on the back of Ellen's neck stood on end.

"Good gracious! You look positively gorgeous!" the redhead gushed, a hand on Seth's arm as she eyed him appreciatively. Whether or not she was a previous client, one thing was certain: she was eager to renew their acquaintance. Like Jeannie, Liza was ogling Seth with obvious interest. For the second time that day, Ellen was convinced that if he had been a piece of fudge, he would have been devoured.

As if suddenly remembering that Ellen was at his side, Seth gave her arm a reassuring squeeze and said, "Ellen, this is Liza Carson. She's a reporter who's been in the Middle East for the past year. Liza, Ellen Richards, Rebecca's mother."

With stilted motions, Ellen shook the warm hand the woman offered. Despite the smile on her face, Ellen knew that Liza was sizing her up. The question was, would she guess that Ellen had paid for Seth's company?

To her credit, Liza behaved in a very cordial manner, commenting on how lovely Rebecca was and how lucky her second cousin Roger was to have her for his bride. If it came as a disappointment that Seth was there with Ellen, she hid it well.

"This is such a coincidence. Do you know I almost didn't come tonight?" she said to Seth, then turned to Ellen to say in an aside, "I hate being an unattached woman at these things."

Ellen's uneasiness grew. Convinced now that Liza was a previous client of Two's Company, she stood mutely by while the reporter brought Seth up-to-date on her recent assignments. To Ellen's dismay, Seth listened with the same attentiveness he had shown her. Ellen, on the other hand, didn't hear a word the woman was saying. She was too preoccupied with concocting explanations as to why she had to hire a man to be her date for the wedding. For she was certain that Liza was going to tell someone that Seth was nothing but her paid escort.

Ellen had no choice but to make an abrupt exit. With a hasty "If you'll excuse me," she tossed etiquette to the wind and headed for the women's lounge. Before she could reach it, however, she felt a hand on her shoulder.

"What's wrong?" Seth demanded as she turned around.

"Nothing's wrong," she lied. She would have moved, but he was holding on to her arm.

"Liza thought you looked a little pale."

"Maybe that's because I haven't been riding camels in the desert," she answered sarcastically.

"Did Liza say something to upset you?" he asked, a totally bemused look on his face—as if the vampy-looking Liza could never upset anyone.

"Who is she?"

"I told you. She's a reporter. Why?"

"Did you used to date her?"

"We've gone out a couple of times." He looked at her curiously. "Is that what's bothering you?"

"Of course it's bothering me. The last thing I need is for one of your previous clients to be here," she whispered impatiently, looking around nervously to make sure no one could hear their conversation.

"She's never been a client," he told her. "I make it a policy to never date the women I meet through Two's Company."

"Oh" was all she could think of to say. If Liza hadn't hired him as an escort, she had to be an old girlfriend. The thought brought little comfort to Ellen.

"I don't just date women for money," he said smoothly, and she felt a flush spread over her. "I do have a personal life."

"Does Liza know what you do for a living?"

"You mean, does she know I work for an escort service?" he asked.

Ellen nodded.

"Probably not, since I've only been doing this for about six months and only on a part-time basis. But even if she is aware of it, I doubt she'd say anything. What would be the point?"

Ellen wanted to tell him that women like Liza Carson would do just about anything if it meant catching their prey. She had looked at Seth as though he were wearing a sign that said Hunting Season Open, and

Ellen had a feeling that the game she was after was her date.

"Look, if you're uneasy about it, I'll talk to Liza myself and make sure she doesn't spread the information around," Seth offered. "But I really don't think you have anything to worry about."

Ellen accepted his assurance, but she still wished that Liza Carson would disappear from the party. There was little chance of that happening she realized a short time later when the band began to play and the dancing started. Despite being a woman without a date, Liza didn't lack dance partners.

During the bridal party dances, Seth was the perfect escort. He waltzed Ellen around the floor in a most gentlemanly manner. He gallantly danced with the bride while Ellen danced with her new son-in-law, and he even suffered a fox-trot with Mrs. Townsend while she partnered Mr. Townsend.

It wasn't long, however, before the traditional music was abandoned for pop. Several fast rock numbers were followed by a series of slow tunes. One was a love song, a sensuous ballad that Ellen remembered from the '70s. It was a song that had special meaning to her; it had been a favorite of Kenneth's, and despite his aversion to dancing, it was the only song that could get him out onto the floor.

Automatically, Ellen's eyes surveyed the ballroom in search of him. When she found him he was staring at her. It was only a matter of seconds before he was on his feet and coming toward her.

"Would you like to dance, Elle?" He stood before her dressed in another Western-style suit, this one brown.

Before Ellen could answer, Seth reached for her hand and guided her to her feet. "I'm afraid you're too late. The lady's already promised this one to me." He nodded at Kenneth, then ushered Ellen out onto the floor.

"Why did you do that?" she asked when they were facing each other.

"You hired me to make him jealous, and judging by the look on his face, I'd say he'd like to stomp his snakeskin boots all over my body," Seth told her as he pulled her into his arms.

Ellen didn't know whether she should feel annoyed or relieved. "This song is special."

"For him or for you?"

"For both of us."

"Then he's really going to be green by the time we're finished." Instead of dancing in the conventional manner, Seth lifted her arms to his shoulders and gathered her in at the waist so that there was no space between their bodies.

Ellen had always loved to dance, and as the evocative voice of the female singer filled the ballroom, she felt as though she were fifteen again and dancing in the high school gym. Only this time her partner wasn't stumbling awkwardly through the number but moving with a fluidity and form that complemented hers.

Dancing had always been a particularly loved form of celebration for her, and tonight she felt especially uninhibited in her movements. As the band updated the old song with a Latin beat, Seth's hip motions made the dance an intimate ritual for two. No longer were they two strangers acting out a part, but mates sharing a silent exploration of each other's bodies through the rhythm of the music.

Time slipped away, as did more of Ellen's inhibitions. Shamelessly, she pressed her body closer to Seth's, reveling in the knowledge that she had a partner who was as attuned to her movements as she was to his. It was only when the music came to an end and she realized that her lips were only seconds away from touching his that the erotic undercurrents of their dance caused her to blush.

At that moment, as she stared into Seth's eyes, she knew instinctively that lovemaking with him would be wonderful. She had an idea that he knew it, too; he had the same look in his eye she had seen earlier when he had almost kissed her on the park bench.

When she would have pulled her hands down from his shoulders, he held her tightly. "Want to stay here and wait for the next one?" he asked in a throaty whisper.

She would have said yes had it not been for Rebecca's appearance.

"Mom, I need to talk to you for a minute," she said anxiously.

Reluctantly, Seth released Ellen. There was a promise in his eyes that told her he'd be willing to resume where they had left off as soon as she returned.

"What is it?" Ellen asked her daughter as they walked toward the exit.

"Dad wants the band to play country music."

From the pained expression on Rebecca's face, Ellen deduced that the idea was appalling to her daughter. "Are they going to?"

"No, they're not going to!" she retorted irritably. "Mom, they're an orchestra, not a country band."

"Did you tell your father that?"

"Yes, but he didn't care. This is so embarrassing!" she exclaimed in an exaggerated drawl.

Ellen was about to ask what would be all that embarrassing about playing a couple of songs in honor of her father when Rebecca said, "You know he's only doing this because of Tina. She's the one who wants to line dance."

Any sympathy Ellen had for Kenneth evaporated into thin air. "Line dancing?" she repeated with her own frown of distaste.

"Mom, none of my friends are into that. What am I going to do? I mean, I feel sorry for Tina. She's hardly danced all night, but..." She trailed off with a frown on her face.

Ellen glanced over to where Tina sat beside Kenneth. She looked bored stiff. Ellen wanted to gloat about that, but strangely she found herself feeling sorry for the younger woman. As hard as she had tried to dislike her replacement, the truth was she had found her to be quite sweet. Having lived with Kenneth for seventeen years, Ellen knew that Tina had no bed of roses, either.

"There must be a simple solution," Ellen said thoughtfully.

"Maybe you could get Seth to ask Tina to dance a couple of times," Rebecca suggested, her eyes brightening at the thought. "Then she wouldn't be so determined to line dance."

Ellen didn't like that idea at all. "I can't tell Seth who he should dance with," she answered, not feeling one bit of guilt at the fib.

"Oh, no! He's going up to the stage!" Rebecca whimpered as she caught sight of her father crossing the dance floor. "Mother, what am I going to do?"

"I think you're worrying over the trivial, darling. Leave it up to the musicians to decide what to do," she said gently. "You might be surprised at how many of your guests are country fans."

Ellen thought it was rather ironic that for the second time in two days she was defending her ex-husband's actions. Maybe time had finally mellowed her emotions.

It wasn't long before she realized just how wrong she was. Kenneth cornered her and said, "Elle, I don't know how to tell you this, but I forgot my checkbook back at the hotel. Could you pay the caterers with your credit card and I'll bring you a check over tomorrow?"

CHAPTER SIX

ELLEN DIDN'T BELIEVE she'd ever see the money again. She had been stiffed by her ex-husband and there wasn't a thing she could do about it. Everything had changed between them, yet nothing had changed. Once more she was going to have to borrow a pile of money to pay for his extravagance.

As the last of the wedding guests drifted out of the ballroom, Ellen felt more alone than she ever had in her entire life. The time had come for Rebecca to assume her role as a wife; after her honeymoon she would be setting up her own house instead of returning to hers. For weeks Ellen had been mentally preparing herself for this moment, yet nothing could prepare her for the emptiness gnawing inside.

She tried to smile as guests said good-night, but eventually her melancholy caught up with her. When Seth approached her and said, "It's getting pretty late," she nearly lost what little control she still possessed.

"So what does that mean? You need more money to stay longer?" she snapped at him.

"No, I only meant it's late and you should go home. You look exhausted."

The compassion in his eyes did little to comfort her. "Thank you for your concern, but I don't need it," she said stiffly.

He looked around the deserted ballroom. "You have another way of getting home that I don't know about?"

"I'll get a cab, thank you."

"Are you sure you can afford one?"

Ellen spun around to face him, her face ashen. "Were you eavesdropping on my conversations?"

Seth rubbed a hand across the back of his neck. "You've paid me to be at your side all evening. You can't expect me not to hear what's going on."

"Well, your obligations are finished as of this moment," she informed him coolly.

"Ellen, wait." He followed her as she hurried toward the front door. "I want to take you home."

"I told you, it's not necessary." They had reached the main entrance where a bellman hovered discreetly.

When Ellen asked for a cab, Seth told the uniformed man it wasn't necessary and pulled her by the arm toward the parking ramp. Too tired to argue, Ellen gave in.

The ride home was accomplished in silence. As soon as the Explorer pulled into the semicircular driveway in front of her home, Ellen hopped out of the car. If she thought she could easily dismiss Seth, she was mistaken. He followed her onto the front porch where she fumbled with her keys.

He took them from her and opened the door for her. When she tried to slip inside without inviting him in, he placed a hand on the door to prevent her from closing it.

"I hope you found Two's Company's services satisfactory," he said with a practiced smile.

"If you're worried I'm going to call up Bernice and report you for being unprofessional, you can relax."

"Unprofessional? Just what was it about this evening you found out of place?" His blue eyes searched her face for an answer.

"You tried to kiss me, for one thing," she said primly.

"You're wrong about that. If I had tried, I would have been successful."

The look in his eyes sent delicious shivers up and down Ellen's body. She decided it was best if she looked at the door while she talked to him. "Consider your duties completed. Everything was fine. You fulfilled your end of the bargain." Again she tried to dismiss him, but he was not about to be sent home.

"Then why do you look so unhappy? I would think you'd be delighted. The Colorado Kid couldn't take his eyes off you tonight."

Annoyed, she blurted out, "Would you please not call him the Colorado Kid?"

"Why are you so defensive about this guy?"

"I'm not."

"Yes, you are."

A large insect flew under the light. "You shouldn't hold the door open. You're going to have all sorts of bugs flying around inside." He stepped around the door and into the foyer, allowing the screen door to swing shut.

"It's late, I'm tired and all I really want to do is go to bed," she said wearily.

"I'll leave in just a minute. But first I have something to give you." He reached into his suit coat and pulled out a small stack of napkins.

Ellen glanced at them curiously as he handed them to her. On the top napkin was a cartoon drawing of a bride. She thumbed through the others and saw that each one was different. With only a few pencil strokes, Seth had captured the personalities of everyone in the wedding party.

"You drew these?"

He grinned a bit sheepishly. "I draw a bit."

Before she could say anything else, he leaned toward her and brushed her lips with his. There was no force, no aggression, just a gentle, tantalizing pressure that produced a flow of warmth over Ellen's body.

Without even being aware of it, she softened against him, seeking more contact. She savored the sweet sensation the brief intimacy created and felt a bit bereft when it ended.

"Good night, Ellen," was all Seth said before slipping out the door.

"I was told Two's Company escorts didn't kiss their dates," she called out to his retreating figure.

He paused on the step. "They don't. I was off duty. Anyway, I didn't kiss you because I was your escort. I kissed you because I like you, Ellen."

She didn't know what to say. Her heart was beating in her throat, her skin tingling as if she were fifteen and had just been kissed for the first time.

"My phone number's on the back of one of those," he told her, pointing at the stack of cartoons. "If your ex sticks around and you need me to put in another appearance, give me a call. I'd be delighted to do it . . . free of charge." And with a wave he was gone.

Long after he was gone Ellen sat looking at the cartoons. When she went to bed that night, she lined them up on her dresser. She thought about the man who had drawn the caricatures. He had said he liked her. The question was, did she dare believe him? After all, the man was a professional charmer.

Not that it mattered, she decided only moments before she fell asleep. She would never see him again. She couldn't afford to. She'd have to settle for the likes of Ned Pickett and leave the Seth Holloways to the Liza Carsons of this world.

WHEN A DOZEN long-stemmed white roses arrived from Seth the following afternoon, Ellen did what any woman would have done. She sniffed them appreciatively, put them on the credenza in the foyer where she'd see them often, then rushed upstairs to call the man who had sent them.

As she dialed, the words on the enclosure card echoed in her mind. "I hope you enjoyed last night as much as I did."

A warmth spread through her as she remembered the way their date had ended. Could it be that he had been sincere when he had said he'd kissed her because he liked her?

Her optimism turned to pessimism when a teenage boy answered the Holloway phone and informed her that Seth wasn't home.

Ellen was about to leave a message when the boy asked, "Is this Rita?"

"Uh, no, it isn't," she stammered, then abruptly ended the phone call.

How could she have been so foolish? He was an escort for hire, not a man who was interested in her as a woman. He probably went through women the way she went through panty hose.

She wouldn't think about their interlude at Lost Lake or the way their bodies had responded to each other's while they had danced or the way her mouth had felt beneath his lips. She was a client, nothing more, nothing less. Relief spread through her as she realized that she was lucky she hadn't reached Seth. Otherwise she might have embarrassed herself by misreading the meaning of the flowers.

Like Ellen, Seth, too, was having a hard time remembering that they had been together for professional reasons and nothing more. Not once in the six months he had been working at Two's Company had he wanted to pursue a relationship with a woman he'd met through the escort service. Not until he'd met Ellen, that is.

It was a rather unsettling feeling. One of the reasons he had agreed to work for his mother at Two's Company was to have a social life without any of the complications that normally went with dating. As a paid escort he could go out with women who were eager to share his company yet weren't looking at him as a prospective husband.

Ever since Laura's death he had been lonely, yet the thought of developing an intimate relationship with another woman held no appeal for him. It still didn't, he told himself. The only reason he had sent Ellen the roses was because he felt guilty about her paying for his services when she had been instrumental in saving his life.

And that was why when Matt informed him that a woman had called while he had been out for his morning run, he hoped that it was Ellen calling to tell him that she needed his services again. After a quick shower, he pulled on a pair of khaki slacks and a navy blue polo shirt, then went to see her.

Any doubts he had about the wisdom of his decision were put to rest when he climbed into the Explorer and found a wilting corsage. He recognized it as

Ellen's and smiled to himself. He now had a valid excuse to see her again.

As he drove to her house he gave little thought to the fact that she might not be at home or that she might not be alone. When he knocked on her door and she answered, he felt his heart skip a beat.

"I wasn't expecting you," she said, stepping aside so that he could enter the house.

"You left this in my car," he told her, holding up the wilting orchid.

"Oh! You could have tossed it in the trash."

Did that mean she wished he hadn't come to see her? "I thought it might have sentimental value." Again, he was reminded of how different she was from his wife. Laura had pressed every flower she had ever received and saved them in an album.

Ellen shrugged as she took it from him. "I suppose I could put it in the refrigerator. It's what Rebecca would do if she were here."

Seth noticed the roses and said, "I see the flowers arrived."

Ellen glanced at them. "Yes. They were a nice touch. Two's Company thinks of everything, doesn't it?"

Seth felt a ripple of annoyance. He had called all over town to find someone who would deliver the flowers on a Sunday, only to have her assume the service had sent them. He thought about correcting her but changed his mind.

"Does this mean you were satisfied with the service you received?"

"Most of it," she answered cryptically. There were several moments of awkward silence before she asked, "Would you like something cold to drink?"

"Only if you're going to have something," he answered politely.

She indicated he should sit down, then disappeared into the kitchen. The sound of a blender whirring made him wonder just what she was concocting. While she was out of the room, Seth took the opportunity to examine the photos lining the fireplace mantel.

Nearly all of them were of Rebecca at various stages of her life. To Seth's delight, none of the family photos included Kenneth. The photo that caught his eye was of four women: Rebecca, her grandmother, her aunt Jeannie and Ellen. The resemblance among them was strong, but Seth thought Ellen was the most interesting. She wasn't exactly beautiful, but there was a quality about her that set her apart from most women.

"Where's Ellen?"

Startled, Seth turned to find Kenneth glaring at him from the doorway. He hadn't liked the man the minute he had set eyes on him and had found it a challenge to be cordial, especially knowing that Ellen had been married to him. And the thought that she still had feelings for him stirred all sorts of conflicting emotions in him.

He knew he should have been polite, but the wedding was over and his services completed. He didn't want to pretend anything.

"Do you always enter someone's home without knocking?" Seth asked, returning the hostile glare.

"I paid for this house, in case you've forgotten," Kenneth reminded him in a tone that was clearly intended to stake a claim to more than the house.

"That may be, but since you no longer live here it would probably be a good idea to knock before you enter." Seth took the liberty of sitting down on the sofa and throwing his arm across the back, as if he belonged there. "You might find you're interrupting something and feel a little awkward."

"Just what are you doing here and where's Ellen?" Kenneth demanded irritably.

"It doesn't take a rocket scientist to figure out that I'm here for the same reason you are. I want to be with Ellen."

Seth thought it was fortunate that she chose that moment to return, for Kenneth looked as if he were going to pop a snap on his Western-style shirt.

Ellen carried a silver tray that bore two glasses with creamy orange liquid in them. Her face paled when she saw Kenneth, and Seth had the urge to boot his cowboy butt right out the door.

"I didn't realize you were here." She carefully set the tray down on the coffee table.

"He didn't knock," Seth pointed out with a smugness that had Kenneth's lips tightening.

He moved closer to Ellen. "I need to speak with you, Elle. Alone."

Ellen's glance slid between the two men. "I have company."

Seth could see that she was extremely uncomfortable. But whether it was because he was there and she wanted to be alone with Kenneth or because Kenneth was there and she didn't want to talk to him, he had no way of knowing.

Since it was obvious Kenneth wasn't going to leave, Seth did the only thing he could do. "Would you like me to come back later?" he asked, wishing that she would tell him to stay and Kenneth to go.

She didn't. "Would you mind?" She looked at Seth beseechingly.

"No problem," he answered, wishing he could wipe the gleam of satisfaction from Kenneth's face.

Since he couldn't, he did the next best thing. He grabbed Ellen by the shoulders and kissed her long and hard on the mouth. Although it had been motivated by Kenneth's smug attitude, the kiss soon took on a meaning of its own.

Ellen's lips were warm and moist beneath his, and the flowery smell of her filled his head, making him want to move his mouth against hers slowly and deliberately. She must have sampled the creamy concoction in the glasses, for she tasted of oranges. When her lips parted, he took advantage of the softening of her mouth to deepen the kiss.

Ripples of unexpected longing surged through him, generating an ache in parts he had been trying to ignore for the past two years. When he would have eased the pressure of his mouth on hers, her tongue slipped between his lips, demanding a response.

Just as they had when they'd been dancing, their bodies once again promised a second-to-none intimate encounter. When she murmured a soft moan of pleasure, he pulled her even closer, a magical feeling swirling inside him.

It was only when Kenneth cleared his throat that each of them remembered what was happening. Ellen's cheeks were flushed, her lips swollen as Seth lifted his mouth from hers.

"I'll call you later," he murmured, wondering just what it was that had happened between them. As he walked out of the house, he knew there was no way he would not phone her, Kenneth or no Kenneth.

Ellen was just as shaken from the kiss as Seth was. Feeling unsteady, she sank down onto the nearest chair and reached for one of the glasses.

"How long have you known that guy?" Kenneth asked.

She took a sip of the frothy orange juice, hoping to regain some of her composure. "Why do you want to know?"

"Because there's something phony about him."

Ellen nearly choked. "There's nothing phony about Seth," she insisted, wondering if there was any way Kenneth could have found out that Seth was an escort for hire.

"Of course you wouldn't think so. Every time he's around you he smiles and says all the right things." His tone was that of a petulant child. "But I'm telling you, Elle, I've talked to him man to man, and he's not what you think he is."

"Believe me, I know exactly who he is," she answered neatly. "Besides, it's really none of your concern. My friends are none of your business."

"They are if they're a bad influence on my little girl," he reminded her.

"Becca's not a little girl! She was just married, for heaven's sake."

"That doesn't mean you should behave recklessly in front of her," he chastised her.

Ellen could feel her blood pressure rise. "Recklessly?"

"Everyone in that ballroom saw the way the two of you were rubbing up against each other like a couple of teenagers."

Ellen couldn't stop the blush. Not because she was embarrassed by what he said but because she remembered exactly what effect Seth Holloway had on her.

"We were only dancing," she told him, knowing perfectly well that more than dancing had transpired between them.

"I suppose he sent you the roses." He nodded toward the crystal vase on the table.

"Does it matter?"

From where they sat she knew he could read the florist's card lying on the table. Judging by the way he was raking a hand through his thinning hair, she figured he assumed that Seth had stayed the night with her.

"I just hope you know what you're doing," he told her.

"If the only reason you came over here was to warn me about Seth Holloway, you shouldn't have gone to the trouble."

He surprised her by saying "That's not the reason why I'm here." He reached into his pocket and pulled out his wallet. "I came to settle the matter of the reception expenses."

Ellen could hardly believe her eyes. Was he going to actually pay her?

"I settled the hotel account this morning, so I was able to get back the original invoice you signed." He passed her a slip of paper.

"There should be nothing charged to you," he explained as Ellen stared at the credit-card slip. "I thought it would be easier if I simply asked for the original invoice and returned it to you. I also had an extra copy of my receipt made so that you would have proof that the bill's been paid in full just in case there are any computer glitches and you end up getting billed for any of the expenses.''

Ellen found herself at a loss for words. The last thing she had expected was that he would actually keep his promise to pay for the wedding reception. Could it be that Rebecca was right? That Kenneth was a success in his new business venture? That he really had changed?

Suddenly a great weight was lifted from her chest. She wouldn't have to borrow any money from the loan company. Nor would she have to get a second job to pay it back.

"I told Rebecca that if there were any other outstanding expenses she wanted me to take care of, she should let me know," he continued, tucking his wallet back into his hip pocket.

Ellen could tell by the way he was eyeing her that he was waiting for her to comment on his generosity. When she didn't, he said, "I'm thinking about giving the kids a down payment on a house."

With a supreme effort, Ellen hid her amazement. She slowly sipped the orange juice, then said, "I'm not sure a house is in their plans at the moment."

"Probably not if they don't have the money. That's why I want to give it to them."

"Money isn't the only consideration. They're two college students. They don't have time for a house."

"What are you trying to say, Elle? That I shouldn't help them out?"

She shrugged. "It's your money. You can do what you want with it."

"That's right, and like I always said, what good is money if you can't spend it?" he asked with a challenging stare.

It was a familiar question Ellen had heard often during the seventeen years they had been married. Kenneth had never had any trouble spending money. His trouble had come in earning it, although judging by his manner he no longer had a problem with that, either.

"You're a big-time businessman with money to burn. Do what you want with it," she said testily, then immediately regretted the comment. What she didn't want to do was allow him to provoke her into an argument. "Maybe you should go. You came here to settle the wedding expenses and they're settled."

But it was obvious that a fight was the last thing Kenneth wanted. "I don't want to go, Elle."

She looked at him and saw something in his eyes she hadn't seen in years. Desire. For months and months after he had left she had fantasized that he would return and look at her in such a way. Now he was here and he was looking at her as if she was the most desirable woman on the face of the earth. Contrary to what she had expected, it didn't please her.

"I need to know if you're happy. I mean, really happy."

Ellen shifted uncomfortably. "What makes you think I'm not?"

He shrugged. "I guess it was just wishful thinking on my part. I was hoping you felt the same way I do."

Her heart began to beat in double time. "I don't know what you're talking about."

"Don't you?" A tiny smile touched his lips.

"No."

"There's always been that special feeling between us. Can you honestly tell me that when you saw me for the first time Friday you weren't overwhelmed with memories of the good times we shared?''

Ellen's discomfort level shot up. She tried to dismiss his comments with a gentle toss of her head. "You're talking about nostalgia. Everyone feels that way at weddings.''

"It wasn't nostalgia, Elle. When I saw you come out of this house I knew I had made a mistake leaving you when I did.''

There was a deafening silence and Ellen thought even he must have heard her heart beating in her chest. She moistened her lips with her tongue, then said, "How can you say that? You're married to another woman.''

"I shouldn't be.''

Ellen could only stare at him in stunned silence.

"She's too young for me, Elle. And I don't love her the way that I loved you.''

Ellen felt sick to her stomach. How could he say such things? She wanted to scream at him, You didn't think she was too young for you three years ago! But the shock of hearing him now say what she had once so desperately prayed to hear robbed her of any words at all.

"She's so busy doing her nails and coloring her hair she forgets to do the laundry and grocery shopping. And she's been talking about having a baby. I don't want another kid at my age.''

Finally, Ellen found her voice. "You shouldn't be telling me this.'' She bumped the coffee table as she stood, nearly spilling the orange juice.

"I had to tell you. For the past forty-eight hours I haven't been able to stop thinking about the way things might have been if I had never met Tina.''

Ellen had started toward the door but stopped to face him. "If you hadn't met Tina there would have been some other woman." As painful as it still was to admit, she had to say, "You didn't want to be married to me."

His recollection of the past differed from hers. "That's not true. I loved you. It's just that I was in a midlife crisis."

"So what are you trying to tell me? That your crisis has passed?" She faced him with hands on her hips.

"Three years ago I got a little crazy. Now I can see that it was just a period of restlessness in my life." He reached for her, but she flinched.

"I think you'd better go," she said quietly, hugging herself tightly.

"There was a time when you would have begged me not to leave."

Ellen could feel emotion choking her. How many nights had she dreamed of this very moment? Now it was happening and all she could wish was that he would leave her alone.

"Those times are gone," she said solemnly, then opened the door for him. "I want you to leave."

"I know I've hurt you, Elle, and I'm sorry. A lot has happened to me since we split up. I've changed. I'm not the man I used to be." He reached into his pocket and pulled out a business card. He grabbed one of her hands and placed the card on her palm. "If you ever need anything, give me a call."

"Please go," she whispered, unable to say just what was really on her mind.

He hesitated, standing only inches from her. Finally, he stepped through the doorway. "We were good together, Elle. Rebecca is proof of that."

Ellen trembled as she closed the door behind him. She pressed a hand to her stomach and she leaned back against the wooden door.

Her plan had worked. The visits to the gym, the blond highlights in her hair, the hired escort. Her and Jeannie's carefully plotted scheme had gotten results, only Ellen was feeling no satisfaction in triumph. If anything, she was feeling miserable. Contrary to what she had been thinking, she didn't want Kenneth. No way, no how.

If she had been suffering a divorce hangover for the past three years, she had finally found the cure. Kenneth's visit had been like a dose of raw egg in tomato juice, cleansing her system of all the toxins that had been there ever since he had left her.

Three years or maybe even six months ago she might have been ecstatic with his declaration of love. She might have welcomed him back with open arms. But not now.

On wobbly legs, she climbed the stairs to her room and plopped herself down on the pale pink comforter. She closed her eyes and tried to sleep, but images of the past weekend spun a dizzying collage across her mind.

Eventually, she must have fallen asleep, for she awoke to the sound of the phone ringing beside her bed. It was Seth.

"Is everything okay?" he asked.

"Why are you calling?" she asked groggily.

"I said I would."

"I thought you only said that for Kenneth's benefit."

"Is he still there?"

"No. He's gone."

"Oh." He paused, then said, "Is there anything I can do?"

"That won't be necessary. I believe he's going back to Colorado this evening."

"I see."

"Thank you for the offer, though."

"You're welcome. Ellen . . ."

"Yes?"

"I really did enjoy last night."

She wondered if maybe he wasn't hinting that he'd be interested in dating her again if she wanted to use Two's Company's services another time. First the roses, then the follow-up visit, and now the phone call. But what about the kiss? She flushed warm at the thought.

"You did a good job," she said evenly, believing his attention was all flattery.

There was an awkward silence, then Seth finally said, "Well, I just wanted to call and see if you needed me to come over and rescue you from the Colorado Kid."

"No, that won't be necessary. Your job has been completed." And as she hung up the phone, she couldn't help but feel regret that it was true.

CHAPTER SEVEN

ELLEN PUT THREE of the long-stemmed white roses in a skinny vase and took them with her to work on Monday morning. When her co-workers automatically assumed they were flowers left over from the wedding celebration, she didn't bother to tell them anything different.

As it was most Mondays, the clinic was busy, much to Ellen's relief. It meant there was little opportunity to dwell on what had happened during the weekend.

When she went home that evening, she was exhausted and grateful for the demands of her job. As she sorted through her mail, she noticed an envelope without a stamp or a postmark. Curious, she opened it before the others.

Inside was a gray sheet of stationery folded in three. As she unfolded the paper, money drifted to the floor.

With her heartbeat increasing, she read the message on the stationery. In very neat printing were the words, "I can't accept money for the pleasure of your company."

Ellen bent down to pick up the crisp bills. Seth had refunded the money she had paid Two's Company— right down to the exact dollar.

Not quite sure what to make of the gesture, Ellen called the escort service and asked to speak to Bernice Benson.

"I'm so glad you called, Ellen," the older woman greeted her enthusiastically. "Normally we send out evaluation forms to all of our clients, but in your case, I also wanted to speak to you personally."

"I wanted to speak to you, too."

"First, let me apologize for changing escorts at the last minute. I know you had specifically requested Clarence, but as you know, he was injured in a motorcycle accident and we really had no choice but to send Seth."

"I understand, Mrs. Benson."

"I only hope it didn't cause any inconvenience?"

"No, none at all." It wasn't a lie. Seth might have wreaked havoc with her emotions, but he hadn't inconvenienced her.

"That's good, but you should know that since we didn't fulfill our end of the contract, Two's Company is prepared to refund your money in full if you were in any way unhappy with the service you received."

Ellen stared at the currency in her hand. Obviously, Seth had given her the money out of his own pocket and hadn't told his boss. The thought sent little goose bumps up and down Ellen's skin.

"That won't be necessary, Mrs. Benson. Seth was the perfect escort," she said without hesitation, realizing it was true in more ways than one.

"I'm delighted to hear that."

Ellen thought she could almost hear the woman beaming.

"He is a rather unique personality and not all of our clients appreciate his sense of humor."

"I found him to be charming," she said honestly.

"Then you were satisfied with our service?"

"Yes, I was."

"That's wonderful! We'll be sending you an evaluation form to fill out, but if you have any comments you'd like to share with me, I'd be happy to hear them."

"Everything was quite nice, thank you. I especially liked the flowers. They were a lovely touch."

There was a pause on the other end of the line and Ellen asked, "Are you there, Mrs. Benson?"

"Yes, yes, I'm here," she answered, although Ellen was certain she had been distracted by something or someone. "I was just making a note here that you liked the flowers. What kind did you say they were?"

"Roses. White roses."

"I see. Well, I'll make sure I mention to Seth that you enjoyed them." She was very businesslike as she said, "I hope you'll keep us in mind should you have another occasion for which you might like to use our services."

After assuring Bernice that she would indeed call again should the need arise, Ellen said goodbye. But she didn't move away from the phone. She sat staring at the money in her hand and the white roses on the table.

What did it mean? For all she knew, he could have returned the money because she had come to his rescue when he was having his allergy attack.

"I make it a policy never to date the women I meet through Two's Company." The words echoed in her mind. Did the refund of the money mean he didn't consider her to be a customer of the dating service? Or was it only wishful thinking on her part that he wanted her to be more than a client of Two's Company?

She sighed. He was occupying far too many of her thoughts. Chances are she would never see him again and if she were smart, she'd forget all about escort services and men like Seth Holloway.

"WE'VE GOT one of the kids from the summer school program at Lincoln Junior High in room three with burns on his hands."

Ellen looked up from her keyboard to find one of the nurses leaning over her work station.

"What happened to him?"

"He had an argument with a Bunsen burner and he lost."

Ellen grimaced. "Is it serious?"

The nurse shook her head in amazement. "He'll be fine, but he needs help filling out the new patient form. His father's on his way, but we should get the medical history, if possible."

Ellen picked up a clipboard. "I'm on my way. What's his name?"

"Brian Holloway."

Ellen stopped in her tracks. "Did you say Holloway?"

"Yeah. You don't suppose he's related to your Seth, do you?"

Several of Ellen's co-workers had been at the wedding and all of them had been introduced to Seth. Ellen hadn't realized at the time that they would take such an interest in her guest.

"I don't think so," she answered truthfully, trying desperately to recall Seth's sons' names. He'd told them to her the afternoon of the wedding. It would be too much of a coincidence if Brian were one of them. What could the odds possibly be that in a metropolitan area with over two million people she'd run into a kid who was related to the man she had hired as her escort?

Pretty good, Ellen thought a few moments later when she opened the door of the examining room and saw a young boy with sandy brown hair. He was thin, lanky and, like most fourteen-year-olds, looked down at the floor, yet there was something familiar about him. He had eyes as blue as the sky and a dimple in his cheek.

"Hi, Brian. I'm Ellen. I hear you've hurt your hands."

His response was more of a grunt than a yes.

"I need to get some information from you." She sat down on the doctor's stool and ran through the list of questions concerning his medical history. When she came to name of parent or guardian, she was surprised when his answer was "Stanford."

"Is that your father's first or last name?"

"First."

"And his occupation?"

"He works for the paper. He's an editorial cartoonist."

"Your father is the Holloway who draws the editorial cartoons in the paper?"

"Yeah."

Ellen had always enjoyed the wit and sensitivity of the artist who drew the humorous yet poignant cartoons on the editorial page of the local newspaper. She enjoyed laughing at the antics of political figures and felt an affinity to the man, for his work always touched her in an emotional way. Could it be that the man who had drawn caricatures on wedding napkins was the one who had touched her heart on so many social issues?

"Brian, what about your mother's name?" She forced herself back to the issue at hand—filling out the medical form.

"She's deceased," he stated matter-of-factly.

"I'm sorry to hear that," she said gently. "Do you know what kind of medical insurance your father has?"

Before he could answer, the door opened and Ellen gasped—just a tiny little gasp, but a gasp all the same. Standing in the doorway was Seth, his face white. He stood motionless for several moments, then reached for his son and embraced him.

"Dad, you're scrunching me," Brian complained, shrugging out of his father's grip.

Seth grinned as he released him, expelling an obvious sigh of relief. "What happened? When the school called, all they told me was that you had been injured in a science experiment."

"One of the guys knocked a beaker off a Bunsen burner. I tried to catch it before it hit the floor."

"You always did have quick hands," Seth told him with a lift of his eyebrows. "What do they look like under those bandages?"

Brian shrugged stoically. "They're not so bad."

Seth looked to Ellen for confirmation, but she could only shake her head apologetically. "I didn't see him when he came in."

"He is going to be all right, isn't he, Ellen?" Seth had moved closer to her, closing the distance between them so that they appeared to be on a familiar basis.

"Why don't I get the doctor? He can answer your questions better than I can," Ellen told him, eager to be out of the room and away from Seth's watchful eyes.

"What about the insurance stuff?" Brian asked as she moved toward the door. "Don't you want my dad's card?"

Ellen looked at Seth. "If you would stop by the desk on your way out I'll get the numbers and you can sign the necessary forms." She tried to sound as professional as possible, but the way Seth was looking at her made her voice sound a bit breathless.

As she closed the door behind her, she heard Brian say, "Do you two know each other?"

"Why do you ask?"

"Because you called her Ellen."

"That's her name... unless she's wearing someone else's name tag."

Ellen quickly moved away from the door, not wanting anyone to think she was eavesdropping. Back at her desk she entered all the information on Brian Holloway into the computer, including his father's name. Stanford. Where had Seth come from? she wondered. And why was he working as an escort when he was an editorial cartoonist for the newspaper?

They were questions she probably shouldn't find the answers to, at least not here in the clinic. The last thing she wanted was for anyone at work to learn that she had hired Seth to escort her to Rebecca's wedding.

"Well, is he related to your friend?" the nurse interrupted Ellen's musings.

"Yes, as a matter of fact he is." Ellen was saved from having to elaborate when one of the clinic doctors instructed her to arrange a hospital visit for a patient. By the time she was finished, the nurse was busy doing lab work.

Any hopes Ellen had that Seth could leave without anyone noticing him were dashed when she looked up and saw Betty escorting Seth and Brian to the front desk.

Ellen was on tenterhooks while Betty commented on the wedding and how much fun she'd had. Ellen could see the curiosity in Brian's face, and she wondered if he was going to say something that would give away her secret.

Fortunately, it was a busy day and Betty didn't have time to spend chatting. Ellen knew, however, that word had spread among the staff that Seth was there, for the lab technician, two of the other nurses and even the office manager paraded past the reception door—all to get a glimpse of the man they thought was Ellen's boyfriend.

Ellen was certain that her face was beet red the entire time Seth was at the counter. When he sent Brian out to wait for him in the car, she wondered if he had done so because he had sensed her discomfort or if he didn't want his son to learn how they had met.

"What do you need me to sign?" he asked Ellen after giving her his insurance card.

Ellen marked an X on the form she set before him. As he signed the form, she couldn't help but notice that he wore a gold band. He was a widower, yet he still wore a wedding ring. Which meant that he was not yet over the death of his wife.

When he handed the insurance form back to her, Seth saw the three white roses on her desk. His eyes moved from the flowers to her face.

"They were so lovely I hated to leave them at home," she told him.

He smiled then and said, "I'm glad you're enjoying them." As he tucked his insurance card back into his wallet he asked, "Do I need to pay the portion of the bill the insurance doesn't cover?"

At the mention of money, Ellen remembered the money he had sent her. "No, er, yes. Actually, why don't you wait until you see what the insurance company pays? I'm sure the school will submit a claim, as well."

He smiled again. "Sounds fair enough."

Ellen knew she had to say something about his returning her money. She also knew that more than one set of ears could hear everything they were saying. If she was going to bring up the subject of Two's Company, she needed to ask to see him away from the office.

"Well, if that's everything, I suppose I'd better get Brian home," he announced.

Ellen knew she couldn't let him leave because then she'd have to call him, and if there was one thing she had never become accustomed to doing, it was calling men. Summoning up all her courage, she asked, "Do you think you could stop over this evening?" She felt a wave of relief after the words were out.

Unfortunately, they were of little use, for Seth answered, "I'm sorry. I can't this evening. What about tomorrow night?"

"I can't tomorrow." Ellen knew the women in the office were watching and listening, even though they pretended to be busy. She could feel her body growing warmer by the minute.

"Why don't you call me and we'll work something out?" he suggested.

"All right," she reluctantly agreed.

"Great." He gave her a warm smile and left.

"Just great," Ellen murmured dryly after he had gone. She turned around to see two of the nurses give her the thumbs-up sign. *If only they knew,* Ellen thought to herself. *If only they knew.*

ALL THE WAY HOME Seth thought about his conversation with Ellen. Why of all nights did she have to ask him to come over tonight? If he hadn't promised Kelly he'd check out the house she wanted to rent near the campus, he could have been sitting in Ellen's living room drinking a frothy orange something and listening to her tell him what?

Why had she invited him over? Did she want to use his services again or was that her way of expressing her interest in him as a man?

It was something he wondered about until he arrived at home and found several messages from his mother. However, every time he tried to call her she was out of the office. It wasn't long before he learned the reason why. She was at his back door.

"How bad are his hands?" was the first thing Bernice said to him.

"He's going to be all right. Won't be playing basketball for a while, though," he told her as he led her into the kitchen to where Brian was sitting at the table drinking a soda. "Heck of a way to get out of doing dishes, wouldn't you say?" he remarked as Bernice fussed over her grandson in a grandmotherly way.

"Haven't you two had dinner yet?" she asked, looking around the kitchen with a critical eye.

"We're waiting for Kelly. She promised to do the honors since later this evening I'm taking her over to look at that place she wants to rent." He pulled out a chair for her. "I'm surprised to see you here. I thought you were playing bridge tonight."

"Wanda's taking my place. I have too much paperwork to catch up on." She patted the bulging briefcase at her side.

"You need to hire more help, Mom," he told her, pulling two Pig's Eye beers from the refrigerator.

"I can't get good help. I don't know what I'm going to do when Kelly goes back to school."

"You can't expect the family to always be there," he warned.

"Is that your way of telling me you're no longer interested in helping out?"

He set one of the beers in front of her, then hooked his leg around a chair and sat on it, facing backward. "I'm getting too old for this late-night stuff."

"Old? You're only forty-three. And since when is midnight late?"

"He didn't get in until almost three last Saturday," Brian piped up.

"Three?" Bernice's face wrinkled with surprise. "Were you with the Richards woman all that time?"

"It was her daughter's wedding. I had to stay," Seth said without any emotion in his voice.

"Just like you had to send her the roses?" Bernice inquired in a sugary-sweet voice.

"She told you about the roses?"

"She thought it was a nice touch on Two's Company's part."

"And you didn't tell her any differently?"

"Was I supposed to?"

He shrugged nonchalantly and took a swig of beer. "She seemed a little put out that Clarence hadn't shown up, so I thought it'd smooth things over."

She looked at him over the rim of her glasses. "Well, it's nice to know you'll go that extra mile for the company's sake."

Seth glanced at his watch. "I wonder where Kelly is."

"I'm hungry," Brian interjected, his bandaged hands in front of him.

"Would you like me to fix dinner?" Bernice started to get to her feet, but Seth stopped her.

"It's all right, Mom. I'm sure Kelly will be here shortly."

"Why don't we just put a pizza in the oven?" Brian suggested a short while later when there was still no sign of his sister.

Seth vetoed the idea until the phone rang and it was his daughter.

"Dad, hi."

"Where are you?"

"I'm at Calhoun Square."

"What are you doing there?"

"I stopped on my way home to pick up a book from Borders and I accidentally locked my keys in the car."

"You did what?" Seth's voice rose in disbelief.

"I locked my keys in the car and I don't know how to get in. A couple of guys from school tried using a coat hanger to get the lock open, but it didn't work."

"Just terrific." Seth closed his eyes and counted to ten.

"I'm sorry."

"Where exactly are you?"

"I'm on the second level of the parking ramp toward the front."

"All right. I'll be there in about twenty minutes," he told her and was about to hang up when she raised her voice.

"No, Dad! You don't have to come. Trent's brother works for a gas station that has a tow truck with one of those gizmos that can get your door open. He's on his way right now."

"Who's Trent?" he wanted to know.

"One of the guys from school."

That was of little comfort to Seth. "How long is it going to be before you get home?"

"Probably at least another hour."

"What about dinner?"

"Maybe you and Brian should make that frozen pizza that's in the freezer. Matt's working until ten and I'm probably going to grab something here."

"What time are you supposed to be looking at that house?" His eyes automatically went to the clock on the wall.

"Oh, I forgot to tell you. The guy called and asked if we could come tomorrow night instead of tonight."

He groaned. "Why didn't you tell me? I could have made other plans if I had known."

"I'm sorry," she said contritely. "Is there a problem with going tomorrow night?"

Again, Seth had to calm himself. "No, but I'm not happy with what's happened here."

As he hung up the phone, he looked at his mother and said, "And you wonder why I think she shouldn't be living in an apartment on her own."

"Locking your keys in the car can happen to anyone," Bernice said in her granddaughter's defense.

Seth didn't comment. It wasn't the keys being locked in the car that had upset him. It was the fact that he could have accepted Ellen's invitation.

Now he wondered if he'd ever see her again. Of course he could always make a few extra trips to the gym and hope that he'd run into her. And there was the matter of Brian's hands needing to be checked at the clinic. One way or another he'd figure out a way, kids or no kids.

"DIDN'T I TELL YOU we'd get fantastic seats?" Jeannie gushed as she and Ellen settled into the front row of the balcony at the Orpheum Theater in downtown Minneapolis. "Once again, His Majesty comes through," she boasted.

"His Majesty" was Jeannie's nickname for her boss, the man who had given her the tickets to the Minneapolis premiere of the Broadway hit *Miss Saigon*. Although Ellen thought Jeannie was overworked and underpaid as his administrative assistant, even she had to admit that her sister's job did have its perks.

"They're great seats, but I'm wondering what His Majesty's going to expect in return," she remarked skeptically.

Jeannie wasn't listening but was gazing through her binoculars to the main floor below them. "Oh, my gawd. This is fabulous. You should see all the celebrities who are here! Look. Isn't that the governor in the front row?" She offered the field glasses to Ellen.

"Don't you think it looks a little odd to be using those things before the play's even begun?" Ellen asked, reluctant to take the binoculars from her sister.

"Just pretend you're focusing on the stage. No one will know the difference."

"You look for me," Ellen insisted, not wanting to draw any attention to herself.

Jeannie continued to peer through the binoculars, describing to her sister everything she was seeing. "That new anchor woman on Channel Five is here in a blue sequined dress that looks like one I saw in Neiman Marcus." She whistled softly through her teeth. "Boy, does she have a gorgeous guy with her."

Ellen glanced through her theater program while her sister rambled on about who was with whom and wearing what. It was a ritual she had become accustomed to. Whenever they attended the theater or symphony, Jeannie would provide a social commentary and Ellen would respond with the appropriate ohs and uh-huhs.

Ellen knew Jeannie took just as much pleasure in surveying the audience as she did in watching the performers. Therefore it came as no surprise to her when her sister planted her fingernails in her forearm and said, "Quick! Ellen, you have to look!"

"What is it? Did you spot Elvis?" Ellen asked, looking up.

"Better," Jeannie answered, shoving the binoculars up to her sister's eyes. "Look in the third row left center. See that woman in red?"

Ellen had no choice but to look through the field glasses. "Uh-huh." She was about to ask, What about her? when she gasped. "Oh, my gawd."

"It's him, isn't it? The guy from the escort service?"

Ellen gently adjusted the focusing bar to take the fuzziness off the image. Seth had stepped out into the aisle so that several other guests could take their seats. Ellen could see that he was smiling at someone. Moving the binoculars slightly to the right, she saw the object of his affection. It was the woman in red—a gorgeous red strapless gown. Long blond hair draped across her shoulders enticingly. She was beautiful and Ellen felt a pang of disappointment. Anyone who looked like that wouldn't need to hire a date. Seth must have brought her because he wanted to be with her.

"How much does that guy go for?" Jeannie asked, only to be quickly shushed by her sister.

"Shh! Keep your voice down or people around us are going to get the wrong idea." Ellen looked around uneasily.

"Sorry." Jeannie lowered her voice. "I was just thinking that I should check into renting him for the company picnic. I'd like to see the expression on everyone's faces if I came with a guy who looked like that."

Ellen found the thought of her sister's dating Seth rather disturbing. "It isn't simply a matter of renting him. You have to go through an interview and fill out a questionnaire to make sure you get a compatible escort," she said discouragingly.

"It would be worth it." Jeannie rolled her eyes. "I'd walk on hot coals for a date that good-looking."

Just then the lights dimmed and the music began. All talk ceased and Ellen turned her attention to the stage where the story was about to begin.

Having come of age during the Vietnam era, Ellen was especially moved by the love story. She was so caught up in the drama that she forgot Seth was in the audience. Therefore, she was surprised when she ran into him in the lobby during intermission. She had just visited the refreshment bar and was carrying two glasses of white wine.

"Ellen...hello!" His mustache twitched as he smiled warmly.

"Hi," she said rather timidly, glancing around for the lady in red. For once in her life Ellen was relieved that Jeannie had rushed off to the ladies' lounge and left her to get the beverages.

"Waiting for someone?" he wanted to know, his glance moving to the two glasses.

"My sister, Jeannie," she said, avoiding his eyes.

"Are you enjoying the play?"

"Uh-huh. It's wonderful," she said sincerely.

"Where are you seated?"

"Up there," she answered, nodding toward the stairs leading to the balcony.

He watched her steadily. "I'm glad we bumped into each other. Ever since I ran into you at the clinic I've been hoping you would call."

"I'm afraid I've never been very good at calling men," she replied in as even a voice as possible, considering that the way he was eyeing her was making her feel anything but poised.

"Then maybe I should call you."

As if he would, Ellen said silently to herself. What cabbage patch did he think she'd crawled out of, anyway? Curious to know who the woman in the red dress was, she couldn't resist asking, "Are you here on business or pleasure?"

"Business."

"I see," she murmured, feeling a tiny twinge of satisfaction that the gorgeous blonde wasn't his real date. Suddenly remembering that she hadn't thanked him for returning the Two's Company fee, she said, "I'm glad I ran into you, too. I never got a chance to thank you for returning my money."

"I think you know why I did it."

A sensual awareness sparkled in his eyes, and Ellen blushed as she remembered what he had written on the note. *"I can't accept money for the pleasure of your company."* She took a sip of the wine to quench her suddenly dry mouth.

"Whatever your reasons, it was very nice of you to work free. Thank you."

"It was hardly work, Ellen," he assured her with a flirtatious grin.

She felt warm and tingly and she knew it wasn't from the wine she was sipping. "I wish you'd told me you're the Holloway who draws the editorial cartoons for the paper."

"Would it have made any difference in the way you behaved toward me?"

"I thought you were a professional escort."

"I am—or at least I am on the occasion my mother needs me to be."

"Your mother?"

"Bernice. You did know she's my mother, didn't you?"

She was about to tell him she didn't when the woman in red walked up to him and slid her arm through his, giving Ellen a once-over that said she didn't see her as any threat.

As soon as the woman was comfortably connected to Seth's side, he made the introductions. "Greta, I'd like you to meet Ellen Richards. Ellen, Greta Hanover."

The blonde smiled politely. Meekly, Ellen returned the polite smile and raised one of the glasses in acknowledgment, murmuring the standard "It's nice to meet you."

Polite small talk followed, until Jeannie came waltzing down the stairs. "Seth! How nice to see you again!" she exclaimed with a bat of her fake eyelashes. Unlike Ellen, Jeannie wasn't intimidated by the blond woman's presence. She chatted on amicably while Ellen stood awkwardly by, sipping wine. She would have liked to excuse herself, but Jeannie was acting as if Greta and Seth were two long-lost friends. Finally, the chime sounded, indicating the play was about to resume. Seth escorted Greta back into the theater while Jeannie and Ellen climbed the steps to the balcony.

"He is such a gentleman!" Jeannie marveled as they made their way back to their seats.

"Of course he is. He's getting paid to be." Ellen couldn't keep the cynicism from her voice.

"I bet he's every bit as nice when he isn't working," Jeannie insisted.

"I wouldn't know," Ellen answered irritably.

"I sure would like to find out." When they were seated, Jeannie directed the binoculars to the main floor. Ellen knew she was looking for Seth, but she made no comment.

When the play was over and the audience began to disperse, neither Jeannie nor Ellen got up right away. Ellen understood her sister's reticence. She, too, was moved by the story and was in no hurry to rush out of the theater. Finally, Ellen turned to her sister and said, "Well, what do you think?"

Jeannie gave her sister a thoughtful gaze, then said, "That does it. I've made up my mind."

"You liked it?"

Jeannie glanced down toward the stage. "Oh, the play was great, but that's not what I made up my mind about."

Ellen gave her a puzzled look.

"I decided that tomorrow I'm going to call Two's Company and get me a Romeo."

Ellen knew it would do no good to argue with her sister. She had that look in her eye that said her mind was made up and nothing Ellen said would make a bit of difference. At this point all she could do was hope that the man Jeannie hired wouldn't be Seth.

CHAPTER EIGHT

REBECCA RETURNED from her honeymoon with the news that she had decided not to return to school in the fall but would join her husband at her father-in-law's manufacturing firm. Ellen wasn't happy to hear that her daughter was dropping out of college to be an employee of the Townsends. The newlyweds already lived rent-free in one of the senior Townsends apartment complexes, and Ellen worried that Rebecca and Roger were becoming too dependent on his family.

When Ellen expressed her concerns about college over lunch, Rebecca dismissed them easily. "It's not like we're not ever going to go back to school," she told her mother between bites of a Reuben sandwich. "We just want to take a year off to earn some money so we can get a few things."

"Such as?"

"Furniture. All we have right now is a bunch of garage-sale castoffs."

"That's the way most couples begin their marriage. I had secondhand furniture for the first nine years of my married life," Ellen told her.

"Mom, it's different nowadays," Rebecca responded. "It's hard to entertain clients with junk furniture."

"Clients?"

"Roger's going to be helping his father on the sales end of the business, so naturally we'll have to do some entertaining."

"Naturally," Ellen repeated dryly.

"I like the idea of entertaining," Rebecca stated cheerfully. "So does Roger. That's why we decided to have our first dinner party."

"Without a brand-new dining room set?"

Rebecca missed the sarcasm. She was too busy washing down her food with a sip of her soda. "That's the neat part. You're not going to believe what was sitting in our dining room when we got back from our honeymoon."

"Flowers?" Better to guess on the conservative side, Ellen thought.

Rebecca rolled her eyes heavenward. "No, a dining room set! Roger's folks gave us the most beautiful table and chairs. It is so neat, Mom. It's contemporary, with black straight-back chairs and a marble table."

"I thought you wanted traditional furniture."

She shrugged. "I like contemporary, too."

Ellen wasn't so sure her daughter was as happy with the furniture as she was pretending to be. She felt a spurt of anger toward Dolores Townsend. Couldn't the woman have taken the two of them to pick out the set they wanted?

"Maybe you could exchange it for the one you like."

"Oh, I couldn't hurt Mother Townsend's feelings that way."

Mother Townsend. Ellen didn't miss the endearment. "Anyway, Roger thought it would be nice if we invited family for our first dinner party," Rebecca went on, cheerfully munching away on a pickle. "You know, Mother and Dad Townsend and you."

"What a lovely idea. Have you set a date?" Ellen asked, pushing aside her annoyance for the moment.

"Uh-huh. Saturday. Can you come?"

Ellen smiled at her enthusiasm. "Of course I'll come. Can I bring anything? Hors d'oeuvres, a dessert?"

"No food, just a guest. I was thinking you might like to bring Seth."

"Seth?" Ellen was certain the blood drained from her face.

"Uh-huh." She took another sip of her soda, then said, "I know I wasn't very friendly to him when we first met, and I'm sorry. You'll be happy to know I did a lot of thinking while we were on our honeymoon, and Roger made me realize that I have to accept Tina as Dad's wife and give up this childish dream that you and Dad might get back together someday."

Ellen stared at her pensively. "Can you do that?"

"Yes," she said firmly. "I'm happily married and so is Dad. You shouldn't have to be alone."

"That doesn't mean I need to be married," Ellen told her. "I've gotten used to being alone."

"Come on, Mom. I've heard the way you and Auntie Jean talk about guys," she said with a knowing grin.

"It's just talk," Ellen insisted.

"Maybe. The point is, I'm happy you're seeing Seth and if you don't bring him to the dinner party, I'm never going to be able to make amends for acting like such a geek toward him. Besides, Roger's never going to forgive me for what he called 'conduct unbecoming a bride.' "

Ellen didn't know what to say. "I understand you wanting to make amends, but the truth is..." She paused, not knowing how much of the truth she should actually tell her daughter. Certainly she couldn't say that Seth had been a paid escort. Yet she didn't want to be dishonest with her daughter, either.

"Seth and I aren't seeing each other anymore." It was the only thing she could say.

Astonishment flashed on Rebecca's face. "You broke up? Mom, I've only been gone a week."

"Well, we never were really going together. I told you he was only a friend."

"It certainly didn't look that way when the two of you were dancing together," she remarked with a lift of her brows.

"Becca!" Ellen couldn't prevent the blush that accompanied her admonition. Had she and Seth really made such a spectacle of themselves?

"There's nothing to be embarrassed about, Mom. You two looked good slow dancing."

"Well, there won't be any more dancing—slow or otherwise," she predicted soberly.

"Are you telling me that you don't want to see him again?" Doubt laced her words.

"Why is that so hard for you to believe?"

"Because I saw the way you act around him. And I also noticed those wilted white roses he sent you are still on the credenza. Any particular reason why you haven't tossed them out?"

"I've been busy," Ellen said defensively.

"Mom, they're dead."

"Thank you for pointing that out to me. I'll be sure to toss them this evening," she said stiffly. "Now, could we please change the subject?"

Rebecca complied with her mother's wishes, but if Ellen thought the subject of Seth Holloway was dead and buried she was in for a surprise.

When Rebecca went home that evening she called directory assistance to get the phone number of a Seth Holloway. The operator told her there was an S. Holloway on France Avenue and Rebecca jotted down the number.

SETH WAS READING his daily stack of newspapers when the call came through. When Matt informed him a woman was on the phone, his first thought was that it might be Ellen. Subsequently, when he heard the voice at the other end, he felt a rush of disappointment.

"This is Rebecca Townsend—Ellen Richards's daughter."

"Rebecca, hello."

"Hi. I hope I'm not disturbing you," she said politely.

"No, not at all. What can I do for you, Rebecca?"

"Well, actually, this is a little awkward, but..." She paused and Seth would have helped her out, but he wasn't sure how to do that.

"I wanted to talk to you about my mother. She says the two of you aren't seeing each other anymore."

"I'm sorry to say that's true."

"You're sorry?"

"Yes. I like your mother, Rebecca."

"I'm glad to hear that because I think she likes you, too, and I don't think she's happy that you're not seeing each other."

"You don't?"

"No. You see, she still has those white roses you sent her sitting on the table. Nearly all of the petals have fallen off, yet she hasn't thrown them out."

That brought a slow smile to Seth's face. He knew for a fact that Ellen wasn't sentimental. "Maybe she forgot about them."

"You don't know Mom very well if you think that. She's a meticulous housekeeper."

"So what are you trying to tell me? That your mother wants to see me again?" he asked, hoping that Rebecca was on the right track.

"Yes, I think she does. That's why I want you to come to dinner on Saturday."

Seth didn't know what to say. It was obvious from the short time he had spent in Rebecca Townsend's company that she wasn't overly enthusiastic about his relationship with her mother. In fact, her behavior had bordered on the ill-mannered.

"You want me to come to your place for dinner so I can be with your mother?" he repeated, just to make sure he understood her correctly.

"Uh-huh. Are you interested?"

"Well, yes, but . . ." He paused, not knowing quite how to tell her of his reservations.

"But you're wondering why I'm trying to put the two of you together, right?" Before he could answer, she launched into an explanation. "I feel responsible for what's happened."

Seth wondered if she knew just what had really happened. Her next words proved she didn't.

"You see, if I hadn't reacted the way I did when she introduced us, she wouldn't have gotten the idea that I objected to her dating again."

"Do you object to her dating?"

"Not now, but it was a bit of a shock to see her with someone who wasn't my father."

"I can understand that," he said solemnly, appreciating her honesty.

"So I think what happened was, she decided it was easier to stop dating you than it was to risk having friction in her relationship with me. So if the two of you are having problems because of me, I'm really sorry." There was a sincerity in her voice that Seth found rather touching.

"Have you told your mother all of this?"

"I tried to, but I'm sure she didn't believe me. Which is why I want you to come to dinner Saturday night. If she sees I've arranged for you to be there, she'll know that I have absolutely no objections to the two of you dating. So now the question is, do you want to come?"

Seth's first instinct was to say no. The last thing he needed was to get involved with a woman who was still crazy about her ex-husband, and especially not one who had been a client of Two's Company.

Yet the memory of the way Ellen had responded when they had kissed sent blood flowing to parts of his body he had trouble ignoring. She was one sexy woman. Was it so wrong of him to want to spend one more evening with her?

He hesitated only for a moment before saying, "What time do you want me to be there?"

"Dad, are you going out on a real date?" Brian questioned his father from the bathroom doorway.

"What makes you ask that?" Seth wanted to know, his attention on the mirror as he pulled a razor across his right cheek.

"I saw *Holloway's House.* You've got George going out on a real date."

George was the main character in Seth's comic strip. A father of three teenagers, he had become Seth's alter ego, and as his children knew, his cartoon escapades often mimicked Seth's real life.

"You don't think he's ready to date?" Seth asked, not taking his eye from the razor that was scraping shaving cream from his jaw.

"He hasn't wanted to, has he?"

Seth rinsed his razor in the bowl of hot soapy water. "I'm not sure he does now. This is just a little experiment for him."

"So who's the babe?"

Seth was about to shave under his jaw but stopped to stare at his son. "She's not a babe, Brian. She's a woman and her name is..." He paused, realizing he hadn't thought up a name for George's cartoon date.

"Well?" Brian looked at him expectantly.

"I don't know yet."

"You're going on a blind date?" Brian screeched in disbelief.

"No!" Seth quickly finished his shaving and rinsed his face with clean water. "I'm not George. I know who my date is," he told his son, then patted his face dry with a hand towel.

"Who is your date?"

"A woman I met a couple of weeks ago," he answered, wincing as he splashed after-shave lotion over his clean face.

Brian waved his fingers in front of his nose and made an exaggerated face. "Whew! Dad, I really think you should go easy on the foo-foo juice."

"Would George?"

"No, but the point is this. You want to impress her, not gag her."

"Don't you have someplace to be this evening?" Seth asked as he stepped around him to get into his bedroom.

"Nope. Jessie's got to go to some dumb family reunion thing and Kyle's on vacation."

Seth slipped into a freshly laundered shirt. "Have Kelly and Matt gone out already?"

"Yup."

"It figures," he mumbled, winding a silky dark tie around his neck. "Can I trust you to make yourself something to eat or should I have something delivered?"

"Grandma said she'd bring me something."

He grimaced as he knotted the tie. "Your grandmother's coming over tonight?"

"She didn't think I should be alone with my hands and all."

Seth gave him a look of disbelief. It was more likely that she wanted to find out where Seth was going and with whom. Ever since he had told her he couldn't work tonight, she had hounded him to find out why.

He slid his sport coat on and straightened his tie one last time. "Well, I gotta go. Tell your grandma she might as well go home early because I'm not talking."

THE MORE ELLEN SAW of Dolores Townsend, the less she liked her. Even though Roger and Rebecca had only been married for two weeks, she was already firmly ensconced in their lives, and Ellen didn't like it one bit.

Not that she could do anything about it. She had promised herself that she wouldn't interfere in her daughter's marriage, yet she was sorely tempted to tell Rebecca that if she didn't stand up to her mother-in-law, the woman was going to be running her life for her.

After an exceptionally busy week at work, Ellen didn't look forward to spending Saturday evening listening to Dolores dish out advice for the newlyweds. She would have liked nothing better than to plead a headache and skip the entire dinner party, but she knew she couldn't disappoint Rebecca.

Because she was tired, Ellen didn't fuss much with her appearance, choosing to slip into a cotton sundress and pull her hair back from her face with a couple of combs. It had been unusually hot all week, and knowing that Rebecca would want to sit outside on the balcony, she decided against hosiery and simply slipped her bare feet into a pair of sandals.

Despite her daughter's assurances that it wasn't necessary for her to bring anything, Ellen had made a spinach dip for an appetizer and a caramel-filled angel food cake for dessert.

Finding no parking space in the lot adjoining the apartment complex, she had no choice but to leave her car on the street, a block away. Several ominous-looking clouds had her glancing warily at the sky as she locked her door. She had an umbrella in the back seat, but trying to balance the cake in one hand and the spinach dip in the other was enough of a challenge without holding an umbrella.

She would walk fast and pray that the rain didn't start until she was at the front door. Her prayers went unanswered. When she was halfway down the block, the skies opened up.

Just before she reached the apartment building, she spotted someone coming toward her with an umbrella. At the sound of her name being called out, she knew it had to be either Roger or Mr. Townsend. Bless her daughter's heart! She had had someone watching for her.

It was only as the figure drew near that Ellen realized it wasn't her son-in-law or his father, but Seth Holloway! He quickly pulled her under the umbrella, relieving her of the cake plate.

"What are you doing here?" she demanded, too stunned to move.

"Come. We have to get inside," he answered, hurrying her toward the door.

Ellen allowed him to usher her up the steps and inside the lobby of the apartment building. Puddles of water pooled at her feet as she stood watching him gently shake the rain from the umbrella. A bolt of lightning lit up the sky across the street and Ellen looked at him.

"Now you know why I was hurrying you."

Ellen could see her reflection in the plate-glass window. She didn't just feel like a drowned rat...she looked like one, too.

"What are you doing here?" she asked, wishing she could make him disappear.

"Rebecca invited me to dinner."

"And you came?"

"Why wouldn't I?"

Ellen didn't have an answer but stood staring at him in horror. Finally, he said, "You're soaking wet. We'd better get you inside." He buzzed Rebecca's apartment as though he were the one familiar with the building, not Ellen.

He hung the umbrella from his wrist, then took both the spinach dip and the cake in his hands. Ellen meekly followed his instructions and held the door for him. When she would have climbed the stairs to the third floor, he motioned for her to take the elevator.

"Are you okay?" he asked when they were alone inside.

She nodded weakly. "I'm sorry you got roped into this."

"I didn't get roped into anything," he said with a devilishly handsome grin. "I wouldn't have come if I hadn't wanted to."

He was looking at her as if she were to-die-for gorgeous, which only made her even more suspicious, for she knew she had to look a mess. What little makeup she'd been wearing must have been washed away and "bad hair day" was an understatement to describe the condition of her own hair, even *before* the rain.

Feeling awkward, she said, "I told Becca we weren't seeing each other."

"I know. She told me."

"Then why didn't you tell her the dinner wasn't a good idea?"

"Because I think it's a great idea. I've been looking for an excuse to see you again. I've been at the health club every day for the past two weeks hoping I would run into you."

Ellen felt her body grow warm, despite her damp clothing. "I quit going," she said weakly. She felt tongue-tied and didn't know how she was going to get through the dinner party with Seth looking at her as if she was the main course.

When they reached Rebecca's door, Ellen paused. "This isn't going to work," she whispered, trembling from the cold, wet clothing clinging to her.

"Do you want me to leave?"

Ellen's insides warmed as she remembered the way his mouth had felt on hers. He was looking at her with those amazingly blue eyes that were so full of concern, and she didn't want to say anything but "No."

He smiled then and gave her arm a gentle squeeze. "Good. Now relax. Everything will be fine . . . I promise." He tucked her arm in his, hugging it close to his side and sending a current of emotion through her.

Just then the door opened and Rebecca ushered them inside, fussing over her mother's wet clothes. She dragged Ellen past the Townsends who were seated in the living room and into the bedroom in order that she could change.

Once they were away from the ears of the others, Ellen demanded to know, "What is Seth Holloway doing here?"

"I invited him. You'd better take off that dress. It's clinging in all the wrong places."

Ellen looked down and was appalled. The wet cotton revealed more than she wanted anyone to see. No wonder Seth had looked at her as if she were edible.

"What am I going to put on? You and I have never been able to share clothing."

"That's because you have a chest. I would have to take after Dad's side of the family." Rebecca sighed as she pulled out a purple shirt and matching leggings. "This is probably the only thing that'll work." She handed the outfit to her mother.

Ellen put her fingers between the waistband of the leggings and stretched them apart. "You can't possibly think I'll fit into these."

"They're not as small as they seem. They stretch."

"That may be, but all my lumps are going to show. Women my age look ridiculous when they squeeze themselves into these things."

Rebecca's look was one of admonishment. "You have a better figure than a lot of women half your age." She gave her a gentle shove. "Now go put those on. Feel free to use anything you need. Hair dryer, makeup...whatever."

When Ellen finally saw her full reflection in the bathroom mirror, she groaned. And this was what Seth had ogled? she wondered in amazement. But then a glance down at her chest revealed the reason for his having done so. Her breasts were clearly outlined through the wet cotton.

Ellen pulled off the offending sundress and threw it on the floor. Next she opened several drawers on the vanity until she found Rebecca's hair dryer. Doing the best she could under the circumstances, she squeezed and twisted her damp hair into shape.

Although she would have preferred not to borrow any of her daughter's cosmetics, thoughts of Seth in the other room had her poking into the rows of jars, bottles and tubes lining two drawers in the vanity. By the time she was finished, she was wearing some exotic-sounding shade of blush and making a mental note to look for it the next time she went to the mall.

As she glanced in the mirror for one final look before joining the others, she thought she looked better now than she had when she left the house. Rebecca had been right. The leggings did fit, and as long as she was wearing the oversized top, no one would know that she had lumps beneath. Maybe the rain had been a blessing, after all, she thought to herself, musing that she might also want to buy something purple the next time she went shopping.

All eyes turned in her direction as she entered the living room. Ellen, however, was conscious of only one startlingly blue pair. They had the power to make every nerve ending in her body stand at attention. It was starting to become a familiar feeling, the thrill she experienced whenever he looked at her with those eyes. And what was even worse was that she liked the feeling. Any uneasiness Ellen had experienced at discovering Seth was a guest at the dinner party disappeared as she realized that none of the others suspected their relationship was anything but normal. To them, he was simply a friend of hers and welcomed as such.

To Ellen's surprise, she enjoyed dinner. Although Roger and Rebecca did spend most of the evening telling everyone about their honeymoon, there was something heartwarming about their dewy-eyed enthusiasm.

Because Ellen had had so many reservations about the marriage, it was a relief to see that they appeared to be off to a good start. Yet personal experience had taught Ellen that the first few weeks of married life were a bit like playing house. She, too, had once been a dewy-eyed newlywed.

When Rebecca asked her mother to help her with dessert, Ellen took the opportunity to compliment her daughter on her efforts. "This is a terrific dinner party, Becca. Everything tasted very good."

"Thanks, Mom, but I cheated. Don't tell Roger's mother, but I ordered most of it from Byerly's deli," she said in a near whisper.

Ellen gave her a conspiratorial wink. "Your secret's safe with me. What's important is that your table looked lovely, the food was delicious and the conversation was interesting. It's good to see you and Roger so happy." She gave her daughter's shoulder a gentle squeeze.

"Thanks, Mom. Why don't you make another pot of coffee and I'll get our dessert." She opened the refrigerator and pulled out a pie. "This I did make myself," she announced proudly as she held the pie up for her mother's inspection. "It's banana cream—Roger's favorite."

"Looks perfect!" Ellen exclaimed, watching her daughter carefully set the pie on the counter. "Would you like me to cut it?"

"Uh-uh. You do the coffee. I'll take care of this."

While Ellen filled a carafe with cold water, Rebecca rummaged through her cutlery drawer in search of a knife and pie server. "You know, Mom, the more I get to know Seth, the more I like him," she said as she fingered the blade on a serrated knife.

"He is nice, isn't he," Ellen remarked as she measured coffee into the basket filter.

"He's really sweet. You should have seen how worried he was about you when that storm came up so suddenly. He stood by the window watching for your car so that he could meet you with the umbrella." She carefully spread whipped cream over the pie.

"I guess chivalry isn't dead, after all."

"You didn't tell me he has a daughter my age. I told him I'd like to meet her someday. What's she like?"

Ellen was saved from having to answer when Rebecca tried to lift a piece of the pie from the pan. Instead of having a thick custardlike texture, the pie's filling was as runny as water. By the time she had deposited it onto a plate, all that was left was the crust and a layer of whipped cream.

"Oh, no! It flopped!" she cried out in dismay. "I can't serve this!" She threw the pie server onto the counter in disgust.

"It's not that bad." Ellen tried to calm her agitated daughter by spooning the runny custard filling onto the plate. "This has happened to me lots of times. It looks bad, but it still tastes good."

"You've never served pie that looks like that!" she said accusingly. "What did I do wrong?" She looked to her mother for an explanation.

"Did you give it enough time to set?"

"I made it this morning. The cookbook said three hours was all it needed to become firm."

Ellen suspected that her daughter might have misread the recipe and either didn't put in enough cornstarch or didn't boil the mixture the necessary amount of time. She decided, however, that it was better not to question Rebecca's culinary skills at this time and said soothingly, "I've noticed that the humidity can affect the texture."

"What are you saying? That I shouldn't try to make a banana cream pie when it's summertime?" She sounded like a petulant child.

Ellen gave Rebecca's shoulder a gentle squeeze. "I'm saying you have to expect there are going to be times when whatever it is you're cooking is going to fail. Now, the good news is, I brought your favorite caramel cake."

Rebecca sank down onto a chair. "I know, but Roger's expecting banana cream pie," she said with a muffled sob.

"You tell him you thought you should serve the cake because your mother went to so much trouble to make it...not to mention getting it here in the middle of a thunderstorm. Then, after everyone's gone home, you can show him the pie. He'll love the fact that you went to all that trouble to make it for him. By then you'll be able to laugh about it and you can get a couple of spoons and finish it off together."

Rebecca followed her mother's suggestion and served the caramel-filled angel food cake. Contrary to what Ellen had told her daughter, Roger did seem a bit put out by the fact that they weren't having the banana cream pie and even went so far as to ask if she would cut a piece for him while the others ate cake. Ellen could have kicked him in the shins. To her surprise, however, it was Dolores who came to Rebecca's defense, giving Ellen reason to hope that the older woman wasn't so bad, after all.

That hope disappeared shortly after dinner when Rebecca's mother-in-law announced she had the perfect after-dinner entertainment. Slides and videos.

Ellen was about to plead a headache and make her exit, but from the look Rebecca was giving her she didn't dare leave. Roger was rearranging the dining room chairs while his father set up the screen.

"These are mostly from our trip to Hong Kong," Dolores explained excitedly, as she pulled out a carousel of slides from a square box. "But there are some of the wedding, too. I knew the kids wanted to see them," she said in an aside to Ellen.

"How many slides does a tray like that hold?" Ellen asked as Dolores set it next to the projector.

"A hundred and sixty," she answered, then turned to her husband to ask, "Did you leave the other tray in the car?"

The other tray. Ellen's eyes met Seth's and it was obvious that he had heard. He slowly shook his head, a grin creasing his cheeks. Ellen could only shrug in apology.

Roger had set five chairs in a straight row. The sixth positioned next to the table where the projector sat. Seth made sure he sat next to Ellen. As soon as the lights went out, she leaned over and whispered in his ear.

"I'm really sorry about this. You can leave if you want."

He reached for her hand and held it firmly in his. His breath was warm against her ear and sent a little tingle down her spine. "I don't want to go anywhere. I like sitting next to you in the dark."

CHAPTER NINE

ELLEN DIDN'T REALIZE that travel slides and home videos of Hong Kong could be so entertaining. Of course she sincerely doubted they would have held the same appeal had Seth not been sitting beside her adding humorous remarks to Dolores's commentary.

Ellen knew why he was a such successful cartoonist. His wit and perception allowed him to see situations in a unique way. Ellen wondered if Dolores would have been as outspoken if she had known he was the Holloway who drew the editorial cartoons in the paper.

Even though Seth wasn't Ellen's paid escort for the evening, she couldn't help but feel a bit guilty about keeping his true identity from her daughter and son-in-law. Even though the circumstances had changed from the night of the wedding, they were still acting out a charade and the thought made Ellen uneasy.

When the party ended with Roger giving Seth a strong handshake and an invitation to come sailing with him, she knew she was going to have to put a stop to the deception, and soon. The opportunity came when Seth offered to walk her to her car.

"I'm really sorry that you were drawn into this whole mess this evening," she said as they walked along the damp sidewalk.

"No one twisted my arm, Ellen," he said, a hint of amusement in his voice. "And it definitely wasn't a mess. I enjoyed myself."

"You don't need to say that to be polite."

"I'm not being polite. You know, until tonight, I never understood why my kids liked to watch *America's Funniest Home Videos*.

"They were funny, weren't they," she said, sighing. "I suppose we should be grateful that at least while the video and slide show was happening, no one was asking us any difficult questions we couldn't answer."

"Were you unhappy that I accepted Rebecca's invitation?"

"No," she answered honestly. "But I can't help but feel like I'm caught in this web of false pretense that keeps getting larger and larger."

"Do you regret using Two's Company's services?"

"I never was comfortable with the idea of paying for an escort," she admitted, grateful for the darkness surrounding them. Somehow it was easier to talk about the subject when she didn't have to look into his eyes.

"I thought maybe it was me."

"No." She quickly disabused him of any such notion. "I wouldn't have been comfortable with anyone. I don't like pretending things are not what they really are. And now it's obvious it wasn't a good idea. Look what's happened. One lie has led to another and another until now we have Roger wanting to take you out in his sailboat and Becca trying to arrange a time to meet your daughter."

"We haven't exactly been lying to them."

"We don't need to. They assume things and we don't correct them. Everyone thinks we're going out together because we like each other and that makes me feel dishonest.''

''Then why don't we put an end to the dishonesty? Why do we have to pretend anything? Can't I date you for real?''

They had reached her car and he stepped in front of her so that she had her back to the car and was facing him.

''You're serious, aren't you?'' she said in disbelief.

''Ellen, the work I do for Two's Company is just that. Work. And I've only done it to help out my mother. I've never dated any of the women I've escorted. I've never wanted to—at least not until now.''

Ellen was tempted, and as a result her voice lacked conviction when she said, ''I don't think it's a good idea.''

''Why not?''

Ellen tried to think of reasons, but at the moment all she could think of was how his mustache had felt against her skin when he had kissed her.

''I don't know you very well,'' she said weakly.

''Isn't that what dating is for?'' When she didn't respond, he lowered his voice and said, ''Something happens when we're together, Ellen. I think you feel it, too. We click.''

She leaned back against the car and he put a hand on each side of her, trapping her between him and the door. ''I like you and I want to get to know you better. But if you don't want to see me again, all you have to do is say so,'' he said in a voice that held a hint of a challenge.

If someone had told Ellen earlier that day that she would end her visit to Rebecca's by giving a man a hot, passionate kiss while standing on a street corner not far from her daughter's apartment building, she would have laughed out loud.

But that was exactly what she did. She reached up and planted her lips on his in a provocative manner she'd never known she was capable of.

It was all the invitation Seth needed. He pulled her close to him and ran his hands up and down her back, across her shoulders, through her hair and around her neck until they finally found the two glorious mounds of flesh he had been unable to keep from dreaming about since the night they had met.

As she responded to his touch, the urges he had fought so hard to control all evening refused to be denied. Blood rushed through him, intensifying his need for satisfaction. It had been a long time since he had experienced such a reaction to a woman, and he relished the sensations.

Just as they had done on the dance floor, their bodies clung together in a way that sent a hurry-up message to their brains. It was only when headlights from a passing car shone on them that they separated.

Breathless, she stammered, "I . . . I'd better go."

"Wait! When can I see you again?"

Her expression became thoughtful. "Give me some time to think about this, okay?"

He reluctantly released her, then opened her car door. "You do know that you can call me anytime, don't you?"

"I'm not very good at calling men," she said shyly as she ducked inside the car. Before Seth shut the door, he leaned inside and kissed her—this time softly.

"Then I'll call you." He dropped one more kiss on her lips, then said, "In the meantime, think about what I said."

She nodded, then stuck her key in the ignition. Another car had pulled up behind them and was waiting to take her parking spot as soon as she pulled out.

"I'm up on the next block. Wait for me at the intersection and I'll follow you home," he told her, then closed her door.

Ellen did as Seth had instructed, pulling over at the next street corner to wait for him. All the way home her heart thumped madly in her chest. Every time she glanced in the rearview mirror and saw him behind her, she grew warm and tingly as if he were still kissing her.

Once she was home, she pulled the car into the garage while he waited out front with his engine running and his lights on. When she was on the front porch and had her key in the lock, she waved for him to leave, but he waited until she went in before driving away.

Ellen was disappointed that he had left. She would have liked him to come inside. She could have made him some coffee and they could have talked and gotten to know each other better.

Liar. A tiny voice in her subconscious didn't believe for one minute that she had wanted him to come inside to talk. She had wanted him to come inside so that he could hold her and caress her and make her feel wonderful all over.

It had been a long time since any man had been able to elicit such a reaction from her. She closed her eyes to block out the memory of the feelings he had aroused, but later, as she lay in bed unable to sleep, she could think of nothing else.

She glanced at the digital clock. One a.m. Seth had told her he often worked into the wee hours of the morning. Would he still be awake? There was only one way to find out. She switched on the bedside lamp and found the paper napkin with his phone number on it.

She picked up the receiver and started to dial, only to slam it back down on the cradle. What was she thinking? She couldn't call him at this hour. He had a family, the members of which were probably fast asleep.

But then she thought about the way their bodies had hugged together and the sexy way he had said, "You do know that you can call me anytime, don't you?" Before she could change her mind, she punched in the numbers. He answered after only one ring.

He didn't sound as if he had been sleeping. "It's Ellen. I'm sorry about calling so late."

"No, it's all right. I'm glad you called." His voice was like a warm and soft blanket, cocooning her with layers of blissful serenity.

"I wanted to tell you that I've thought about what you said and I agree. We won't know if it'll work until we try."

There was a silence for several moments, and Ellen wondered if maybe he had been sleeping, after all. But then he said, "I'm glad to hear that."

Something in his voice made her tremble in anticipation.

"Should I call you tomorrow?" he asked.

"Maybe you'd like to come over for breakfast and we could talk."

"Sure. What time?"

Ellen glanced at the clock. "Want to come now?"

Seth looked down at the bulge in his briefs. "I'm on my way."

TWO YEARS, thought Seth. It had been two years since
Laura had died and all that time his hormones had
been in a coma. Grief did that to a person. It redi-
rected one's energy. He had been able to stay up half
the night and work, yet he hadn't had any interest in
sex. At least not until now.

Now, the hormone coma was over and he was ready
to be a man again. Oh boy, was he ready. He was so
ready that he practically flew out of the house. He was
about to back his Explorer out of the garage when another car pulled in behind him, blocking the driveway.

It was Kelly coming home from a date. Seeing her
father about to leave, she jumped out of the car and
rushed over to his window.

"What's wrong? Why are you leaving?"

"I'm just meeting a friend for some coffee," he told
her, feeling like a kid sneaking out in the middle of the
night.

"Dad, do you realize what time it is?"

"Yes, it's past your curfew."

"I'm not the one leaving," she reminded him.

"So what's your point?"

"You always tell us kids that we have to let you know
where we are when we're out after midnight."

"I told you. I'm meeting an old friend. We're going
to drink coffee and reminisce about the good old
days." He was growing impatient with her inquisition.

Kelly gave him a suspicious glare. "Something's not
right with this picture."

Seth glanced to where Kelly's date sat revving his
engine. "You'd better say good-night to your boyfriend. He's getting restless."

Slowly, she walked back to the idling car, looking
over her shoulder at her father in a disapproving way.

"Don't worry about me. I'll be fine," he called out through his window.

He felt a momentary stab of guilt. Kelly had been right. He probably should have told her where he was going, but he wasn't ready to have her dissecting his relationship with Ellen.

The more he thought about it, the guiltier he felt. Not only about his daughter, but about Laura. For two years he had remained faithful to her memory, yet he had made the decision to be with Ellen without so much as giving Laura a thought.

It wasn't as if he was being unfaithful to her, he told himself as he drove. After all, he wasn't going to make love to Ellen, exactly. He hadn't known her long enough to love her, though he had a very powerful suspicion that he could very well end up loving her one day. No, tonight he was simply going to have sex with her. He had wanted to from the first time he had seen her in the gym.

He pressed the gas pedal closer to the floorboard and sped down the deserted city streets. Suddenly, he heard a siren. A glance in his rearview mirror told him he was being pursued by a cop. "Oh, brother," he moaned, pulling over to the side of the road. While he waited for the officer to get out of his squad car, he dug out his registration papers and his license, handing them to the officer when he appeared at his window.

"Step out of the car, please," the officer instructed, shining a beam of light into his eyes.

Seth complied with his order. "What's the problem?" he asked.

"You were doing fifty in a thirty," the officer answered brusquely, examining the license under the flashlight beam. Any hope Seth had that he would simply write him a ticket and let him go was dashed when he said, "Come with me."

He led Seth over to the police car where he put him in the back seat while he climbed in front and called headquarters.

"The car's mine and there are no warrants for my arrest," Seth told him, but the officer paid no attention.

The whole process took an unusually long time, or at least to Seth it seemed to be an abnormal amount of time. Since the officer seemed reluctant to talk to him, he didn't bother to try to make any conversation, but sat quietly in the back seat, trying not to look at his watch.

"Have you been drinking?" the officer demanded over his shoulder.

"No...er, yes...I mean, I had a glass of wine at dinner." Seth realized the mistake he had made a few minutes later when he was put through the sobriety checks. He should have lied. Telling the truth was only going to prolong his detention.

When he had finished walking a straight line, touching his nose with his index finger and blowing into the breathalyzer, the officer put him back in the squad car to wait some more. Seth was running out of patience.

"Can't you just give me the ticket and let me go?" he asked, a question he was convinced only made the officer's movements more deliberate.

More time elapsed and finally the all-clear came over the police radio. Seth was tempted to say, "I told you so," but wisely kept quiet. He took his speeding ticket and went back to his Explorer, where he stuffed the piece of paper into his glove compartment.

He couldn't possibly use this scene in *Holloway's House*. The kids would have a field day with this one if they found out about it. For the first time in his life he had gotten a speeding ticket, and it was all because of raging hormones.

As he drove the remainder of the distance to Ellen's, he started to have second thoughts about what he was doing. He was, after all, a forty-three-year-old father who was about to go to bed with a woman he had known less than a month. A woman he hadn't actually dated . . . yet. Was he really ready for this? Again, thoughts of Laura made his doubts swell.

By the time he parked his car in Ellen's driveway, he had made a decision. Sex was out. They'd talk, get to know each other, share a few kisses, maybe even do a little heavy petting, but he wouldn't become intimate with her. Not yet.

IT HAD BEEN THREE YEARS since Ellen had cooked breakfast for a man. Gone were the days when she had fried hash browns and eggs, pancakes and sausages. Breakfast to her was a toasted English muffin or a bowl of oatmeal.

So when she stared into her refrigerator, she saw no bacon, sausages or ham on the shelves. Actually, there wasn't much of anything. Living alone, she seldom stocked much in the way of groceries and it would be a challenge for anyone to find the makings of a good breakfast in Ellen's nearly empty refrigerator.

She did a quick inventory and came up with half a carton of skim milk, seven eggs, a rusty head of lettuce, a block of Cojack cheese and two tomatoes. Possible omelet ingredients.

Scrounging around in the pantry cupboard produced a jar of mushrooms. She checked her bread drawer and saw that there were several slices of stoneground wheat she could toast. She breathed a sigh of relief. Mushroom-and-cheese omelets with toast looked like a possibility.

If he wanted to eat. Ellen wasn't deluding herself into thinking Seth had accepted her invitation because he wanted to taste her cooking.

The memory of the way they had kissed outside Rebecca's apartment sent a rush of heat through her. She had forgotten what it was like to want a man so badly that nothing else seemed to matter. Now, she found the situation terribly exciting.

It was the reason she had slipped the washed-silk skirt and blouse over bare skin. It was also the reason she had put lace-trimmed sheets on her bed and misted them with her perfume atomizer.

She just wondered why it had to be Seth she wanted. For the hundredth time that evening she told herself that he wasn't simply a professional escort. He was a well respected cartoonist and the father of three teenagers. She wasn't making a mistake getting involved with him.

Still, the doubts lingered...until she opened the door to him and saw him standing in the glow of the porch light. There was something in the way he looked at her that confirmed her suspicion that he hadn't come to have breakfast.

"I'm sorry I took so long," he said as he stepped inside.

"It's all right." She closed the front door and flicked off the porch light. They stood in the entry, the gently whirling ceiling fan sending a cool draft of air down on them.

"I...I didn't know when you'd get here, so I waited before starting breakfast," she told him, feeling absolutely no shame at the open invitation she was giving him.

"Nothing's cooking?"

She shook her head. "Uh-uh."

Seth knew he should suggest taking her out to breakfast. It would be safer and wiser. However, with the way the silky blue material was clinging to her curves, he was having trouble thinking in terms of safe and wise.

His mind didn't want to do much thinking at all. He tried to call up the name of even one restaurant he knew was open twenty-four hours but he drew a blank. It had to be Ellen's fault. She looked good, she smelled good and he knew she would taste good.

Nor did his mind want to remember the conversation he had had with himself or the resulting resolution he had made. His mind didn't want to do much of anything except step aside and let his raging hormones do the talking.

"I'm kinda glad nothing's cooking 'cuz that means we can do this," he said, pulling her close and covering her mouth with his.

From the moment their lips met, all guilty thoughts disappeared. So did reason. And caution. This time their kisses were deeper, wetter and hotter than they had been earlier that evening, and Seth's body trembled with longing. The quivering response he felt as she pressed her body closer to his told him that she wanted the same thing as he did. When she started to grind her belly into his hardness, he could barely keep his hands from undressing her on the spot. Reluctantly, he lifted his mouth from hers. "I think we're playing with fire," he said hoarsely.

"I know. Isn't it fun?" she said temptingly. Then she took his hand and placed it on her breast. She wasn't wearing a bra beneath the silk shirt, and her nipple was hard and erect as his fingers closed around it.

Seth couldn't resist the temptation. He fondled and caressed her through the silk until her breathing was as ragged as his. The pictures his mind was conjuring up of what she must look like beneath the shirt nearly drove him crazy. He wanted her. All of her.

When she loosened the buttons on his shirt and placed her hands on the warm flesh inside, he pulled away from her.

"Are we sure about this?" He needed to know, for in a very short time he would be past the point of asking.

For an answer she led him up the stairs to the second floor, not stopping until they were in her bedroom. It was a woman's room, with lots of lace and floral patterns on the walls, the draperies and the bed linens. A small ginger-jar lamp with a pink lampshade gave off a rosy glow.

As Ellen pulled him into the room, she smiled shyly.

"Still sure?" Seth asked when the smile became a nervous giggle.

She turned the tables on him. "Aren't you?"

For an answer he pushed her down onto the bed and pinned her beneath him, looking into her wide eyes. No part of him moved except for his right hand. It started at her left shoulder and worked its way down her arm to her hip where it lifted the washed-silk skirt until it was bunched about her waist.

Flesh met flesh as his hand found her thigh. As tempted as he was to look at that naked thigh, he kept his gaze locked on hers while he moved his hand upward ever so slowly.

Ellen's eyes darkened, and her breathing quickened as he enticingly stroked her warm flesh. A groan of satisfaction escaped him. He was the one setting the pace, calling the shots, and he wasn't going to rush any of it.

But it had been too long since he had made love with a woman. If he wasn't careful, it could be all over in a matter of minutes. And as his hand gradually slid upward, he realized that she had thrown him a curve ball.

She wasn't wearing any underwear.

A triumphant sparkle shone in her eyes at his discovery. As his fingers lost themselves in the hairy mound between her legs, she whimpered. Instinctively her hips lifted, her legs spreading apart in a seductive invitation Seth couldn't ignore.

Slowly and gently, he pressed his finger deep into the core of her womanhood. She was incredibly soft and wet, and he could feel his own control rapidly slipping away.

He closed his eyes, willing his body not to rush such an extraordinary experience. He didn't want to take his pleasure until he was sure she would reach the peak of satisfaction, too. But she was moving beneath him in a rhythm that had him reacting, not thinking.

He eased his finger out of her and opened his slacks, freeing his swollen flesh. When he entered her, she shuddered with pleasure. Again he closed his eyes, wanting to prolong the rapture of the moment, but he knew it would be impossible. His body ached so badly that he couldn't wait another minute.

"You feel so good. I can't hold back," he said hoarsely.

"I don't want you to," she told him, tightening her inner muscles around him.

He sank deeper into her, the heat building between them as their bodies moved together with an urgency that was as natural as breathing. Being inside her was like no other experience he had ever had in his life. Lustfully, she matched his ardor, stroke for stroke, until he felt the heat and tension drain from him in a rush.

When coherent thought returned, Seth was beside her, waiting for his breathing to return to normal.

"My gawd, we didn't even undress," he said huskily, glancing down at his pants, which were bunched at his ankles.

"We didn't need to," she told him with a feminine smile that smacked of satisfaction, but he didn't see it, for they were lying side by side, staring up at the ceiling.

"I feel like I put the cart before the horse." He turned his head on the pillow and studied her face.

"I'm not complaining."

Seth thought she had every right to. Although he had felt the spasms rock her body just as they had his, it had all happened much too fast. He wanted to tell her that it was only because he hadn't been with a woman for so long that he had behaved like a teenager.

"But getting naked is part of the fun," he said on a sigh.

"Parts of us were naked," she reminded him.

He looked down and saw that her skirt was still hiked up to her waist. He felt a quick jolt of excitement and again his soft flesh started to harden.

When he looked up at her, he saw that her eyes were closed, a blissful expression on her face. She had no idea of the effect she was having on him simply by being there. He leaned over and kissed her.

She looked up at him as he lifted his mouth from hers and he whispered, "I think we should get naked all over."

"More fun?"

He shifted so that she could feel his arousal pressing against her hip. "I think the horse should pull the cart."

He stood up and she watched him as he undressed. When she, too, stood and began to unbutton her silk shirt, he stopped her.

"Let me," he instructed, crawling across the bed to reach her. "That's part of the fun."

Slowly and with great pleasure he removed the twisted skirt from around her waist. Then he unbuttoned the shirt, unable to resist slipping a hand inside to cup a breast before pushing the silk away from her shoulders.

"You're a beautiful woman, Ellen," he said when she was naked before him. Then he began kissing her again, his hands skimming over her shoulders, her breasts and her hips.

He eased her down onto the bed, caressing her breasts until they swelled with passion. When his mouth closed over her nipple, she moaned and clutched at his shoulders. Seth felt a desire he had never known before, a desire so overpowering that it made him feel as though some part of him had always known it would be this way.

This time when he entered her, his movements were careful and controlled, yet he was moving in a way that was new to him; there was an intensity, an awareness of every sensation, that made his journey toward the release they both were seeking almost mystical. When it happened, both of them cried out in wonder and joy.

Exhausted and insanely happy, Ellen closed her eyes as he slipped out of her and rolled onto his back.

"Pinch me and tell me that wasn't a dream," Seth said with a sigh, his breathing still ragged.

Ellen slipped her fingers around his penis and asked, "Where do you want me to pinch you?"

"Not there," he said with a halfhearted chuckle.

She smiled, and moved her hand up to his chest where she flattened her palm against his damp hair. They didn't say anything for several moments, both content to bask in the afterglow of their lovemaking.

As their bodies started to cool down, Seth reached for the scented sheet and pulled it up around them. Ellen moved her head so that it lay on his shoulder, and he covered the hand she had on his chest with his own.

After several minutes of blissful silence, he said softly, "I can't stay the night. I didn't tell my kids where I was going."

"Then you should go," she told him, unable to keep the disappointment from her voice.

He lifted her hand to his lips and kissed the knuckles. "I don't want to leave you. I'd like nothing better to fall asleep right here and wake up in the morning and love you all over again."

She looked up at him then. "We could set the alarm," she suggested, then quickly shifted away from him, her face coloring as she realized how bold she had become.

He put a finger beneath her chin and forced her to look at him. "I like the fact that you want me as much as I want you." He pressed a kiss on her mouth. "It was good tonight, Ellen. I can't stay till morning, but we can prolong this moment for a little longer."

It felt so right to be with him. She sighed and allowed him to pull her back into his arms. Resting her head on his shoulder, she smiled, content to listen to the beat of his heart.

Seth closed his eyes, allowing his senses to fill with her scent, his body to rest in her warmth. Before either one realized what was happening, they were asleep.

IT CAN'T BE MORNING, Ellen told herself when the faint beeping of the alarm interrupted her sleep. She was too tired, she was too warm, and she was too comfortable to get up just yet. So instead of waking up, she did something she very seldom did. She pushed the snooze feature on the alarm. Not once, but twice. It was only when the alarm beeped for the third time that she forced herself to face the fact that it was morning.

She was going to have to get up. As she began to roll over, she realized that something was wrong. For one thing, she was naked beneath the covers. And there was an arm wrapped around her middle. A man's arm.

Immediately, she looked back over her shoulder and saw Seth's sleeping face. A shadow darkened his jaw and his hair was mussed, but he was every bit as handsome as he had been last night. Memories of what had happened only hours ago came flooding back, and her body began to tingle as she recalled all the pleasures they had shared.

Then she remembered that Seth had said he couldn't stay the night. She glanced at the clock. Why was he still here? She reached over and gently nudged his shoulder.

"Seth? Seth?" she repeated, a bit louder the second time.

When he stirred, he tightened his hold on her, his hand reaching up to fondle a breast. A smile creased his face as he played with her nipple, his eyes still closed. "Umm. What have we here?"

"Seth, it's seven-thirty," Ellen answered, trying not to ignore the sensations she was feeling as his fingers toyed with her.

Suddenly, his eyes were open. He looked toward the window and saw the slivers of sunlight between the draperies and the wall. Then he looked at her naked body next to his and groaned.

Before swinging his legs over the side of the bed, he bent over her and pressed a trail of kisses across her breasts. He stopped briefly to suck on a rosy nub, sighing in appreciation as he circled it with his tongue.

"You are so beautiful," he said with a husky moan, then he kissed her firmly on the lips. "I love you, but I have to go."

Ellen watched as he pulled the shirt on over his flat stomach. Her desire for him must have shown in her eyes, for he said to her, "Don't look at me like that or I'm not going to be able to leave."

Blushing, she climbed out of bed and slipped on a soft green terry robe. Part of the reason she had been staring at him had to do with the fact that she was fascinated by his body and her own body was aching for him. But most of her amazement had to do with the fact that he had said, "I love you, but I have to go."

She wasn't so naive as to think it was a declaration of love, yet she didn't want to think that he would use the word love lightly. Whether or not she was ready to admit it, she had fallen more than a bit in love with him. The thought brought a worried frown to her face and she turned so that he wouldn't notice.

But he had already seen the play of emotions crossing her face. As soon as he had zipped his pants, he went to her and took her in his arms. "I love the way you look at me, but I have to leave."

"I know and I'm sorry. I didn't mean to make it difficult for you," she apologized.

He kissed her again, this time tenderly and without any urgency. "You don't need to apologize for being a woman," he said, holding her tightly in his arms. "I need to get home and straighten out a few things. Next time we're together, there'll be no rushing and no hasty goodbyes, okay?"

She nodded, not knowing whether she should trust herself to speak.

"Good." He slipped on his shoes, then with one last kiss said goodbye. Ellen walked him to the door and only hoped that he was sincere when he said, "I'll be back."

CHAPTER TEN

IT WAS ONLY after Seth left that Ellen remembered it was Sunday. She glanced at the clock and grimaced. Jeannie would be coming to pick her up for church in less than twenty minutes.

If she hurried she could at least shower before her sister arrived. She rushed up the stairs and was heading for the bathroom when the phone rang.

It was Rebecca.

"Hi, Mom. I know you're getting ready for church, so I won't keep you, but I wanted to make Roger some hash browns. How do I do it?" she asked in a rush that only made Ellen more aware of how far behind schedule she already was.

"You just add a little green pepper and onion as you fry the potatoes," Ellen answered. "Look, I really hate to cut this short, but I'm running a little behind this morning and Auntie Jean's on her way."

"But, Mom, I need to know how long I have to cook them."

Ellen almost snapped, If you had shown any interest when you lived at home you'd know the answer, but she really didn't want to argue with her daughter over potatoes. Instead, she sighed. "Fry them until they look done."

"In butter?"

"I use butter, but you can use margarine, if you like."

"How much salt and pepper do you add?"

"I don't have a set recipe, Becca," she said shortly. "I season them to taste. Just give them a try and see what happens."

"That's easy for you to say. Everything you make tastes great. You should have seen my fried eggs yesterday morning. Roger said they were so rubbery he could have used them to patch his tires."

"Good cooks aren't born, they're made. Practice makes perfect." Ellen found herself quoting her own mother, something she had vowed she would never do. "Now I really must go or I'll be late for church."

"Wait! Before you hang up, you have to tell me what you thought about last night."

"I already told you. Everything was lovely," she said, unable to keep her eyes from glancing at the clock radio.

"Mom," she drawled a bit impatiently. "I'm not talking about everything. I'm talking about you and Seth Holloway. Did you have fun?"

Ellen glanced at the rumpled bed sheets and felt her body grow warm. "Yes. We had fun."

"We?" Becca didn't miss that her mother included Seth in her response. "Does that mean you're going to see him again?"

"I think so, but in the future, I would appreciate it if you wouldn't try to arrange any dates for me." She wanted to make her voice sound admonishing, but deep down she was happy that Rebecca had invited Seth to dinner. "Now I really must go."

"Okay, Mom. I'll talk to you later."

"Good luck with the hash browns," Ellen said before hanging up. She looked one last time at the tousled linens, smiled broadly, then headed for the shower.

She had just finished drying herself off when the doorbell rang. It was Jeannie.

"What happened to you? Did you oversleep?" she asked when Ellen answered the door in her robe, a towel wound around her head turban-style.

"Yes, I'm sorry. You'll have to go without me," Ellen replied. "I can't possibly get ready on time."

"You never oversleep." Jeannie eyed her suspiciously. "What happened at Becca's?"

Ellen wondered what her sister would say if she told her that she had fallen in love with Seth Holloway last night. "Nothing happened," she said, toweling her hair to avoid Jeannie's inquisitive eyes.

"Did Becca say or do something that kept you awake last night?"

"Uh-uh. To be honest with you, her dinner party was rather nice. We ate, we talked about the wedding and Becca's honeymoon, and then the Townsends showed slides of their trip to Hong Kong."

"And you call that nice?" Jeannie looked at her as if she had said she enjoyed having her teeth extracted without novocaine.

"Yes, it was nice."

Jeannie shoved her fists to her waist. "Are you sure you're feeling all right? Yesterday you were complaining about not being able to sit through dinner with Dolores Townsend. Now you're telling me you had a nice time watching her vacation slides."

Ellen shrugged. "What can I say?" She draped her towel across her shoulders and finger-combed her hair away from her face. "Look, there's no reason why both of us have to miss church. Why don't you go without me?''

"Uh-uh. I hate sitting alone in church." Jeannie made herself at home in the living room. "If you're going to miss, so will I. Besides, I have some news to share with you. Get dressed and I'll treat you to breakfast.''

"What news?" This time it was Ellen wearing the suspicious look.

"While you were listening to old lady Townsend ramble on about her trip to Hong Kong, I was out with the most gorgeous man. Not an eight, not a nine, but a ten," she boasted, counting on her fingers.

Ellen had a sinking feeling in the pit of her stomach. "You didn't hire an escort from Two's Company, did you?"

"Yes, and he was every bit as wonderful as yours was. His name is Zeke and he models part-time for the Conrad Agency. He's your classic tall, dark, handsome." She swooned as she leaned her head back against the sofa. "Actually, last night was our second date.''

"You've been out with him before?''

"Yes, and I'm going to date him again if I can," she replied enthusiastically. "You know how much I hate going to His Majesty's summer barbecue alone. Well, this year I won't have to. And when Judy from the claims department gets married in August, I'll take Zeke. And there are several other occasions I wouldn't mind having him at with me."

"Jeannie, it's going to cost you a small fortune if you use him for a steady date."

"So what? He's worth it if it means I won't have to be alone. Do you know how many bums I've dated in the past ten years? At least he's kind, considerate and makes me feel pretty.''

Ellen's uneasiness grew. Wasn't that exactly what she thought about Seth? Doubts rushed in once more, weakening the fragile bond of trust that had started to develop between her and Seth. She pushed them aside, telling herself that Jeannie's circumstances and hers were entirely different.

''Besides, we get along so well that I think it's only a matter of time before we date on a personal basis.'' Her eyes glowed with anticipation.

''Jeannie, it states right in the contract you sign with Two's Company that escorts are prohibited from dating the clients on a personal basis.''

''You can't honestly think that none of those guys date the women they meet?'' She gave her sister a dubious look. ''Go get dressed and dry your hair so we can get something to eat,'' Jeannie ordered, reaching for a magazine that rested on the coffee table.

Ellen did as she was told, but this time when she saw the rumpled sheets on her bed, she didn't grin. Had she fallen so easily into Seth's arms because, like Jeannie, she was lonely and looking for someone to make her feel pretty? No, she thought a moment later. She may have been lonely, but she hadn't slept with Seth out of desperation. She wasn't the type to go to bed with a man after only a couple of dates, but with Seth everything had seemed so natural.

And he wasn't just another escort for hire. She wasn't paying him for anything, as Jeannie was still paying her Zeke. Seth was special. Very special.

By the time she had dried her hair and finished dressing, she had convinced herself her situation and Jeannie's were as different as night and day. Seth was sincere, not acting out a part, and she was silly to even make comparisons between the two men.

There was no way she was going to allow her sister to spoil the joy she was feeling. What she needed to do was to keep her relationship with Seth private—at least for a while. Eventually, Jeannie would find out about it, but until Ellen felt more secure with it herself, there was no reason she needed to discuss Seth with her sister. And with that thought firmly in place, she went downstairs.

SETH COULDN'T BELIEVE that he had fallen asleep in Ellen's bed. He understood why it had happened, but he wished he could turn back the clock. Sneaking out at one o'clock in the morning had been bad enough. Sneaking back in at eight was even worse.

He only hoped that his teenagers would sleep until noon and not realize that he hadn't been home last night. As he pulled his Explorer into the driveway, he noticed the Sunday paper wasn't lying on the front step. A bad sign. Someone was up.

His instincts were right on target when he stepped into the kitchen and found Kelly sitting at the table, leaning over the want ads. When she saw her father, she crossed her arms and gave him a pointed glare. "Must have been some coffee break."

"What are you doing up?" Seth asked, an edge to his voice. What he didn't need at eight o'clock in the morning was his daughter's disapproval. Self-recrimination had been creeping up on him all the way home.

"I'm meeting some friends for breakfast." She eyed him suspiciously.

"Oh." He couldn't think of another thing to say.

"Oh," she repeated sarcastically. When he would have walked right past her, she stopped him with "Is that all you have to say to me? Oh?"

Seth shoved his hands into his pockets and thought about his cartoon strip, *Holloway's House*. What would George say in such a situation?

"I don't think a father owes his daughter any explanations in an instance such as this." As soon as he had said the words, he knew he would never have written them in a cartoon bubble.

"You stay out all night without telling any of us where you're going and we shouldn't worry about you?" Her voice rose an octave.

"I'm sorry. After meeting with Hank, I went down to the paper to catch up on some work. I should have called home, but I didn't want to wake anyone."

"You were working?"

She didn't believe him and he couldn't blame her. He never went in to work in the middle of the night, but he couldn't admit that to her. "There are people who work all night at the paper," he said, then quickly left the room.

"You should have called," she reminded him, following him out of the room.

"I know. I've said I'm sorry."

"I suppose now you're going to go to bed," she commented as he started up the stairs.

He paused on a riser. "I thought I'd shower, then have some breakfast. What time are you leaving?"

"In about half an hour."

The suspicion in her face made him uneasy and he continued up the stairs, calling back over his shoulder, "Would you make me a pot of coffee before you go?"

"Sure," she answered, watching him pad up the stairs. "By the way, we found another apartment."

Again, he paused, this time at the top of the stairs. So that was her strategy. She was going to use his guilt to score points in the apartment battle. Well, it wasn't going to work.

"Who's we?"

"The kids I'm rooming with."

"I think we should discuss this subject another time."

"Fine, but I thought you should know I'm going to go see the apartment later today."

"You agreed to wait until we could go together," he reminded her.

"If I wait around for you, I'll never get a place."

The anger juices were burning in Seth's chest once more, only this time he didn't have any antacids handy. He wanted to say more, but thought better of it. "I think it's best if we discuss this later." He turned and continued toward his room.

Just before he reached his door, he heard her call out, "By the way, you buttoned your shirt wrong."

Seth glanced down and felt the blood rush to his face. Sure enough, in his haste to leave Ellen's, he had left an extra buttonhole at the top of his shirt. No wonder she had looked at him so suspiciously.

As soon as he reached his room, he practically ripped off the offending shirt and tossed it into the corner, cussing under his breath. He felt guilty. He couldn't help it.

He stepped into the shower and let the water pelt his skin. He watched the soapsuds disappear down the drain, wishing he could wash away his guilt so easily.

He turned the water up a notch so that it burned as it struck him. But no matter how hard he scrubbed or how hot the water was, he couldn't rid himself of the feeling that he had done something wrong. Last night in Ellen's arms everything had seemed so right. Yet now...

He closed his eyes, not wanting to think about his relationship with her. Still, he couldn't blot out the memory of telling her he loved her. The words had tumbled out spontaneously. He hadn't thought about them, hadn't rehearsed them, hadn't wanted to say them. They had simply happened.

Could he have meant them? At one time he had thought there would be only one woman he would ever love. Laura. Now he had discovered an intense passion that had left him feeling euphoric but guilty because for the first time since Laura had died another woman had a piece of his heart.

Was he ready for such a relationship? It was a question he couldn't answer because his hormones said one thing and his brain said another. By the time he had finished shaving and dressing, he had come to a decision. Even if he was a little in love with Ellen, it wasn't a good idea to be intimate with her until he was sure of where their relationship was heading.

Instead of reading the paper or watching CNN as he usually did in the morning, he grabbed a cup of coffee, picked up his sketch pad and found his favorite spot on the couch. He needed to work on *Holloway's House.* He drew several strips: George sneaking out at midnight, George getting stopped by the cops and George falling into the arms of a beautiful woman. However, each effort became a crumpled ball he tossed into the miniature basketball net perched on the rim of his trash can.

Finally, by midafternoon, he had drawn a strip he liked. Caught in a tiny white lie, George promised to always be honest with his teenagers.

When he showed the strip to Brian, the fourteen-year-old asked, "Aren't you going to tell what happened when George went out on his date?"

"It didn't work out as he planned" was Seth's response. He hoped his son would take the hint and not ask any more questions about the previous night. Like George, he didn't want to lie to any of his kids.

"I think your readers are going to want to know what happened, Dad."

Seth pondered his son's remark for several moments, then said, "*Holloway's House* doesn't have any readers."

"What about us?"

"I guess you'll just have to wait and see what I decide to do." It was a cop-out. He knew it, but he didn't want to talk about Ellen. Not yet. He was having a hard enough time understanding his feelings himself.

That was why, when his mother called, pumping him for information about the mystery woman in his life, he lied. And when Matt asked him if what Kelly said was true, that he had stayed out all night with a chick, he lied again.

By the time he went to bed Sunday night he felt like one big liar. And the worst part was that all he could think about was doing it again.

EVEN THOUGH SETH COULD DO much of his work at home, he often went over to the newsroom because he liked the energy and excitement of it. Stuff happened and he liked being around people.

Normally he ate lunch with a couple of guys from the editorial department, but on Monday he decided to call Ellen. He figured that the sooner he saw her and straightened out what had happened between them, the better.

His schedule was flexible enough that he could pick her up and take her to a restaurant near the clinic. She suggested they eat at a bar that was in the oldest building on the block. It was dark and hazy inside, and had a smell that only old bars with wooden floors and leather booths had.

"This place is interesting," Seth commented, glancing around as the waitress seated them in the back.

"I know it's not much to look at, but the food is wonderful," Ellen told him, passing him one of the menus from behind the salt and pepper shakers. "And they serve Pig's Eye beer," she added with a knowing grin.

Seth returned her smile, then forced his attention to the menu in his hands. It was difficult to think about food when all he wanted to do was stare at her. Ever since he had picked her up he had been having trouble keeping his eyes off her, especially since one of the buttons on her uniform had come undone. Although not much was revealed through the tiny gap, Seth knew what treasures lay beneath the white fabric, and the image was an enticing one.

"What do you recommend?" he asked, unable to resist looking in her direction.

"The mushroom burger is good, but my favorite is the Philly cheese steak—if you like green pepper and onions."

Seth loved green pepper and onions. When the waitress appeared he ordered two Philly cheese steaks, a Pig's Eye beer for himself and an iced tea for Ellen.

As soon as the waitress had left, she said, "I'm glad you called this morning. Mondays are always crazy at the clinic and it's nice to be able to get away for a while."

Her white uniform seemed out of place in the 601 Club, yet she didn't seem the least bit uncomfortable. He was the one who was fidgeting with the condiment tray and looking at everything but her bodice.

"I wanted to see you, Ellen." It was the truth. She had preoccupied his thoughts for the past twenty-four hours and then some.

"I'm glad," she said, a ghost of a grin curving her lips.

With each smile she gave him, it became harder to broach the subject he needed to discuss. He wanted to say, We need to talk about what happened Saturday night, but the way she was looking at him made him feel as though his thought processes were being zapped. And when she brought up the subject of Saturday night, he had a brief, strange sensation that she could see into his head.

"Everything happened so fast between us Saturday night, I wasn't sure if it was real or not," she said with a shyness that he found endearing.

He reached across the table and took her left hand in his right. "It was very real." Her hand was warm and soft in his, causing him to remember how she had touched him. He gave it a gentle squeeze, then released it at the same time the waitress appeared with their beverages.

While they waited for her to finish setting the table, they sat in silence. Seth wished he could find the words to tell Ellen what was really bothering him, but the longer he sat across from her, the less he wanted to bring up anything that would distance him from her. Telling her he didn't think they should be intimate in the future was not going to produce any smiles.

"You didn't run into any problems at home, did you?" she asked, as soon as the waitress had disappeared.

"No," he lied, then immediately wished he hadn't. He didn't want any pretense between them. "Actually, that's not true. My daughter, Kelly, was up when I got home and I don't think she believed me when I said I had been working all night. My shirt was buttoned wrong."

Ellen's eyes met his and the twinkle he saw reminded him that they shared an intimate memory. "You did leave in a hurry."

"Not by choice," he reminded her, his look conveying another silent message. He took a sip of his beer, then said, "Because of my rather sudden departure, we didn't have much time to talk."

"Is that what this lunch is for?"

It was the opening he had been waiting for. The opening he should have taken. But the way she was looking at him made his blood dance. So instead of saying, Yes, I think we need to discuss what happened Saturday night, he found himself saying, "This lunch is for you and me to get to know each other better and I think that'll be easier to accomplish if I do this."

He pushed his beer mug across the table, then slid his body across the U-shaped leather bench seat until he was sitting next to her. As he moved closer to her, he caught a hint of the scent that had filled her bed on Saturday. He felt a quick jolt of excitement and had to fight the urge to drape his arm around her shoulder.

"Does this mean I can ask you personal questions and you'll answer them?"

"Ask away," he said with a lift of his mug.

She took a sip of her tea, then asked, "How did you get the nickname Seth?"

"My complete name is Stanford Edward Thomas Holloway. When I first started cartooning, I used my initials which spelled S.E.T.H. Once I started drawing political cartoons I decided to use Holloway as a signature."

"When did you start drawing cartoons?"

He shrugged. "I can't remember ever not drawing them. When I was a kid I used to sketch all the time. I'd draw large chalk characters on the playground during recess, copy the funnies on my notebook." He shook his head in reminiscence. "It got me into trouble on more than one occasion."

"Why was that?"

"I'd punch out anybody who'd step on the chalk drawings on the playground. I think my teachers thought I was a rebel." He liked the way his body felt sitting close to hers. It was so natural, as if next to him was where she belonged.

"What did your parents think?"

"My father was of the opinion that art was not work, so when I said I wanted to be an artist, he told me I better get a real job first and have cartooning as my hobby."

"Did you get a real job?"

"I drew maps for a while until a small paper in Wisconsin hired me as an illustrator. I managed to convince the editor to let me slip an editorial cartoon in every now and then, and before I knew what was happening, I was getting picked up by *Newsweek* and some of the other major magazines.''

"What's it like being a cartoonist?"

"Truthfully?" When she nodded, he said, "It can be exhilarating and it can be frustrating. Even though I have days when coming up with an idea is like sweating blood, most of the time I love my work."

"You're lucky," she said with a wistful smile. "Not many people can honestly say that."

"Can you?"

"I wouldn't say I love it, but I enjoy it. I've always been interested in the medical profession and the clinic is a nice place to work."

"You would have made a good doctor," he told her.

She tilted her head when she looked at him. "What makes you say that?"

"Because you're good with people. And you're not easily frazzled—something for which I will always be grateful," he told her with a knowing grin. "If you were a doctor, I'd trust you with my life." He paused, then said, "I do trust you with my life."

Suddenly the atmosphere became charged with an intimacy that was broken only by the arrival of their waitress with their food. While they ate lunch, their conversation centered on their children, with Seth's confiding in her his reservations concerning Kelly's moving into an apartment, and her telling him of her own concerns about Rebecca's marriage.

"You were right. The food is great," he told her nudging his empty plate aside. "I'm glad you came today, Ellen."

"Thank you for inviting me." She gave him a pert grin.

"I'd like there to be more lunches like this."

"I'd like that, too," she said candidly.

"How about tomorrow?"

"You want to have lunch again tomorrow?"

"Yes, do you?"

She nodded. "But unfortunately, I have to say no. I have an appointment."

"What about Wednesday?"

"I'm sorry, but I can't on Wednesday, either. I always meet my sister for lunch on Wednesdays."

"And Thursday I have an appointment," he said with a sigh. "And of course Friday's the Fourth of July."

The thought of not seeing her for another week brought a slight frown to his face.

"Have you already made plans for the Fourth?" she asked.

"Not really. What about you?"

"We always have a family picnic. It's sort of a tradition."

He nodded in understanding. "We used to go camping, but now that the kids are older..." He trailed off with a shrug.

"Sometimes it's nice to break away from traditions," she said, looking at him over the rim of her cup.

"Does that mean if I were to invite you to spend the day at the Taste of Minnesota Festival you'd skip the family picnic?"

"Is that an invitation?"

"Yes. Are you accepting?"

"Yes." She said simply, then looked at her watch. "Oh. I have to get back."

Seth stood, then offered his hand as she slid out of the booth. "Ellen, about Saturday night..." he began once more.

"What about it?" she asked with a directness he found refreshing.

He paused, not knowing how to tell her that he wasn't going to rush into an intimacy he wasn't ready for, that he wanted the two of them to get to know each other better. But the more he thought about it, the sillier it sounded. After all, he had already made love with her, and despite the short time they had known each other, he felt a connection to her that went deeper than he would have ever expected it would.

Seeing the expectant look on her face as she waited for him to continue, he finally said, "I just wanted you to know how special it was for me."

She smiled at him and said, "It was special for me, too, Seth."

CHAPTER ELEVEN

"WHY DIDN'T YOU TELL ME you saw Seth Holloway at Becca's Saturday night?" Jeannie wasted no time in getting to the point when she phoned Ellen later that day.

"Because it was no big deal."

"That's not what Becca said. What is going on?" Jeannie demanded.

"If you talked to Becca, then you already know what happened," she said shortly.

"She thinks the two of you are really seeing each other."

"We are," Ellen admitted, knowing that sooner or later she was going to have to tell her sister the truth.

"Ellen! Since when?"

"Since Rebecca decided to play matchmaker." She tried to keep her voice from sounding defensive.

"And you weren't going to tell me? You let me go on and on about Zeke at breakfast yesterday, yet you never said a word."

"Because there really wasn't much to say." Ellen tried to minimize their relationship.

Her sister made a sound of disbelief. "Well, I don't want to hear you criticize my relationship with Zeke when you're going out with someone from the same dating service."

"Jeannie, it's not the same thing."

"You don't think so?"

"No. I'm not paying Seth to take me anywhere."

"So what are you trying to say? That I have to pay for my dates and you don't?" There was a hint of envy in her sister's tone and Ellen bristled uncomfortably.

"I'm just saying be careful with this Zeke. Don't expect more than professional services from him."

"In other words, it's okay for you to get involved with a man who works for an escort service, but not me. Is that it?"

"Look, I don't want to argue with you." Ellen deliberately softened her tone. "Please be careful, all right? That's all I want to say."

"Ditto, big sister," Jeannie crowed irreverently. "Now before you hang up, we need to talk about what we're bringing to the Fourth of July picnic."

There was a small silence before Ellen said, "I'm not going."

"Why not?" Before Ellen could answer, she said, "Oh, let me guess. You've made plans to go out with Seth Holloway on the Fourth."

Ellen's fingers played with the phone cord as she said, "He invited me to go to the Taste of Minnesota Festival. But even if he hadn't, I wasn't planning on going to the picnic this year. I thought this might be a good time to try something different, especially now that Becca's not going to be there."

"Hey! You don't need to explain it to me. I don't blame you for accepting a date instead of going to a picnic with a bunch of your relatives. I just wish that I had an alternative."

"Then you're not bringing Zeke?"

"I asked him if he wanted to drive up to Uncle Albert's with me."

"And?" Ellen prodded when her sister didn't continue.

"He wanted to come with me and he would if he hadn't already made plans to visit his folks in Wisconsin."

Ellen wondered if Jeannie would have had to pay for his company but decided not to ask. Besides, her sister did have a point. Who was she to question Zeke's motives when she wasn't questioning Seth's? They did, after all, work for the same escort service.

Actually, Seth was thinking of ways to remove his name from the list of eligible escorts at Two's Company. He had spent the better part of an afternoon jotting down reasons he could give his mother for no longer wanting to work for her.

None of them included Ellen, even though he knew deep in his heart that she should head the list. If he was going to put on a tuxedo and lavish attention on a woman, he wanted it to be Ellen, not someone he would never see again. If he was going to dine at a fancy restaurant and order expensive wine, he wanted Ellen to be sitting across from him, not someone who was paying for his company.

When Bernice called him early that evening to see if he could take a client to dinner on Thursday, he knew the time had come to tell her he intended to resign from Two's Company. "Mom, I'll take the assignment this time, but I should warn you. I think my escort days are about over."

"What?"

She sounded as if he had just told her he was slitting his throat with a kitchen knife. "I think the time has come for me to stop working for you."

There was a silence, then she asked, "Who is she?"

He feigned innocence. "What are you talking about?"

"The woman you've been seeing. You wouldn't tell me her name the other night, but now that you're quitting Two's Company, I think I have a right to know."

"I'm not quitting Two's Company because of a woman," he denied, looking at his list of reasons for not working as an escort. "You know that the biggest reason I agreed to help you out was that you were shorthanded. You've had more than enough time to hire more people."

"But no one is as good as you are. The clients love you! You're the perfect escort," she crooned.

"That's because I learned everything I know from you." Seth flattered her, hoping a little gallantry would soften the blow.

She dismissed his flattery with a click of her tongue. "I know it's a woman. Kelly told me you snuck out in the middle of the night and didn't get home till morning."

Seth moaned. "I wish she hadn't done that."

"Why? You think I'm going to scold you or something?"

Seth could feel his cheeks burn, and he rubbed a hand around the back of his neck. "It's not what you think, Ma," he told her, even though he knew it was exactly what she was thinking.

"Well, I guess I should have known it was bound to happen sooner or later. It was only a matter of time before you came out of the deep freeze."

"Deep freeze?"

"You haven't been interested in women since Laura died. That's why you found it easy to date so many different ones. It was just a job to you. But now you've found one who's managed to thaw that ice wall you've had around your heart and you're no longer interested in being anyone's date."

"Aw, Ma, it's not like that at all," he countered, uneasy with how well she understood him.

"You still haven't told me her name, this woman who has you sneaking around in the middle of the night."

Seth knew there was no point in keeping it a secret. If he continued to see Ellen, his mother was bound to find out. "It's Ellen Richards."

"Refresh my memory. Isn't she the one who hired you to make her ex-husband jealous?"

"Her ex is no longer in the picture," he said a bit irritably, wishing his mother hadn't reminded him of the reason Ellen had used Two's Company's services. He preferred to think she didn't have any feelings for the broken-down cowboy.

"Well, how soon do I need to find your replacement?"

"Soon."

Bernice sighed. "All right, but can you give me a couple of weeks? I think I'm going to have to let one of the recently hired men go."

"Which one is that?"

"Zeke Paulson. I have a suspicion that he's looking to make extra money on the side, and you know how hard we work to keep our reputation squeaky clean."

"All right. I'll stay till you find his replacement."

"Oh, and one other thing. Promise me you won't do anything foolish where this Richards woman is concerned, okay?"

"Foolish? Mother, I'm forty-three years old," he reminded her, snuffing out the memory of Saturday night. "Besides, I'm not looking for a replacement for Laura. Ellen's a friend. That's all."

"Uh-huh," she murmured absently, making him feel like a child.

He hated it when his mother treated him as if he needed to be reminded that he was an adult. What was even more maddening was when she was right to be concerned about him.

This was one of those times. He hadn't wanted to admit that his behavior Saturday night had been a bit risky, but the more he thought about his impetuous actions, the greater was his worry that one night of pleasure would have lasting consequences.

How many times had he preached to his kids to be careful in their relationships? Safe sex. He had said the words often enough, yet when the time had arisen for him to practice what he preached...

He shook his head in reproach. All he'd thought of at the time was making love with Ellen. Nothing else had mattered. The zombie hormones had done battle with his brain cells and won.

And what was even worse was that when he had met her for lunch, he couldn't tell her he wanted a platonic relationship, not a sexual one. He laughed with self-derision. Safe sex? The only way he would be safe would be to stay away from Ellen. Period.

And that was something he knew he wouldn't do.

WHEN SETH AROSE early on the Fourth of July to go for his daily run, he found Kelly waiting for him outside. "Oh, good. You are going," she said, as he came out of the house in his shorts and T-shirt. "I didn't think you were up." One foot was propped against the concrete riser, the other on the lawn so that she could stretch her leg muscles.

"You're going to join me?"

"Uh-huh. I'm thinking about running cross-country at school this fall."

Seth regarded her suspiciously. He found it rather difficult to believe that someone who found sweat disgusting and rarely left the comforts of air-conditioned edifices would suddenly want to run in humid heat.

"This might not be a good day to start. It's really hot," he warned.

She shrugged. "I can handle it. I've been running on the track at the U."

"You have?"

"Yeah. It's much better than using the sidewalks around here. Another reason why an apartment on campus would be a good idea."

So this was going to be another sales pitch for moving out, Seth thought as he started down the walk. "Are you ready?"

"Sure. Let's go," she answered, and they were off, running side by side through the residential area. He kept the pace moderate, making sure she could keep up.

To his surprise, she didn't launch into her "I want an apartment" theme, but jogged beside him in silence. After several blocks and only a couple of comments about the weather, she finally said to him, "Gran said you have a girlfriend."

Seth glanced sideways at her. So it wasn't about moving into an apartment, after all.

"A man my age doesn't have girlfriends," he said gently, the reprimand automatic. It was what Laura would have said. A feminist at heart, she had always corrected her children whenever they referred to women as girls. "Your mother wouldn't appreciate your choice of adjectives."

"All right, you have a woman friend," she amended. "Do you think mother would appreciate that?"

It was something Seth didn't even want to think about, let alone discuss with Kelly. To his surprise, however, he found himself saying, "Your mother always wanted the best for all of us."

Kelly didn't say anything for several moments. "Gran says you met her at Two's Company."

"Uh-huh," he answered, not offering any further information.

"I thought you said you'd never date anyone you met through the service."

"She's not like any of the others."

"You still broke the company rules."

"Technically, I didn't."

"How do you figure that?"

"I gave her back her original fee."

"Gran let you?"

"Gran doesn't know about it. The money I gave her back came out of my own pocket."

They were silent again as they crossed a street, still jogging, and entered a park with a paved hiking path. Finally, Seth asked her, "Does it bother you that I'm dating someone for real?"

"I'm...not...sure," she said, becoming winded from the exercise.

"It has been two years since your mother died," Seth said aloud, for both of their sakes.

They came upon a park bench and Kelly dropped down onto it. "I have to rest for a couple of minutes."

Seth sat down beside her. "Are you okay?" he asked as she massaged her right side with her fingertips.

She nodded. She didn't speak for several moments, then said, "Dad, ever since you stayed out all night I've been thinking about all of this . . . you, Mom, and this faceless woman."

"She's not faceless. You met her the day I had the anaphylactic reaction."

"It's your Florence Nightingale?" Her brows lifted in surprise.

"Her name is Ellen," he said quietly. "And I really hadn't planned on discussing any of this. Not because I want to keep anything from you but because I really haven't gotten to know her well enough to feel comfortable talking about her."

"Does that mean that Matt and Brian and I don't have anything to worry about?"

"Worry in what way?"

"That it's something serious . . . that she'll move in and want to take over where Mom left off."

Seth reached for her hand. "I'm not looking for someone to replace your mother." Again, he said the words as much to convince himself as to convince his daughter.

"Then this really isn't serious?"

"Would it upset you if it was?"

"It might," she admitted honestly, looking down at her hands as she spoke. "I mean, intellectually I can understand why you'd want to get involved with someone, but emotionally it's hard to think of you with anyone but Mom."

Seth released a long sigh. He wanted to tell her that he was fighting the same battle in his own heart. That he couldn't understand why it seemed so natural to be with Ellen yet strange that he loved being with someone who wasn't Laura. He was never one for platitudes, yet all he could think of to say was "Things change. Life goes on."

Several moments of silence followed before she said, "Am I going to get to meet her?"

"When the time is right."

"Then it's really not serious? You're just friends?"

Tell the truth. Tell the truth, a tiny voice echoed in his brain. He couldn't—not until he himself was sure what it was.

"I've only known her a few weeks," he pointed out, evasively.

"Aren't you the one who told me you met Mom on a Tuesday and married her the following Saturday?"

"Yes, but I was young then. I've become much more cautious in my old age."

"How many dates have you had with her?"

"A few," he hedged. "Why?"

"Because I read somewhere that one-fourth of all men fall deeply in love before the fourth date, but only 15 percent of women do. I'd hate to see you get hurt, Dad."

Seth didn't want to think of that possibility and decided it was time to change the subject. "I'll be okay," he told her, giving her shoulder an affectionate squeeze. He stood up and wiggled his limbs. "Are you ready to go?"

"All right," she said, rising to her feet. "Just promise me one thing."

"What's that?"

"That you won't do anything foolish."

Seth rolled his eyes. "I'm not the one who wants to move into an apartment near the campus."

She gave him a playful shove. "You're changing the subject, but that's okay, because it's a subject we need to discuss." And with that, she started back down the jogging path.

THERE HAD BEEN a time following Laura's death when Seth and his children had been inseparable. Although he had advised them to resume their activities and return to their regular routine, they had needed a grieving period and had spent an unusual amount of time together as a family. Gradually, they had slipped back into sports, school activities and part-time jobs, until finally life was once again back to normal—or as normal as it could be in a house with three teenagers.

They were always surprising him. Often the things Seth wanted to do most were the things they wanted to do least. So when he mentioned that he was going to the Taste of Minnesota Festival, he got the shock of his life when all but one of his kids seemed interested in tagging along. Matt had made plans to go waterskiing with friends, but both Brian and Kelly looked at him with eager expressions on their faces, as if waiting for an invitation. Fortunately for Seth, his mother called and invited her grandchildren to spend the day with her. To his surprise, they accepted the offer.

Although Seth thought it a little odd that Kelly wasn't spending the holiday with friends, he was too tantalized by the prospect of being with Ellen to give it a second thought. Nor did he ask his mother where the three of them would be spending the day.

Soon he would be seeing Ellen. Memories of her invaded his senses, the soft sound of her laughter, the sweet smell of her hair, the sensuous serenity that seemed to surround her. In just a few short weeks she had changed his life from ho-hum to oh-boy, and all he could think about was seeing her again.

He had promised himself that he wouldn't let his physical attraction to her cause him to do anything foolish. Which was why he had asked her to the festival. There was so much he didn't know about her, so much he wanted to discover. What better way than by strolling through the rows of food booths at the festival, sampling the various cuisines of the Twin Cities?

After his conversation with Kelly earlier that morning, Seth half expected that his mother would mention his date with Ellen, but to his surprise she said nothing. He heaved a sigh of relief as Kelly and Brian followed their grandmother out to her minivan, their swimsuits and beach towels stashed in their sports bags.

"Don't wait up for us," Bernice called out before climbing inside. "We're going to go to the fireworks if it doesn't rain."

Seth smiled and waved. He glanced up at the clear blue sky. There wasn't a cloud in sight. His grin widened.

He hadn't thought about fireworks until his mother had mentioned them. If he and Ellen stayed until after ten, they could watch the display at the Taste of Minnesota Festival.

He mentally juggled his schedule. Instead of spending the afternoon walking around the Capital grounds and taking Ellen home before dark, he could take her for a cruise down the Mississippi River, then head over to the Taste of Minnesota Festival toward evening.

An hour later he had parked his Explorer on Harriet Island and was escorting Ellen up the plank of the *Jonathan S. Padleford* stern-wheeler, a copy of a nineteenth century Mississippi riverboat.

"Do you know in all the years I've lived here I've never done this before?" she told him as they leaned up against the railings on the passenger deck.

"Good. I like introducing people to new experiences," he said, noticing how the sunshine caught the streaks of blond in her hair. "And I like being on the river."

"There is something soothing about being on water, isn't there," she mused.

"Then you don't mind that I changed our plans at the last minute?"

"Oh, no," she assured him. "This is nice ... and so refreshing."

The wind gently lifted her hair as she gazed out at the passing shoreline. Because she was wearing sunglasses, Seth couldn't see the expression in her eyes, but he knew she was sincere. Her appreciation was there in the way she lifted her face to the wind and inhaled the smell of the river.

Because it was a hot summer day, there were several passengers dressed in bustiers and halters, and even a few wearing bikini tops in order to catch the powerful tanning rays of the sun. Ellen wore a sleeveless denim shirt tucked inside a pair of white shorts, and Seth thought she looked sexier than any other woman on the boat.

"What are your kids doing today?" she asked.

"Two of them went with their grandmother, and Matt—he's the seventeen-year-old—went waterskiing with some of his friends."

"After I accepted your invitation, I was worried that I might be taking you away from the traditional Fourth of July family activities."

"You mean like painting my house?"

"Is that what you did last year?"

Seth nodded. "Yes, and it was hot and none of the kids stuck around to help." He sighed at the memory. "When Laura was alive, we used to go camping over the holiday weekend, but now that the kids are teenagers, they've lost interest in roughing it. They want to go to Valleyfair Amusement Park or to the wave pool or tubing on Apple River... and not with their father, but with their friends."

"It's a tough reality all parents must face. There comes a time when your child would rather be with a friend than with you."

"Actually, it's not so much the kids' fault. We can't manage to coordinate our schedules for family activities. It seems the older we get, the more often we find ourselves drifting in different directions." He sighed. "Sometimes I wish I could just miniaturize all three of them so we could do the things we used to do." Suddenly realizing how sentimental he was sounding, he shook his head in regret. "Listen to me. You'd think I didn't have a life of my own."

As he said the words aloud, he realized just how true they really were. For two years he had lived his life through his children and his memories of Laura. He hadn't wanted a life of his own, not if it meant closing the door on the past.

"I think you're a man who's being honest about how difficult it is for parents to nurture their children for so many years and then suddenly have to let them go out into the world," she said in understanding.

"It is tough, isn't it?"

She nodded soberly. "Maybe even tougher for those of us who are single parents." She shrugged. "Maybe not—who knows." She shoved a strand of hair back from her face. "I only know it's not easy."

He reached for her hand and entwined her fingers in his. "How are you coping with Rebecca's absence?"

This time she was the one who sighed. "I'm slowly getting used to it. Believe it or not, there are some advantages to having your children leave." To Seth, it sounded as though she was still trying to convince herself as much as him.

"Such as?" he gently probed.

"Like today, for instance. Ever since Becca was young we always went up to my uncle's cabin for the Fourth of July holiday, which meant I could never do any of the celebrations planned here in the cities."

"So you've never been to the Taste of Minnesota Festival?"

"No, but now that Becca's married and spending the holiday with her in-laws, I'm finally free to choose where I go and with whom."

Her words made him feel rather special. He gave her hand a gentle squeeze. "I'm glad you chose to be with me, Ellen. This is much better than painting."

She smiled. "I think it is, too. You're a nice man, Seth Holloway."

He had the overwhelming urge to kiss her right there in front of everyone. He chose, however, to lift her knuckles to his lips. He knew exactly why he was so attracted to her. When they were together, he felt as if everything was right in his world.

He was slowly discovering who she was and as the pieces of the puzzle came together, he liked the picture they created. She was unlike any woman he had ever known. There was a gentleness about her that evoked his protective instincts, yet he knew that she had an inner strength that could see her through any crisis.

As hard as he tried, he couldn't stop himself from comparing her to Laura. He didn't want to do it, it simply happened. And the better he got to know Ellen, the more he realized how very different she was from Laura.

His wife had been a bundle of energy—sometimes too much energy. By the end of their very first date she had joyfully recounted her life history to him, and in all the years he had lived with her, she had never been at a loss for words.

Ellen, on the other hand, revealed little about herself voluntarily. She had a quiet way. He never thought he'd find that attractive in a woman, yet there was a sweet feeling in the silences they shared.

Seth knew it was going to be tough to stick to his resolution to keep their relationship platonic, for every time he looked at her he wanted to touch her. He settled for walking hand in hand with her on the deck of the paddle wheeler, and then later, through the rows of food booths at the Taste of Minnesota Festival. By nightfall they had sampled a variety of exotic foods, quenched their thirst with Pig's Eye Pilsner and listened to Molly and the Haymakers perform country music on the outdoor stage.

It was a wonderful day for Seth, and when the last of the fireworks exploded in the night sky, he knew that he was only fooling himself if he thought his attraction to Ellen was a passing fancy. He had thought that he would never love again, yet what he felt for Ellen was every bit as intense as his feelings for Laura had been.

Could it be that he was in that 25 percent of the male population who knew they were in love after only four dates? He didn't need to think very long for an answer. Now the only question needing an answer was this: was Ellen in the 15 percent of women in that same category?

Probably not, he decided, judging by the distance she kept between them as they strolled through the festival grounds. He wished that she would initiate contact with him, make some overture indicating she wanted his touch as much as he wanted hers. Yet she didn't, and he wasn't sure if it was because of her reserve or if she was subtly telling him that he was moving too fast.

Then there was the possibility he hadn't wanted to consider—that she was still hung up on her ex-husband. The sole purpose of their first date had been to make the Colorado Kid jealous. Memories of how she had looked defending Kenneth Richards the night of the wedding rehearsal brought a frown to his face.

He slowly shook his head. Could it be that he had finally found a woman who could make him forget about Laura and that woman was still in love with someone else? He remembered the sadness that had been in her voice when she told him Kenneth had returned to Colorado.

Thank goodness his competition was gone. What he really needed was time. No matter how much he wanted to sweep her into his arms and confess his feelings for her, he couldn't do it. All of his life he had behaved impulsively. This time it would be different.

When he took her home that night, she suggested he come in for a nightcap. He was about to accept her offer and ignore his resolution not to put himself in a situation that might lead to intimacy when she led him by the hand into the living room.

"Take a seat and I'll get us something to drink," she told him and headed for the kitchen. Just as she was about to open the refrigerator, the phone rang. She answered the kitchen extension.

"Elle, it's me."

Kenneth didn't need to identify himself. After seventeen years of marriage and the fact that he had called her Elle, Ellen automatically knew it was her ex-husband.

"Why are you calling?" she asked, her heart beating unevenly.

"I just wanted to hear your voice."

Ellen grimaced. "This isn't a good time. I have company."

"I won't keep you long. I just need to talk to you for a few minutes. I've been thinking about you a lot since Becca's wedding."

"You shouldn't be," she told him, peeking around the door frame to check on Seth.

"I can't help it. Ever since I got back I can't stop thinking about us."

"Us? There is no us," she reminded him sharply.

He sighed. "I know and it's my fault. I should never have left you, Elle."

Ellen's spine stiffened. "We shouldn't be having this conversation, Kenneth. You're married to another woman."

"I shouldn't be married to her," he admitted regretfully. "Like I told you when I was in for Becca's wedding, she's too young for me. And I don't love her the way I loved you."

His words made her stomach churn. She couldn't believe what she was hearing. Not so long ago she would have practically died to hear him say such a thing.

"Elle, all she's been talking about is having a baby. I really don't want another kid at my age."

Ellen didn't want to hear about his problems with Tina. "This is really none of my business."

"Don't say that, Elle. You were always there for me when I needed to talk."

"That was when you wanted me to be a part of your life. You left me, Kenneth. Or have you forgotten? We're divorced."

"Three years ago I went a little crazy and I'm sorry. Good Lord, you don't know how sorry I am."

Ellen didn't think she wanted to hear what was coming next. "Look, Kenneth. There's no point in us talking about this. You're married to another woman, and I'm not looking to take a walk down memory lane. Now I really have to be going. I have a guest." And with that she abruptly said goodbye and hung up the phone.

As she set a bottle of sparkling wine and two glasses on a serving tray, she couldn't stop thinking about Kenneth and Tina. Was their marriage really in jeopardy? She felt a strange sort of emotional numbness now in regard to her ex-husband. Maybe it was a self-protective reaction to keep her from being drawn into a relationship with him again. Or maybe it was the reaction of a woman who was truly over her ex-husband. She hoped it was the latter.

When she returned to the living room, Seth noticed the change in her mood immediately. The sparkle in her eyes had been replaced by a worried look. He took the tray from her hands and set it on the coffee table.

"I'm sorry it took so long. I had a phone call," she said as she sat down beside him, her voice sounding a bit brittle. "Why don't you open this?" She handed him the wine.

He could see that her smile was forced, and he had a pretty good idea of the reason why. The phone call had been from the Colorado Kid. The house was small enough that he had heard bits of her end of the conversation, and it was obvious that Kenneth Richards could still tug on Ellen's emotions.

The thought was a sobering one for Seth. He definitely was going to have to give Ellen more time before he rushed into any further intimacy. Instead of opening the bottle of wine, he held it up and said, "It's late. Why don't we save this for next time?"

When she would have protested, he silenced her with a kiss, then forced himself to leave before his impulses made him forget all about his good intentions. "Don't worry. I'll be back," he called out to her as he walked toward the Explorer.

CHAPTER TWELVE

ELLEN KNEW Rebecca's honeymoon was truly over when her daughter phoned one evening and the first words out of her mouth were, "Mother, you wouldn't believe how inconsiderate he is."

"Who, dear?" Ellen asked innocently, knowing perfectly well that it was her son-in-law who was the object of her daughter's scorn.

"Roger. We were supposed to be meeting everyone at Champps Sports Bar a half hour ago, and he hasn't even picked up the phone to call and tell me he's going to be late."

"Maybe something important has come up and he can't get to a phone," Ellen suggested, trying to calm her daughter's ruffled feathers.

"He has a cellular phone, Mother," she snapped impatiently.

"Oh. Well, do you think he might have his signals crossed and is meeting you there?"

"If he were there, he'd call and find out why I wasn't," she said stubbornly. "I can't believe how he's changed since we've been married."

In the course of the next twenty minutes, Ellen heard how her son-in-law didn't appreciate her daughter's cooking, was a workaholic who was seldom home and who, when he did manage to quit working at a decent hour, became a couch potato interested in an intimate relationship only with the TV remote control.

"I swear, Mother, he's not the same man I dated."

"Yes, he is," Ellen said placatingly.

"Oh, no, he's not!"

"Maybe it doesn't seem like he is because you're in a period of adjustment." Ellen tried to keep her voice calm. "All couples go through it. You have to get used to each other's habits and little quirks."

"Quirks?" she repeated in disbelief. "Mother, he doesn't rinse the dishes before he puts them in the dishwasher!"

"Did you tell him he should?"

"Of course I did . . . not that he listens to anything I have to say. I can't tell you the number of times I asked him not to put the salt and pepper shakers in the cupboard, that they should be on the table. I bet if I were to open my cupboard they'd be inside." There was a pause and she said, "See. There they are."

Ellen couldn't help but smile. "Maybe you should be in charge of cleaning up in the kitchen."

"I'm not cleaning up in the kitchen!" she declared indignantly. "We decided before we ever got married that this marriage would be a fifty-fifty proposition. It wouldn't be fair if I had to do the cooking and the cleanup."

Ellen wanted to tell her that she didn't think there was a marriage in the world with better than an eighty-twenty ratio when it came to housework, but she didn't need to hear her daughter get on her soapbox regarding gender inequities. "Maybe you could trade him another task for kitchen duty . . . like laundry or something."

"Are you kidding? He has twice as many clothes as I do. If I let him do the laundry I won't have a clean pair of underwear until he's down to his last dirty sock."

Ellen decided it would be prudent to change the subject. "So tell me how your job is going."

"I hate it," she said sullenly.

"Why? I thought this was what you wanted? To get away from studying and out into the workplace?"

"Well, I guess it wouldn't be so bad if I got a little help at our apartment. But I come home too tired to cook and when I ask Roger to take me out to eat, he says, 'We can't afford it. Why don't you make something simple?' Mom, he's missing the whole point. I don't want to cook when I'm tired."

"Join the club," Ellen drawled sympathetically.

"He doesn't want to take me anywhere. All he does is work. We haven't even been to the movies since way before the wedding."

Ellen sighed. "Darling, your life-style changes when you get married. I tried to warn you but you wouldn't listen to me."

"Oh, please, Mother. I hope you're not going to say 'I told you so.'"

Ellen wanted to. The words sat on the edge of her tongue like a cat ready to pounce on a bowl of cream. "What I'm going to say is that it's normal for newlyweds to experience a period of adjustment. It's sort of like growing pains for a marriage."

"That's real comforting, Mom. I'm miserable and you tell me it's normal."

Ellen sighed. "Oh, Becca. What do you want me to say? Just a few months ago you were accusing me of being too critical of Roger. Now you want me to find fault with him?''

"Oh! There's someone at the door, Mom. I think it's him. I've gotta go.''

"All right, but listen to me, Becca. He's your husband. Talk to him. Tell him what's bothering you. It's important that you're honest with each other.''

"All right, all right. I will,'' she promised, exasperation in her voice.

"And I thought Dolores Townsend was going to be her biggest problem,'' Ellen mumbled to herself as she hung up the phone.

THROUGHOUT THE MONTH of July, Seth stuck to his game plan. He and Ellen dated often, much to his delight. They attended concerts in the park, strolled through art galleries and went to a film festival of Alfred Hitchcock movies.

The more he saw her, the harder it was to stop thinking about what it had been like the night they had made love. It was only with a supreme effort that he was able to keep his resolution to give her time to get over her ex-husband. By now he was certain he was prepared for an intimate relationship with someone other than Laura. Ellen, however, had given him no indication that she wanted things to be any other way, so he had no reason to believe she was unhappy with their relationship as it was.

Little did he know that the more often they dated the more confused Ellen became. She had assumed that after their passionate night together that they would become lovers, yet Seth hadn't made one move in that direction. Instead of finding opportunities for them to be alone, he went out of his way to make sure that when they were together there were always other people around. What she didn't understand was why he had withdrawn from her physically when emotionally they were growing closer.

Seth's apparent lack of sexual interest in her had her questioning whether he really had enjoyed making love with her as much he had proclaimed he did that night. Having lived with Kenneth for seventeen years, she knew her self-confidence in the area of intimacy wasn't the greatest, but she had been almost positive that Seth had enjoyed her as much as she had enjoyed him. Men didn't fake it—or did they?

The longer they dated and the less anxious he was to become intimate with her, the more she worried that Kenneth had been right when he had told her she didn't have what it took to keep a man satisfied.

But deep down, she knew it was irrational to even entertain such a thought. Kenneth was a jerk. And what good were all her months in therapy if she was going to revert to the same self-defeating behavior that had traumatized her after the divorce?

There was a reason for Seth's not pursuing a sexual relationship with her. A good reason. She just needed to be patient and wait for him to tell her that reason. She only hoped that it wasn't because he only wanted a friendship with her and not love.

As ELLEN AND SETH grew closer, Rebecca and Roger appeared to be drifting apart, much to Ellen's dismay. It was becoming routine for Rebecca to call her mother and complain about every little thing that went wrong. Ellen could only hope that what Rebecca and Roger was going through was a period of adjustment and not true marital strife.

When Rebecca called to tell her mother she couldn't go shopping one Saturday morning because Roger was taking her sailing, Ellen felt a wave of relief. She pushed all thoughts of there being any serious trouble between the newlyweds out of her mind and drove herself to the mall in search of a new dress for the party Seth was taking her to that evening.

After several hours of sifting through the clearance racks in search of a bargain, Ellen found the aroma of freshly baked cookies too great of a temptation to resist and followed the scent to the food court. It was while she was waiting for the clerk to get her order that she noticed a familiar face at one of the tiny wrought-iron tables out front.

It belonged to a young woman with long, straight dark hair who smiled when she noticed Ellen's interest. Ellen's wave was tentative as she searched her memory for a clue as to why the girl looked so familiar.

With a cup of coffee in one hand and a macadamia nut cookie in the other, Ellen turned to get a better look at the young woman and realized that she was Seth's daughter, Kelly. She had moved her packages from a nearby chair and was gesturing for Ellen to join her.

"Hi. You are Ellen, right?" she asked, as Ellen set her coffee on the tiny table.

Ellen nodded as she sat down.

"Oh, good. It would have been embarrassing if you had been a total stranger." She smiled and a dimple creased her cheek in the same place it did her father's. She wiped her fingers on a napkin, then extended her hand to Ellen. "I'm Kelly Holloway."

"Yes, I know." She smiled as she shook her hand. "It's nice to see you again. How are you?"

"Fine, thanks. I wasn't sure if you'd remember me. We only met that one time and I was sort of freaked at what was happening to my dad."

"Anaphylactic reactions can be scary," Ellen remarked, wondering if Seth's wife had been as dainty and as delicate looking as this beautiful girl was.

She had an animated face and Ellen couldn't help but warm to her as her eyes widened expressively. Except for the dimple, she didn't share many traits with Seth, and Ellen could only assume she must have taken after her mother. If that was the case, it was obvious the late Mrs. Holloway had been a beautiful woman.

"Is that macadamia nut?" Kelly asked as Ellen broke her cookie into two pieces before taking a bite.

"Uh-huh. Would you like a taste?"

"Oh, no, that's all right. I already had mine." Instead of coffee, she lifted a small carton of milk to her lips. "They make the best cookies here. No matter how hard I try, I can't walk past without stopping."

"Me neither," Ellen confessed, wondering now if some of the animation wasn't nervousness, for Kelly was folding her paper napkin into accordion pleats.

"Maybe it was destiny that we were supposed to meet at the cookie counter," Kelly said with a laugh, and this time the uncertainty was definitely there.

Ellen's brows rose slightly. "Maybe it was." She took a sip of her coffee, wondering what it was that Kelly wanted to say to her, for it was obvious there was something on her mind.

"I'm glad we did meet because I've been hoping I'd get a chance to talk to you."

Uh-oh, here it comes, Ellen thought and mentally prepared herself for an inquisition. All she could think about was that Kelly knew her father had spent the

night at her house. It was a thought that made her want
to squirm.

"I thought my dad would have brought you over to
the house by now, but I don't think he's ready to share
you with the family just yet."

"We haven't known each other very long," Ellen
pointed out as gently as possible.

"I know, but..." She hesitated, her fingers pleat-
ing yet another paper napkin.

"You wanted to check me out before your father got
seriously involved with me?" Ellen supplied.

Her cheeks turned a light pink. "My brothers and I
are a little curious, but I think that's only natural. You
are the first woman my dad's actually dated since my
mother died. I mean, besides the professional dates
he's had at Two's Company, and this Liza person he
knew from work, although they weren't actually dating."

"Really?"

"Uh-huh. You look surprised."

"I am. Because of the kind of work he did for Two's
Company I assumed he was..." She trailed off, not
sure how to delicately say what she was thinking.

"That he was what? Some kind of playboy or
something?"

Ellen shrugged. "Not exactly a playboy, but maybe
something of a ladies' man."

Kelly burst out laughing, easing the tension. "I'm
sorry. You don't know how funny that sounds to me. I
mean to hear my dad being called a ladies' man."
Amusement danced in her eyes.

"He is very charming and he has had a lot of experience dating women," Ellen said in her own defense.

"There's a difference between going out with someone for professional reasons and dating."

"That's true, but I'm not sure the public always makes that distinction."

"You're probably right," she conceded. "Grandma's always telling me how tough it is for Two's Company to establish a professional reputation when there are so many escort services out there that aren't legitimate."

Ellen thought about her own initial reaction to Two's Company and nodded in understanding. "How long have you worked for your grandmother?"

"Just since the first of June. I'm only filling in for one of the employees who's away on maternity leave. Grandma has a way of getting us to help out even when we really would rather not do it, you know what I mean?"

Ellen nodded. "I suppose it's hard to turn her down."

"I know it is for my dad. But he finally told her he's quitting."

Ellen was thrilled to hear it. But she forced herself to focus on Kelly. "What about you? Do you like working at Two's Company?"

She shrugged. "Actually, it's kind of fun. I'm hoping I'll be able to use my experience for psychology papers or something. My dad probably told you I'm a student at the U."

"You're going to be a sophomore, right?"

"Uh-huh. I'm hoping to get an apartment close to the campus. This past year I commuted and it was a real pain." She rolled her eyes. "I suppose my dad also told you he's against me moving out."

"He did mention it," she admitted honestly. "It's hard for parents to acknowledge that their children are no longer children. But there comes a time in every parent's life when they have to let go."

"Tell that to my father," she said wryly.

"I already have." She smiled sympathetically.

"You know we've been battling over this, don't you?"

Ellen nodded. "He's mentioned it to me."

"And do you think it's foolish for me to want to move into an apartment when I could live at home?"

"Not at all. My daughter went away to school, so she had to live in a dorm, but if she had stayed here and attended the U, I would have wanted her to be on campus."

"You have a daughter my age?" she asked with interest.

"Yes. She's nineteen, but almost twenty. And she's married."

"Whoa! Already?"

Ellen's brows lifted. "Unfortunately. Maybe that's why I can understand why your father's having trouble accepting that you want to move away from home. I'm having trouble letting go, too."

"But you didn't try to stop your daughter from getting married, did you?"

"I don't think I did but if you talked to her, she'd probably say something different," she answered with a crooked smile. "Sometimes, Kelly, it's hard for parents not to want to protect their daughters."

"But that's the problem. My dad's overprotecting me. When my mother was alive, she always said that the greatest gift she could give us kids was to teach us to be strong capable adults. My dad's totally forgotten that. He's treating me like I'm twelve years old and I can't be trusted to take care of myself."

Ellen took another sip of her coffee, then asked, "Do you honestly think that if your mother were here she'd support you on this issue?"

Kelly thought for a moment before saying quietly, "I really think she would, but every time I try to tell that to my dad, he gets all hostile."

Ellen felt a rush of sympathy for Seth and the delicate-looking teenager sitting across from her. It was obvious that they were having trouble communicating, and she wished there was some way she could help. Yet considering her own precarious relationship with Seth, she didn't feel she was in a position to presume that her help was either wanted or needed.

"Is it difficult for the two of you to talk about your mother?"

Kelly shrugged. "Not really, but we hardly ever do."

"Why is that?"

"Probably for the same reason he hasn't published *Holloway's House*."

"*Holloway's House?*" That roused Ellen's curiosity.

"It's a cartoon strip he created after my mother died. It's about a single father with three teenage kids and all the funny little problems they encounter."

"It's based on your family?"

"Dad says it isn't. He named the main character George and the teenagers are two girls and a boy—just the opposite of us, but we all know it's our family."

"And he hasn't submitted it for publication?"

"Uh-uh." She drained the remainder of milk from the carton, then squashed it and tossed it into the trash receptacle nearby. "He says it's not ready, that it's not fully developed yet."

"Maybe it isn't," Ellen suggested, looking at her over the rim of her paper cup.

"Oh, yes, it is. I've seen it. And if the syndication people looked at it, they'd snap it up in a minute."

"He must have his own reasons for not selling it," Ellen said in Seth's defense.

"Oh, he does," she said cryptically.

Ellen didn't want to ask, but she couldn't stop herself. "You think it has something to do with your mother?"

"I know it does. You see, she was always after him to create a comic strip based on family life and he always told her the same thing. 'I'll start it tomorrow.' Well, before tomorrow came, she became sick and died."

"What happened to her, Kelly?" Ellen asked softly.

"It was a virus that struck her heart. We thought she had the flu, then suddenly she was in the hospital and then..." She broke off, her voice choking with emotion.

Ellen reached across the table and covered her hand with hers. "I'm sorry. That must have been a terrible experience for you."

She nodded, then bit down on her lip. "It was, especially because it all happened so fast."

"So when did your dad start drawing the strip?"

Kelly took a deep breath before answering. "It was at least three or four months later."

"So you think that in his mind it's sort of a tribute to your mother?" she probed gently.

"In a way. He misses her so much." Again her voice cracked with emotion. "I'm sorry. This isn't the kind of stuff you want to hear. I mean, you're dating my dad." She looked away in embarrassment.

"Yes, I am, but I realize he has a past. You don't ever need to apologize for being happy that your father and mother had a good marriage."

"Did you have a good marriage with your first husband?"

"No, I didn't," she said candidly.

"I'm sorry. It's none of my business. I don't know why I'm asking you all of these personal questions," she said a bit nervously.

"Because you care about your father," Ellen supplied the answer for her. "I do, too, which means we already have something in common."

Kelly's lips curved ever so slightly. It was a smile—a small smile, but a smile just the same, and Ellen knew she had crossed one bridge without falling into the water. It was only after she and Kelly had parted company that Ellen realized the full significance of their conversation. Seth's children were in no way responsible for the stall in their relationship. If there were any obstacles blocking their road to happiness, they had come from another source—Laura Holloway.

Seth had been so devoted to her that he didn't want an intimate relationship with any other woman.

It would explain why he hadn't made any attempt to make love with her since that night of Becca's party. It would also explain why someone like Seth would work as a personal escort. Maybe Two's Company had been a sort of protective device to keep him from getting emotionally involved with a woman.

It could very well be that all he wanted from women was companionship. Maybe there wasn't a woman alive who could compete with the memory of Laura Holloway.

All the way home Ellen was troubled. As much as she had enjoyed talking with Kelly, she wished she hadn't seen the young woman, for now she had the uneasy feeling that she had fallen in love with a man obsessed with his dead wife.

SETH HAD ARRANGED to pick up Ellen at seven the following Friday evening to attend Two's Company's annual employee appreciation night. Once a year Bernice Benson arranged the special party for her employees and their guests.

Ellen had looked forward to the evening, not only because she was curious to meet the other members of Two's Company, but also because Jeannie was going to be at the party with Zeke. As far as she knew, her sister was still a client of Two's Company, and it was somewhat of a relief to Ellen to know that she would at least be introduced to him on a night when her sister wasn't paying for his services.

There was no sign of her sister when she arrived at the hotel banquet room where the party was being held. Nor did she show up during the cocktail hour before dinner. Ellen kept an eye out for her as Seth introduced her to the other employees at Two's Company.

When everyone was seated for dinner and there was no sign of either Jeannie or Zeke Paulson, Ellen had the uneasy feeling that her sister's date had either stood her up or Jeannie was sick.

"Are you looking for anyone in particular?" Seth asked as Ellen craned her neck to look around the room.

"I thought my sister Jeannie would be here."

"Oh, really? Why?"

"Because she's dating one of your escorts."

"She is? Who?"

"Zeke Paulson."

Seth's expression changed from surprise to concern. "Since when?"

"I don't know. Maybe three, four weeks."

"Did she meet him through the service?"

"Yes."

He sighed and rubbed a hand across his jaw. "I wish you had told me she was interested in him."

"Why? What's wrong?"

"Zeke Paulson doesn't work for Two's Company anymore. When my mother found out he was asking women for money on the side, she had no choice but to fire him."

CHAPTER THIRTEEN

ELLEN LET her sister's phone ring at least a dozen times before hanging up. She waited for her quarter to be returned, then reinserted it in the coin slot and punched the seven digits in Jeannie's number one more time to make sure she hadn't called the wrong number.

She hadn't. There was still no answer. "Where are you?" she mumbled into the receiver in exasperation, then reluctantly dropped the handset back on the hook.

This was the third time she had slipped out of the party to use the pay phone in the lobby. Ever since Seth had told her about Zeke Paulson, all she could think about was getting in touch with her sister to make sure she was all right.

Throughout the evening Ellen continued to call but without any luck. Despite Seth's attempts to reassure her that just because Zeke didn't meet Two's Company's standards didn't mean he didn't care for her sister, Ellen wasn't convinced that her sister wasn't in for a rude awakening.

If only she knew where Jeannie was. Had she gone out because Zeke had stood her up, or was she with him at this very minute, giving him money so he'd stick around? Maybe now that he had been fired from Two's Company he'd latch on to her sister like a bloodsucker.

It was that last thought that concerned Ellen the most. Jeannie had never had time for smooth-talking men, but with Zeke Paulson she had appeared to lose touch with her common sense. Ellen wanted to believe that when her sister learned what kind of man he really was, she'd show him the door so fast that his head would swim.

It was because Ellen was worried about Jeannie that she asked Seth if he would mind stopping by her sister's house on the way home. When they pulled into the driveway of the small bungalow, there was light showing in several windows.

"Do you want to wait here or come in?" Ellen asked, her fingers clutching the door handle.

"I'll walk you to the door to make sure everything's all right," Seth told her.

As soon as Jeannie answered the door, Ellen had a pretty good idea that Zeke wasn't around, for her sister's eyes were red, her face puffy from crying. She looked surprised to see them.

"What are you doing here?" she asked, glancing from Ellen to Seth and back again.

"I asked Seth to stop so I could talk to you. Are you all right?" Ellen asked.

"I'm fine. Why?"

"When you didn't show up at the party tonight I got a little worried about you."

"Oh! The party." She pushed her hair away from her face. "That didn't work out as we had planned, did it?"

"No, it didn't." Ellen could tell that she wasn't exactly thrilled to see them, and she wondered if maybe she was wrong and Zeke was inside. "Can we come in for a few minutes?"

"Oh, sure." She held open the door, but Seth chose not to go in.

"Why don't I wait for you in the car?" he suggested.

Ellen nodded and gave his hand a grateful squeeze. When she stepped inside, she was relieved to see that there was no sign of Zeke. Ellen doubted whether he had been there at all, for Jeannie's living room was in its usual disorganized state.

A newspaper was spread out across the couch, a jacket was draped over a chair arm and shoes were scattered across the carpeted floor. But it was the pile of used tissues crumpled up on the coffee table that caught Ellen's eye. It was next to a smaller mountain of candy-bar wrappers. Her sister always pigged out on miniature chocolate bars when she was upset.

"So how was the party?" Jeannie asked, using a remote control to flip off the late-night talk show that had been playing on the television.

Ellen shrugged. "You didn't miss much. It was like any other office party. The employees had a great time and the guests walked around pretending to have a great time."

While she talked Jeannie bustled around the room, trying to straighten up a bit. With one sweep of her arm she dumped the candy wrappers and crinkled tissues into a trash can, then scooped up the newspapers from the sofa so Ellen could sit down. "I'm glad Seth didn't come in. This place is a mess."

"Don't worry about it. It looks all right," Ellen told her as she sat down on the leather sofa.

Jeannie continued to put things away. "I guess I should have stayed home this evening and cleaned house."

"Where did you go? I tried calling several times but there was no answer."

"I was out with a couple of new friends. We were celebrating our good fortune."

"Good fortune?"

"Yeah. All three of us are going to save a lot of money in the future."

Puzzled, Ellen asked, "What are you talking about?"

"Well, you see, until today I didn't realize that there were three of us all in the same predicament. We were all pouring money down the drain for a worthless cause."

"Are you talking about Zeke?"

Jeannie dropped down beside Ellen. "His real name is Martin. Zeke is the name he uses when he wants to hustle women. You were right about him all along. He wasn't interested in me personally, only in the money he could make off me."

There was a sadness in her voice that contradicted the flip tone of her earlier comments. Ellen suspected that her sister had given more of her heart to Zeke Paulson than she had intended.

"I'm sorry, Jeannie."

"Yeah, me too," she said with a sniffle. "But I'm not going to cry over him anymore. At least I didn't lose as much as Linda and Denise did."

"Those are the two women you went out with tonight?"

"Yeah. Linda actually believed he was going to marry her, so she hired this private investigator to check up on him and discovered that not only did he have one other girlfriend, but two. Me and Denise."

"Did he meet both of them through Two's Company?"

"Only Denise. Linda he met through a friend who had used Two's Company."

"Well, if it's any consolation to you, he lost his job. Seth told me Bernice fired him when she found out he was trying to make money off her clients."

Jeannie chuckled sarcastically. "I suppose she didn't want money going into his pockets that should have been hers."

"She didn't want him using women," Ellen said in the older woman's defense. "She's trying to operate a legitimate escort service."

"Then she better screen her employees better," she retorted, her face twisting with bitterness.

"I'm sure she's just as upset by this as you are. Don't forget that same silver tongue he used on you he also used on her. Even after he was caught red-handed, he tried to talk her into turning a blind eye to his off-duty adventures."

Jeannie reached for a tissue to blow her nose. "At least I still have my car. Linda loaned him her minivan, thinking he was going to go make travel arrangements for their honeymoon. The police figure he's in another state by now."

The thought sent a chill up and down Ellen's spine. "I don't think Seth knows about that."

"He probably knows a lot more than you give him credit for," Jeannie remarked.

"What's that supposed to mean?"

"Ellen, his mother owns the business. Don't you think he's up on everything that goes on?"

"What if he is?"

She shrugged. "I didn't mean anything by it. I just want you to think really long and hard before you get any more involved with him than you already are. I mean, he works for an escort service. Whether it's legitimate or not, you must have some reservations about him."

"For the record, he doesn't work for Two's Company any longer. Besides, he's not some character who drifted into town. He's a well respected cartoonist for the newspaper," she pointed out, her voice rising in anger.

Jeannie held up her hands in self-defense. "There's no need to get upset about it. I didn't say the guy's another Zeke Paulson. I'm just trying to warn you not to expect more than the man's willing to give."

"I don't," Ellen insisted, although long after she had left her sister's house, she was still thinking about just what it was she wanted from Seth.

Jeannie had raised serious questions, intentional or not, in Ellen's mind concerning her future with Seth. Even though on several occasions he had implied that he wanted them to have a long-term relationship, the truth was he hadn't said he wanted that long-term relationship to be anything more than a friendship.

He had murmured a few "You are so good for me's" and a couple of "I like being with you's" but there had only been one "I love you" and that had come after a night of passion that had never been repeated. Initially, Ellen had interpreted the news of his quitting Two's Company as a sign that he wanted to date only her, but she realized now that it could have meant he was tired of being friendly to strangers and preferred the company of one woman who wouldn't put any demands on his time.

The more she thought about it, the more uneasy she became. After talking with her sister, she realized that she had entered the relationship without any idea of what it was she wanted from him.

Originally, she had thought that it was sex. But for a long time now she had known she wasn't only physically attracted to him. She did want something from him. She wanted to be special to him . . . as special as Laura Holloway had been.

Ever since her conversation with Kelly, Ellen hadn't been able to stop thinking about Seth's wife. Until Kelly had told her that her father had been so devoted to Laura that he hadn't wanted to date for two years, Ellen had thought their one night of lovemaking had been based on a mutual attraction. Now she knew that for him, it might have simply been a matter of physical need.

The "I love you" could have been a slip of the tongue. In the weeks that followed, he had treated her as if he hadn't reached inside and kissed her very soul. Not once had he even come close to losing control again.

She could only conclude it was because what he felt for her was friendship, not love. Always the perfect gentleman, he treated her like a queen, yet he never gave her the one thing that would move their relationship into another dimension—himself.

Maybe Jeannie was right about not expecting anything from a man like Seth—but not for the reasons her sister believed. Falling in love with Seth had been dangerous only because he had given his heart to a woman who had taken it to her grave.

"You've been awfully quiet all evening," Seth commented as he parked the Explorer in front of her house.

"I've been thinking," Ellen answered honestly.

He slipped his arm across the back of the seat and gently nudged her closer to him. "I'm sorry your sister was hurt in this mess with Zeke Paulson. If only I had known she was involved with him I could have done something."

"It's not your fault, or even Two's Company's fault for that matter. I told her not to see him outside of the dating service." When Seth tried to draw her closer to him, she held herself away.

"Have I done something wrong?" he asked when she stiffened at his touch.

"No," she answered quietly, yet she didn't move.

He put his finger beneath her chin and gently turned her face. "I'm not Zeke Paulson."

"I realize that." She struggled to meet his penetrating gaze.

He reached for her hand and carried it palm-side up to his lips. "My intentions are quite honorable," he murmured gallantly and would have taken her mouth with the same delicacy he had used on her palm had she not eluded his touch.

"I'd better go in." She reached for the door, but his arm stopped her.

"Wait!" He pinned her back against the seat, his eyes searching her face for a clue as to what was wrong. "Something's bothering you. What is it?"

She sat perfectly still without saying a word. Then, after releasing a long, pent-up breath of air, she said, "Maybe I'm just tired." She kept her gaze on her hands, avoiding his face.

He let his arm slide away from her, accepting her explanation without any questions. "And it's no wonder, considering what's happened to your sister. Should

I call you in the morning?'' he asked with such tenderness that Ellen felt like a fraud.

She nodded and was about to get out of the car when she realized that the only way she would get any sleep would be to confront Seth with her fears. Seth had already opened his door when she was the one who said, ''Wait.''

He took one look at the expression on her face and pulled his door shut again.

''I'm not just tired,'' she told him, studying her hands. ''Seth, I don't know how to say this....'' she trailed off nervously.

He misread her anxiety. ''Are you trying to tell me you don't want to see me anymore?''

She looked at him then, and the expression on his face was enough to convince her that it certainly wasn't what he wanted. ''No!'' she quickly denied. ''No, that's not it at all.''

''Then what is it?''

''I need to know where I stand with you. What do you want from me? Am I supposed to be a friend? A lover? I thought there was this strong physical attraction between us but...'' She paused, realizing that her voice was so shaky that she sounded as if she was on the verge of tears.

Seth sat in stunned silence until she asked bleakly, ''Don't you want me anymore?''

''Want you?'' he repeated in disbelief, then gathered her into his arms and hugged her tightly. ''Good Lord, Ellen, I want you so badly there are some nights I can hardly sleep.''

If she had any doubts, he soon swept them away as his mouth captured hers in a kiss that had him caressing the curves of her lips while his hands moved slowly down the length of her back. As she opened her lips to the smoothness of his tongue, she made a soft sound.

Shock waves of pleasure echoed through her as the kiss deepened and he let his mouth tell her just how much he wanted her. Ellen felt his body tighten in a sensual reflex that brought her hips closer to his, and his hands slipped under her breasts.

She shivered and made a tiny sound of delight as his fingers worked at easing the buttons open on the front of her dress. The sight of her naked flesh caused his breath to catch in his throat as he said, "How could I not want you? You're so beautiful."

With a groan he bent his head to her chest, and Ellen felt her nipple tighten as he closed his lips around it. She closed her eyes, forgetting about everything except the exquisite sensations he created with his caresses.

When she could no longer keep from touching him, she reached for his belt buckle, only to have his fingers close around hers.

"You're going to destroy my self-control if you do that," he said raggedly, his eyes dark with desire.

"That's my intention," she whispered seductively. "I want you in my bed, Seth." Her fingers teased the warm flesh beneath the waistband of his trousers.

"Are you sure?" he asked, shuddering at the exquisite torture.

"Why do you always ask me that? I'm a grown woman and I know what I want." She teased him by opening and closing his fly. "I want to be loved by you."

He reached for her hands and was about to open the door when headlights shone in the rear window. A car had pulled up behind his.

"What the..." Seth began, squinting at the brightness.

Ellen pulled herself away from him. "It's Becca," she said, panic in her voice.

"At this time of night?"

Ellen groaned as she frantically straightened the bodice of her dress. "Am I buttoned up?" she asked, twisting around so that he could check her dress.

"You look fine, except one of your earrings is missing."

Ellen quickly removed the other one and tossed it into her purse, then climbed out of the car just as Rebecca was getting out of the convertible.

"What are you doing here?" Ellen demanded, a sinking feeling in the pit of her stomach at the sight of her daughter hauling a suitcase from the back seat of the car.

"I've left Roger. I can't stay married to him anymore," she said in an emotional tone.

"What!" Ellen could hardly believe what she was hearing.

"I told you. I left Roger. I'm coming home."

By now Seth was out of the car and was looking inquisitively at Ellen, who could only shake her head and shrug her shoulders helplessly.

She walked over to Rebecca and gave her the house key. "Go inside. I'll be there in a minute." As soon as Rebecca had stepped inside the house, Ellen turned to Seth and said apologetically, "I can't send her away."

"It's all right," he told her, giving her a hug. "I understand."

"But you're the one I wanted to come inside," she said, in agony.

He rested his forehead against hers and sighed. "I know. I wanted that, too."

Evidence of his desire was pressing up against her, and Ellen could only groan in frustration. "I can't believe this is happening. I want to make love with you, Seth."

He pulled her closer to him, kissed her hard on the mouth, then nuzzled aside her blond hair to nibble at her ear and whisper, "Tomorrow night nothing will stop us. I promise." And with one last kiss, he started toward his car.

"What time tomorrow night?" she called out to him.

"I'll call you."

Before he could drive away, she ran over to the side of his car. Leaning into the window, she said, "I forgot to tell you one more thing...I love you."

He reached up and kissed her. "I love you, too. Hold that thought until tomorrow night."

Ellen watched him leave, waiting until his Explorer was out of sight before going inside to confront Rebecca. As she locked up the house she thought about everything that had happened that evening. First there had been the party and the discovery of Zeke Paulson's true identity. She had nursed her sister's broken heart, and then, as a result of her conversation with Jeannie, she had finally admitted her true feelings to Seth. Now she was about to play marriage counselor for her daughter.

She found Rebecca in her old room, unpacking her suitcase.

"Would you mind telling me what is going on?" Ellen demanded, feeling less than sympathetic at the moment.

"I can't live with him, Mother. He's impossible."

"That's not what you were saying two months ago. You told me you couldn't live without him. That's why the wedding had to be in June and why you had to leave school and why you had to take a job from his father."

"So you were right. I shouldn't have gotten married. There. I've said it. Are you satisfied?" she cried out before a flood of tears had her crumpling on the bed.

Ellen knew she had overreacted, but she should have been making love to Seth at this minute, not trying to solve her daughter's marital problems. She reached for Rebecca's shoulder and pulled her into her arms as if she were a small child needing comforting.

"No, I'm not satisfied," she murmured gently. "The last thing I want is to see you unhappy."

"I...I...had to come over here. I...I didn't have anywhere else to go," she told her mother, sobbing.

Ellen felt a rush of maternal feelings. "Why don't you tell me what happened?"

She handed her a tissue and waited patiently while Rebecca blew her nose before starting her explanation. "We were supposed to go to Gloria's for a cookout, but as usual he had to work late. So I decided I'd go by myself."

"Did you tell Roger you were going?"

"No, because he told me he didn't want me there."

"Why was that?"

"Because Gloria had invited a bunch of fraternity guys from the U and he's so jealous he can't stand the thought of me even being in the same room with single men."

"But you went, anyway?"

"Yes. I figured, why shouldn't I? Gloria had offered to send someone to pick me up."

"So then what happened?"

"Roger got home earlier than I expected and came storming over to Gloria's. It was so embarrassing, Mother. He practically dragged me out of the pool...."

"You were swimming?"

"We were playing water volleyball."

"With some of those fraternity guys?"

"Yes, but I wasn't doing anything wrong!"

"I'm sure Roger didn't see it that way," Ellen stated uneasily.

"No, he didn't. Like I said, he made this big scene and when Gloria offered to let me spend the night there, he told me that if I didn't come home with him right then and there, I didn't have to ever come back."

"Oh, Becca," Ellen said with a sigh. "Can't you see what's wrong here?"

"I suppose you think it's all my fault," she said, pouting.

"I think you and Roger need to come to an understanding what each of you expects from marriage. He didn't want you going to that party, innocent or not, without him."

Rebecca pushed away from her mother and stood up, her arms folded across her chest. "You're siding with him."

"I am not siding with either of you," Ellen said, rising to her feet. "I'm trying to make you see that this is a problem you and Roger have to work out together. Packing your bags and coming over here isn't going to solve anything."

"Well, then I'll leave," she said in a huff, throwing the clothes she had just removed back into her suitcase. "I'll go to Auntie Jean's."

Ellen stilled her hands. "You're not going anywhere except home to your husband."

"I can't go home to him. He doesn't want me." Again, the tears fell.

It was then that the doorbell rang. Rebecca pushed away from Ellen's arms and rushed over to peek through the curtains. "It's him! He must have taken a cab," she said, swiping at her tears with the back of her hand. Then she rushed over to the dressing table mirror. "I'm a mess!"

"Do you want me to get the door or will you?" Ellen asked.

"I don't want to see him," she said as she finger-combed her hair.

Ellen gave her a critical look, then went downstairs to answer the door. Standing on the step was her son-in-law, looking like a lost puppy dog.

"I've come to get my wife," he said with false bravado.

Ellen made a sweeping motion with her hand. "She's upstairs in the guest bedroom."

Ellen took a seat in the living room and waited. And waited. And waited. Finally, the couple came down the stairs, clinging to each other as if they were joined at the hip.

"I'm taking Becca home," Roger announced, a protective look on his face.

Ellen looked at her daughter. "Is that what you want, Becca?"

"Yes."

"I'm sorry if we caused you any unnecessary worry," Roger said politely.

"Are you sure it's unnecessary?" Ellen asked.

"Absolutely. I love Becca. I'd never do anything to hurt her," he said sincerely.

"Sometimes we don't realize we're hurting the ones we love, Roger," Ellen said quietly. "I've already told Becca this, but I want to tell you, too. Marriage isn't easy. The best thing you can do for each other is to be honest about your feelings. You need to sit down and talk through whatever it is that's causing the trouble in your relationship."

"We will," Becca promised.

With mixed feelings, Ellen watched them drive away. Were they simply suffering the growing pains of a new marriage or had they married too young? She wanted to think that it was the former, but she had a hidden fear that it was the latter.

THE FIRST THING Ellen did Saturday morning was open the paper to the editorial section and look at Seth's cartoon. It was becoming a ritual with her. And as on every other morning, she took a pair of scissors, and clipped the cartoon from the paper and added it to the pile accumulating on her kitchen counter.

She would have liked nothing better than to spend the entire day with Seth, but it was her mother's birthday. Jeannie had made lunch reservations for the three of them at the Lowell Inn in Stillwater, a historic small town on the scenic Saint Croix River. The town's main street was lined with quaint shops and specialty stores Ellen's mother loved to visit. It would be an all-day event, which meant she wouldn't get to see Seth until that evening.

Ellen hoped that he would call before she left, but when the time came for her to depart and she still hadn't heard from him, Ellen knew she was going to have to do something she dreaded...call him. She was a bit relieved to discover he was out for his morning run and left a message with his son. She told Matt to tell his father that she had to spend the day with her family, but she would be home later that evening and he should call her then.

Ellen tried to enjoy her day with her mother and sister, but as she strolled through shops filled with scented soaps and hand-painted crafts, her thoughts were not on shopping but on Seth and the romantic evening she hoped lay ahead. When they stopped in a tiny store that sold hand-sewn silk lingerie, Ellen was tempted to purchase a skimpy green teddy trimmed with lace. However, noticing the looks on her mother's and sister's faces as she fingered the delicate item, she folded it and put it back on the shelf.

Back in Minneapolis Seth was sharing the same vision of romance. Only he was wondering if it was going to be a reality or not, for all day long he had been phoning Ellen's home but getting no answer. He couldn't help but worry about her. She hadn't wanted Rebecca to get married in the first place and now it was obvious there had been good reasons for her reservations.

Of all the times for Rebecca to decide she needed her mother's advice. He felt a brief spurt of irritation that the young woman hadn't listened to her mother before the wedding. Then he felt a bit contrite.

Here the poor girl was having problems and all he could think about was how his night of lovemaking with Ellen had been interrupted. The important thing was that Ellen had admitted she loved him, which not only meant she no longer had any feelings for her ex-husband, but that they had a future together.

As evening drew near and there was still no answer at Ellen's, some of Seth's optimism began to fade. Why hadn't she tried calling him? Finally, when he could no longer stand the wondering, he called Rebecca's apartment.

A man answered the phone and Seth automatically assumed it was Roger. "Hi, Roger. It's Seth. How's it going?"

"This isn't Roger. I'm Rebecca's father, Kenneth."

There was a silence that was more deadly than an atomic bomb. Kenneth was back? The news hit Seth right in the gut.

"May I please speak to Rebecca?" he said calmly, although he was feeling anything but calm.

"She's not here. Would you like to leave a message?"

"Er...no. You wouldn't happen to know when she'll be home, do you?"

"Your guess is as good as mine."

Which could mean anything, Seth thought as he hung up the phone. Maybe she was still at Ellen's. Maybe she had gone back to Roger and the two of them were out.

Damn. He should have thought to ask for Roger, but the fact that Kenneth Richards was in town had caught him by surprise, and he hadn't thought much except for what Ellen's reaction was going to be when she found out.

Or maybe she already knew. Maybe she had already seen him. Maybe she had sent for him. That thought was enough to send him searching for the bottle of antacid tablets.

Again he called Ellen's house and there was no answer. Then he called his mother and asked her to look up Jeannie's phone number. There was no answer at her place, either.

Just as he was about to get in his car and drive over to Ellen's house, Matt walked in the back door.

"Hi, Dad. What's for dinner?"

"Whatever you can find to eat," Seth answered impatiently. "I have to meet someone."

"Oh, okay. Cool." He opened the refrigerator and stared at its contents. "Did you see this?" He pulled out a slip of paper.

"What is that?" Seth demanded.

"It's your phone message from this morning. I put it in the refrigerator under the juice bottle so you wouldn't miss it."

Any other morning Seth would have had his usual glass of orange juice after his run, but this morning he had gone straight to the shower, pausing only to get a drink of water. He squinted as he tried to read the note. "What does this say? I can't read your handwriting."

Matt took it from him and studied it briefly. "It's from some lady named Ellen. She said to tell you that she was going to be gone all day and that you could call her tonight."

"That's it? That's all she said?"

"Yeah, that was it. Is this the chick you've been seeing lately?"

"She's not a chick, Matthew. She's a woman," he automatically corrected his son.

"Sorry, Dad. I guess I've been hanging out with the guys at the garage too long. So when do we get to meet her?"

"Do you want to meet her?"

"Meet who?" Kelly had entered the kitchen and picked up on their conversation.

"Ellen Richards."

"I already have. She's a neat lady," Kelly stated cheerfully.

"How do you know her?" Seth asked, surprised.

"I was there when she saved your life. Or have you forgotten?" She picked an apple from the bowl of fruit sitting in the middle of the table and took a bite. "I also ran into her at the mall the other day. We had a nice little chat," she said as she munched on the apple.

"You didn't tell me that," Seth said in an accusing tone.

"I've hardly seen you." She reached up and gave him a peck on the cheek. "You're looking a little stressed. Are you having trouble with a cartoon or something?" She took another bite of the apple.

"No, my cartoons are fine. So what was it you and Ellen talked about?" Seth wanted to know.

Kelly shrugged. "Oh, I don't know. Stuff. I think you ought to have her over for dinner so we can get to know her better."

"Are you offering to cook?" Seth asked.

"I bet Grandma would."

"So it's true. You really do have a girlfriend?" Matt looked at his father with wide eyes.

"He has a lady friend." This time it was Kelly who corrected him.

Before either of them could ask any more questions, Seth glanced at his watch and said, "I have to go."

"Where are you going?" Kelly wanted to know.

"Out."

"But what about dinner?"

"Your brother's in charge," Seth tossed back over his shoulder and hurried out to his car before either one could protest.

There was no question in his mind where he was going. He had to see Ellen even if it meant camping on her doorstep and waiting for her to return.

Unfortunately, when he turned down her street, he noticed the front porch was already occupied. The Colorado Kid, all decked out in his boots, jeans and cowboy hat sat on the steps. But it was what was beside him that had Seth's blood pressure on the rise. Luggage.

Seth slowed his Explorer down to a near crawl, finally parking in front of her house. He slammed the door as he climbed out of the car and walked up the walk.

"Well, if it isn't the boyfriend," Kenneth drawled, a nasty grin on his face.

"Where's Ellen?" Seth demanded, stopping several feet from him.

"Not home."

"What are you doing here?"

"Now, I think that's between me and Ellen, but since I can see you think you have a right to know, let me tell you this. I realized that I made a big mistake three years ago and I'm back to make amends."

Seth had to use all his restraint not to grab him by the neck and throw his back up against the wall. "Does she know you're here?"

"What? You think we haven't been in touch with each other?"

Seth knew the man was taunting him, but it drove him crazy all the same. "Tell Ellen I was here," he barked out, then walked back to his Explorer.

"One other thing you ought to know," Kenneth called out to him as he was leaving.

Seth couldn't resist stopping, but he refused to turn around.

"I never make the same mistake twice."

CHAPTER FOURTEEN

THERE WAS ONLY ONE THING on Ellen's mind as she drove home. Spending the night with Seth. While her mother and sister had gone into a pet store, she had gone back to the boutique with the silky lingerie and purchased the green teddy.

When she turned the corner onto her block and saw that Rebecca's red convertible was not sitting in the driveway, she breathed a sigh of relief. Tonight she wanted no interruptions. She was determined that her date with Seth would be the most romantic night of his life. She'd make him forget all about Laura.

As she drew nearer to the house, however, she noticed several suitcases on the porch steps. An ugly feeling settled in her stomach. It couldn't be....

She parked her car and looked for signs of Rebecca, but there were none. The front door was locked when she tried to open it. She walked to the end of the porch and peered around the side of the house, thinking Rebecca might be in the yard. However, it wasn't her daughter she found standing next to her small vegetable garden, but Kenneth.

"Tomatoes look great this year," he said as a greeting.

"What are you doing here?" Shock had her voice sounding shrill.

He ambled over to the porch railing and tilted his hat back to look up at her. "You're looking good, Elle. Real good."

"Kenneth, you didn't answer my question. What are you doing here?" she demanded.

"Do you think maybe we could go inside? I don't exactly feel like telling the world my life story." Two of Ellen's neighbors were outside, glancing curiously in their direction. Ellen motioned for him to come up onto the porch and walked over to unlock the front door.

"You can leave your luggage where it is," she said pointedly when he hoisted his bags in his arms.

"What if someone steals it?"

She hesitated for a moment, then said, "All right. Bring it in."

She stood in the hallway, arms folded, waiting for him to explain why he was at her house. As soon as he had shoved the suitcases up against the wall he asked, "Have you been shopping?"

Ellen took the bag with the teddy inside and tossed it into the front hall closet, then turned again to face him. "Why are you here, Kenneth?"

"Do you think I could get something to drink? I've been sitting outside in that heat for quite a while." He took his hat off and several thin strands of damp hair lay plastered across his bald spot.

"Come into the kitchen," she ordered.

She gave him a glass of water and reluctantly set it on the table. As she watched him sit down and take a drink, she saw lines in his face, lines she was certain hadn't been there the last time she had seen him. Instead of anger, she felt pity toward him.

"Thanks," he said when he had taken a long swallow. "I suppose you're wondering why I'm here."

She remained standing, needing to feel in control of the situation. "Why are you here?"

"Tina and I have split up."

Ellen knew she shouldn't have been surprised by the news. After all, the night of the wedding he had told her he and Tina weren't getting along. Still, it caught her off guard, sending a strange sensation trembling through her.

"Is there any chance for a reconciliation?"

He shook his head in regret. "She wants to marry another man. Some young rodeo rider she met in Las Vegas."

Ellen didn't know what to say. Part of her wanted to scream, It serves you right! but it was not in her nature to take pleasure in another person's misfortune. And he looked so pitiful sitting there.

"I'm sorry." She didn't know what else to say.

He expelled a long sigh, rubbed a hand across the five o'clock shadow on his jaw, then said, "Yeah, well, I guess it wasn't meant to be, which is why I came back home."

"Home?" Ellen repeated in alarm. She thought about the luggage sitting out in the hallway. He couldn't possibly mean her home, could he?

Just then the phone rang and Ellen jumped to get it. It was Seth and he didn't sound happy.

"I've been trying to reach you all day," he said, an edge to his usually good-natured voice.

"Didn't you get my message?"

"Yes, but you didn't say much."

"I'm sorry. It was my mother's birthday, so Jeannie and I took her out for the day," she explained, conscious of Kenneth's presence.

"I was worried about you. I didn't know what had happened with Rebecca."

"Everything's fine." She glanced over at the table and saw that Kenneth was listening to every word she was saying. "Look, this isn't a good time for me to talk right now. Can I call you back?"

"Why? What's wrong?"

Ellen thought about telling him the truth, that Kenneth was there and she needed to get a few things straight with him, but then she remembered how he had taunted her the night of the wedding about her feelings for her ex-husband and she decided it would be better if she didn't mention that he was sitting there in her kitchen. What he didn't know wouldn't hurt him, and she intended to have this whole mess resolved before she saw him again.

"Nothing's wrong," she fibbed, turning her back to Kenneth so that he would hear as little as possible of their conversation. "It's just that I can't talk right now."

"Well, when can you talk?" he asked a bit impatiently.

"Later, I promise."

"What about our date tonight?"

"I haven't forgotten," she assured him. "I just need to take care of a few things first."

"Is there anything I can do to help? I'm free right now if you want me to come over."

"No! It really would be better if you waited until I called you, all right?"

"All right," he grudgingly agreed.

Before he hung up she heard him say, "I miss you."

She would have liked to tell him that she missed him, too, but she wasn't comfortable expressing her feelings with an audience; it was something she just couldn't do.

"Important phone call?" Kenneth asked as she sat down across from him.

She nodded. "It was a good friend."

"Was it your boyfriend?"

"Look, you didn't come over here to discuss my phone calls." Ellen deliberately changed the subject. "I want to know what you meant when you said you had decided to come back home. Back home where?" she asked bluntly.

"To Minnesota. To my family. After living in Colorado for the past three years, I realize how important it is to have people you care about around you."

"What about your business in Colorado?"

"I sold it."

Ellen's jaw dropped open. "Just like that?"

He shrugged. "Profits were down, business was slow. Besides, I heard about a deal back here in Minnesota...." He began to explain, but she tuned him right out.

He was the same old Kenneth, after all. Always looking for a better deal, always moving on when the going got tough. Only it appeared that Tina wasn't going to stand by him and bail him out of trouble.

"So you're moving back to Minnesota," Ellen murmured, making no attempt to hide her disappointment.

"Yup. I'm looking for a place right now. Becca offered to let me stay with her and Roger, but her mother-in-law put a lid on that idea."

"Dolores did?"

He nodded. "She came over when the kids were out doing some shopping and suggested I find another place to stay. She said they were having enough problems without having a father-in-law camped out on their doorstep."

Never had Ellen imagined she would agree with Dolores Townsend, but in this instance she could have easily given the other woman a hug. "Mrs. Townsend said that?"

"Yeah, and when she talks, people listen, including me," he told her with a wag of his finger.

Ellen didn't contradict him.

"So what I want to know is what kind of trouble Becca and Roger are having?" He fixed her with what he obviously thought was an intimidating stare.

"It's nothing serious. Just the usual newlyweds learning to live with each other kinds of problems."

"Are you sure? I don't like to think that Becca's unhappy."

"I don't think she is," Ellen answered honestly. "I think she and Roger are simply going through that period of adjustment every newly married couple goes through."

"You mean like we did?"

She shrugged. "I'm sure we did, but it's too long ago for me to remember."

"I remember it, Elle. We had that tiny little apartment over in Robbinsdale. It had a slanted ceiling in the bedroom that I was always bumping my head on whenever I got up out of bed in the middle of the night."

Ellen was in no mood to listen to him reminisce about the good old days. "You still haven't told me why you're here on my doorstep."

"I was hoping you could help me find a place to put my weary bones to rest for tonight. I started calling the local hotels when I arrived, but everything was booked and then Mrs. Townsend gave me the boot before I had a chance to find anything, so here I am."

Ellen could only stare at him in disbelief. "You expect me to find you a place to sleep?"

"Is that too much to ask? I only need it for the night."

"Well, it's not going to be here!" she told him in no uncertain terms.

He shot her a wounded look. "I didn't expect it would be. I just thought you could help me call around and find a room for the night. Then tomorrow I'll get a rental car and start looking for a permanent place."

Ellen could have easily strung him up by his toes. How typical it was for him to expect someone else to solve his problems. She would have liked to tell him to get lost, but she was afraid that if she did, he'd only end up back at Rebecca's and the last thing her daughter needed was to have her father freeloading at her place. Which is exactly what Ellen expected would happen. He'd go for a night and stay for weeks.

So Ellen did what she had so often done in the past, what she had vowed she'd never do again. She took care of his problem for him.

Finding a hotel wasn't easy, for there were several conventions in town, plus the usual load of summer tourists who had come to shop at the Mall of America and take in the local sights.

But as it turned out, there was a vacancy at one of the downtown hotels. "Great. He'll take it," Ellen told the hotel clerk and promised that he'd be there in thirty minutes.

She wasted no time in gathering up her purse and keys. "We'd better hurry. It looks like it's going to rain," she told him as she glanced outside. She held the front door open for him so that he could carry his suitcases out to the car, but he only picked up a small sports bag.

"Do you mind if I leave the rest of my luggage here?" he asked.

"Why?"

"It'll be a lot easier to take the shuttle from the hotel to the car-rental agency if I don't have to drag all that luggage with me. I promise I'll come by and get it first thing in the morning."

Ellen didn't stop to think about why he couldn't leave his luggage at the hotel. She just wanted him to go. Besides, those weary lines on his face were tugging on her heartstrings. Knowing that it wouldn't hurt anything to have his suitcases sitting in the hall, she said, "All right, but call before you come to make sure I'm home."

By the time she had dropped him off at the hotel, a blanket of thick, dark clouds had obscured the setting sun. On the way home she turned on the radio to hear that the national weather service had issued a severe thunderstorm warning for the entire metropolitan area.

The phone was ringing as she unlocked her front door. She hurried to answer it, her breathing ragged by the time she finally reached it.

"Mom, it's me. Where's Dad?" Rebecca wanted to know.

"He's at the Hyatt downtown."

"You sent him to a hotel?" The criticism in her voice was explicit.

"And just what was I supposed to do with him? Let him stay here?"

"Why not? It's not like you don't have the room."

"Becca, we're divorced!"

"If you weren't going to let him stay there, you could have at least called me to come get him. Even my couch is better than being alone at a hotel when you're as emotionally distraught as he is."

"Emotionally distraught?" Ellen repeated with a frown.

"His wife just walked out on him for another man. Of course he's distraught!"

"He looked tired, but I don't think he's dangerously depressed," Ellen remarked, trying to keep things in perspective.

"I should have known you wouldn't have any sympathy for him. I should have never let Roger's mother talk us into going out to dinner. This is all her fault."

Ellen noticed that "Mother Townsend" was now "Roger's mother" again. "Your mother-in-law is right in this instance, Becca. You two don't need your father moving in with you."

"It was only for one night," she insisted. "And since when are you on Roger's mother's side?"

Ellen made a sound of exasperation. "Why does it always have to be a matter of sides with you, Becca?" She forced herself to stay calm. "Maybe we'd better change the subject before we end up shouting at each other."

"Fine," she answered shortly, giving Ellen the impression that it really wasn't all that fine with her. "Have you spoken to Auntie Jean?"

"Not since I dropped her off. Why?"

"She called here looking for you. She said it was important that you call her as soon as you get home."

"Did she say what it's about?"

"No, only that she needed to talk to you as soon as possible. How was your day with Grandma?"

"It was fine." A whooshing sound alerted Ellen to the fact that a strong wind had come up. "Look, Becca, we'd better hang up. There's a severe thunderstorm warning and it's starting to blow here. Make sure you and Roger keep an eye on things, okay?"

As soon as Ellen hung up the phone, she looked out the window and saw trees bending and debris being tossed around. A neighbor's garbage can was being carried down the street by a gust of wind.

Ellen quickly called Seth, but the line was busy. She waited a minute, then called again, but it was still busy.

Next she called Jeannie. "Hi. Is it storming where you are?"

"It's awful. I can't even see across the street, the rain is coming down so hard. We shouldn't be on the phone. I just saw a big bolt of lightning."

"I just talked to Becca and she said you were looking for me."

"I was. I wanted to tell you that Linda's car was found in Iowa, but there was no sign of Zeke."

"Is she going to get it back?"

"Apparently he had an accident. He smashed up the front end and left it in a cornfield. At least she'll be able to collect on the insurance." Jeannie let out a startled gasp. "Did you hear that thunder? We'd better hang up. I'll call you when this is over."

As soon as Jeannie had hung up the phone, Ellen tried Seth's number again. It was still busy.

Then the rain came, creating tiny streams of water in the streets and small lakes in the residents' yards. Marble-sized hail pelted the roof and Ellen wondered if any of the windows would break from the force.

But just as quickly as it had swept into town, the storm moved to the east, leaving broken tree limbs and leaves in its wake.

When the phone rang, Ellen expected it to be Seth, but it wasn't. It was Jeannie.

"How bad was it at your place?"

Ellen lifted a corner of her kitchen curtain. "I don't think I have any damage, although I suspect my tomato plants took a beating from the hail. What about you?"

"I'm okay, but Mom's car is underwater."

"What?"

"The garage in her apartment complex flooded, and her car's in water up to the steering wheel. To make matters worse, they've lost the electricity in her area."

"Is she all right?"

"You know Ma. She's heard some of the other tenants telling horror stories about what happens when a car is submerged in water, so now she's worried she won't be able to get hers to run again."

"We'd better go over there and see what we can do," Ellen suggested.

"I think that's a good idea. Apparently they're pumping the water out of the garage, but some residents are trying to move their cars. Others are saying she shouldn't move it, and she's in a hissy fit wondering what to do."

"I'll change my clothes and be right over."

Ellen quickly exchanged her rayon split skirt and blouse for a pair of jean shorts and a T-shirt, then slipped her feet into a pair of old worn moccasins. Before leaving the house, she tried to call Seth, but when she lifted the handset, the line was dead.

When she arrived at Jeannie's, she told her sister she needed to call the phone company and to report her phone out of order.

"It's no use. Mine's dead, too. Apparently there's quite a number of them out in this area. We should just be happy we have electricity," Jeannie told her.

"I need to use a phone," Ellen insisted as Jeannie climbed into her car.

"Use Mom's. She's going to have to stay with one of us tonight," she told Ellen as they drove the short distance to their mother's apartment complex.

"You want me to take her?" Ellen glanced sideways at her sister, knowing there would be no night of romance with Seth if she had her seventy-five-year-old mother underfoot.

"I thought you said you had plans for tonight?"

"I can change them if it's necessary." Ellen knew she had to make the offer as much as it killed her to say the words.

Jeannie didn't answer right away and Ellen feared she was going to agree. But then to her relief she said, "No, I might as well take her to my place. She doesn't like to do stairs."

"That's true, but I know this isn't the best of times for you. Are you sure you don't want me to take her?" Ellen knew she had to be crazy to even mention it a second time, but she felt guilty being so happy with Seth when Jeannie was so miserable over Zeke.

"No, it's all right. Just stick around until we find out what's going to happen to her car. I don't think I could take a whole night of her agonizing over a '73 Plymouth," Jeannie said with a sigh.

"It's a deal," Ellen agreed, an agreement she later came to regret. By the time all the confusion at the apartment complex had been sorted out and their mother's car had been towed to a garage, it was late. Ellen wondered if it wasn't too late for her and Seth to be together.

When she had arrived at her mother's apartment, she had found her mother sitting by candlelight next to the phone, waiting for the insurance company to return her call. Fearing that she'd miss the agent if Ellen used the phone, her mother had refused to allow either Ellen or Jeannie to make any calls. Consequently, Ellen hadn't been able to get hold of Seth and let him know what had happened.

Stopping at a gas station not far from her mother's complex, Ellen finally found a phone in operating condition. However, when she called Seth's number, there was no answer.

Little did she know that he was in the car on his way home from her place. As soon as the storm had ended, Seth had tried calling Ellen, only to discover the phone lines were out of order in her area.

Needing to know that she was all right, he had jumped in his Explorer and headed over to her place, only to find she wasn't home. Peeking through the narrow panel of glass beside the door, he could see a portion of the entry. Sitting in the hallway was luggage—several pieces of luggage. The same luggage he had seen alongside Kenneth Richards earlier in the day.

Seth's insides twisted in agitation. What could it possibly mean except . . . He tried to push the thought from his mind but it refused to go away. The harder he tried not to think about it, the more it plagued him. Why would the man be staying at Ellen's house unless she wanted him to be there?

It was an excruciatingly painful thought. As he stepped down from the porch, his shoulders were slumped, his head low.

All the way home he berated himself. He should have seen the warning signs. She had hired him to make her ex jealous, for crying out loud. And every time he had brought up the subject of the Colorado Kid she had defended the man as if he were still a member of the family. Now she hadn't told him her ex-husband was even in town.

Last night he had gone home cursing the fact that Rebecca had shown up when she did. Now he thought it probably was a blessing she had been there. If he had spent one more night in Ellen's arms, he doubted that he would have been able to gracefully walk away when she chose her ex-husband over him. . . .

ELLEN WAS EXHAUSTED when she got home that night. After a day of traipsing around the streets of Stillwater and then spending half the night trying to reassure her mother that her car would be fine—and if it wasn't, her insurance would cover the cost of a new one—she felt as if she could sleep for days.

At least the electricity was back on and there was no damage to her house. As soon as she was inside she picked up the phone. There was still no sound. With a sigh she dropped it back down again. Seth couldn't have called her if he had wanted to.

She went over to the closet and pulled out the package she had purchased in Stillwater. She held up the green teddy and shook her head in regret. "So much for our night of romance," she said aloud. She was about to shove it back in the bag when she changed her mind.

Maybe Seth was still planning to stop over. It might make things a whole lot easier if she was ready for him, she thought with a devilish grin. With the green teddy in hand, she headed for her bedroom.

IT WAS AFTER NINE when Ellen awoke on Sunday morning. She reached for the phone beside her bed and lifted the receiver. There was still no dial tone. She dropped the handset back down on the cradle with a sigh, wondering just when she would hear from Seth.

As if her wishes were being answered, the doorbell rang. Pulling on her robe and sliding her feet into a pair of slippers, she hurried into the bathroom to run a quick comb through her hair and a toothbrush over her teeth.

When the doorbell sounded a second time, she dropped the toothbrush and rushed downstairs to discover it wasn't Seth standing on her doorstep but Kenneth.

"I know you said to call first, but your phone's not working," he said when she looked at him as if he were an intruder.

"Oh, I know," she said, tightening the sash on her robe. "It went out during the storm. I was hoping they'd have it fixed by now, but being it's a weekend I suppose it'll take longer than usual."

"I came to pick up my luggage. Can I come in?"

Reluctantly, Ellen stepped aside. She didn't move away from the door, however, hoping he'd take the hint that she wasn't in any mood for socializing.

"You must have been up early," she commented as he bent over to pick up the luggage.

"Yeah, I couldn't sleep, so I figured I might as well get up and get started on looking for a place to stay," he said, sounding despondent.

Ellen wasn't about to express any sympathy. "Have you talked to Becca? She was looking for you last night."

"Yeah. We're meeting for breakfast. Want to come along?" He paused in front of her, suitcases in hand.

"No, thank you."

Kenneth shrugged. "Whatever." He started toward the car, leaving behind one small bag that he couldn't carry. Ellen, seeing it, picked it up and carried it out to the car for him.

It was at that moment that Seth arrived. After a night of tossing and turning and wondering if maybe he hadn't jumped the gun about Ellen and her ex-husband, he had skipped his morning run and jumped into his car to drive straight to her house.

More than anything, he needed to hear that he had been wrong in his assumptions. That Kenneth hadn't stayed the night. That she no longer cared about her ex-husband. That she loved him and only him.

But when he pulled up in front of her house, the evidence was strong against the case he had built for himself. The Colorado Kid was loading luggage into a car, and Ellen was right beside him in a robe. A sharp pain wrenched his heart. She looked as if she had just got out of bed.

Seth sat motionless. He couldn't move. He didn't want to drive away and he didn't want to stay. He wanted to close his eyes and wake up and find he had imagined the whole ugly scene.

He did close his eyes. He heard a car door slam, an engine start, a car pull away. Still he didn't move until finally there was a rap on the passenger-side window. He opened his eyes and saw Ellen smiling at him.

He rolled down the window. "We need to talk." Was that his voice sounding so gruff?

Her smile faded. "What's wrong?"

He didn't want to look at her, for in that brief moment when she had leaned into the car he had caught a glimpse of a silky green negligee beneath the terry-cloth robe and a pain had stabbed at his heart.

"You can ask me that when your ex-husband is driving away from your home with his suitcases in tow at this time of the morning?" He looked straight ahead as he spoke.

He didn't see the look of bewilderment on her face. She opened the door and climbed into the Explorer. "You can't possibly think I slept with him?" The bewilderment changed to horror as she uttered the words.

"Did you know he was coming? Is that why you wanted me to stay Friday night? So that he would catch us together and be jealous as hell?" he accused in a voice he didn't even recognize as his own.

"Seth! What is wrong with you? How can you even think such a thing?" Her fingers clutched at the lapels of her robe.

"Was he here when I called you last night?"

"Yes, but it's not what you're thinking." She started to explain what had happened but he wouldn't listen.

"Why didn't you tell me you were with him when I called? Instead of telling me you had things to take care of, why didn't you just tell me you didn't want to spend the night with me?"

"Because I did want to spend the night with you!" she declared emotionally. "You've got this all wrong. Why are you acting like this?"

"Acting like what?" He threw up his hands in confusion. "What? I'm not supposed to be upset when the woman who says she loves me spends the night with her ex-husband?"

"I didn't spend the night with him!" she screamed in frustration. "Will you please let me explain?" Realizing that her neighbors could probably hear what was being said, she pleaded with him, "Please come inside so we can get this whole mess straightened out."

"There's nothing to straighten out, Ellen. I think this little scene I witnessed this morning says it all. You made it perfectly clear from the start that you needed me for one purpose and one purpose only—to make the Colorado Kid jealous." He slapped the steering wheel. "Taa daa! Mission accomplished! And the beauty of it is you did it without having to spend any money at all."

It was a low blow, but Seth couldn't help himself. He thought she had been sincere when she had said she loved him. He had thought that last night she would be in his arms and they would be planning their future together.

Instead she had crawled into bed with Kenneth Richards, a man who had dumped her for a woman young enough to be his daughter. A man who would never appreciate what a fine woman she was. A man he'd like to take apart with his bare hands.

"You can think what you like but I never used you," she said between clenched teeth, then jumped out of the Explorer and ran into the house.

Seth didn't try to stop her but simply drove away.

CHAPTER FIFTEEN

ELLEN WAS MAD. Spitting mad. She slammed the front door with a force that echoed through the quiet house. At the sound of rubber screeching on the paved road, she mumbled in disgust, "Good riddance!"

How could Seth possibly think that she had thrown him over for a balding, pot-bellied cowboy? Not only was he insulting, he was stupid. And bad-tempered, she thought, grabbing the vase full of gladioli from the credenza. Seth had given them to her the night of the Two's Company party.

With one hand she whisked the colorful flowers from the glass while with the other, she dumped the water down the drain. With a stomp of her foot, the trash can lid sprung open and in went the flowers.

"That's what I think of you and your accusations, Stanford Edward Thomas Holloway," she said to the stems sticking up out of the trash.

Next she found a half-eaten box of candy he had given her and was about to stuff it down the garbage disposal when she stopped short. "Better not. Chocolate is chocolate."

She swept through the house searching for anything that reminded her of him. She found little. Not being a sentimental person, she hadn't saved any theater programs or movie ticket stubs.

Unfortunately, most of her reminders were engraved on her heart. The way he said her name. The funny sound he made when he had tried not to laugh at Dolores Townsend's slides. The tickle of his mustache when his lips brushed hers.

She shook her head to chase away those reminders. If there was one thing her divorce had taught her, it was that she wouldn't cry over any man ever again. Whatever was meant to be would be. Obviously, she and Seth didn't have a foundation of trust upon which they could build a solid relationship. If they had, he wouldn't have left or she might have stopped him.

That was that. It was over. Kaput. Finis. She would move on with her life. She wouldn't sit around moping over what might have been. She would keep right on living...do things, which was why when Jeannie arrived a short time later, she found Ellen on her knees in the garden, trying to mend the damage the previous night's storm had done.

"So this is where you are. I've been trying to call you for about an hour," she remarked to Ellen's backside.

"I didn't think the phones were working." Ellen didn't want to tell her that she had purposely let hers ring because she hadn't wanted to talk to anyone.

"Yup, and Mom's electricity is on again, too. I just dropped her off." When Ellen didn't look up but continued to chop at the ground with a small hoe, she asked, "What are you doing here, anyway? I thought you'd be out with that guy who was blessed with the perfect tush."

"You were right about him," Ellen said, keeping her eyes fixed on the garden.

"You mean you finally agree he's a ten?"

Ellen tossed a clump of weeds over her shoulder. "I'd say a one and a half would be more accurate."

"Uh-oh. Do I sniff trouble in paradise?"

Ellen sat back on her heels and swiped at her brow with the back of her gardening glove. "There is no paradise." She peeled the cotton gloves from her fingers and tossed them aside. "I'm thirsty. Want to come in for a drink?"

"You mean drink as in alcohol?"

"Why not? It's after noon, isn't it?" Ellen didn't wait for an answer but headed for the house.

Jeannie whistled through her teeth. "I don't understand it. Yesterday you were eyeing sexy lingerie and today you're drinking to his departure? What happened?"

Ellen kept on moving toward the kitchen. Once inside, she opened the refrigerator and pulled out two beers. "You want a glass?"

"Not me." Jeannie eyed the bottle suspiciously. "Pig's Eye? Since when?"

"Since Seth. Luckily I only bought one twelve-pack." She took a long sip and said, "Actually, I kind of like it. Do you want to sit in here or should we go back outside?"

Jeannie parked herself on a chair. "It's too hot out there." She, too, took a long swallow, then asked, "So what are we drinking to?"

"Professional escorts—may they never cross our paths again." Ellen raised her bottle and gently clinked it against Jeannie's, then took another swallow.

"Sounds like a good resolution to me. I know what was wrong with mine. Are you going to tell me what the flaw was in yours?"

Ellen scratched at the label with her thumbnail. "He was stupid."

"Gee, last week he was brilliant. What happened?"

"Kenneth happened," she said sourly.

"Kenneth?"

"He came back. Seth saw him and jumped to all the wrong conclusions and left. End of story."

"Wait a minute." Jeannie raised a hand. "Back up and fill me in. Two plus two isn't equaling four."

So Ellen went over in detail exactly what had transpired between the time she had left Jeannie's until Seth had peeled away in a cloud of smoke that morning. When she was finished, her sister could only shake her head in disbelief.

"This is crazy. What you have here is a misunderstanding, not a reason for going your separate ways," Jeannie argued.

"Not in my book. The way I read it, we go our separate ways," Ellen stated stubbornly.

Jeannie eyed her suspiciously. "Are you sure?"

Ellen had worked nearly half of the label free of the bottle and ripped that portion off. "Since there's no future for us, it's better to end it now."

"But is this the way you want it to end? With some silly misunderstanding over Kenneth?"

"Since you didn't hear the way he talked to me, I don't think you should be rating it as silly," she reprimanded her sister. "Besides, Kenneth is only part of the problem."

"So what's the other part?"

"His wife."

"He's married?" Jeannie screeched, her eyebrows arching.

"No, he's a widower. But that's the problem. He's still in love with his wife, and I'm never going to be able to compete with her memory," she said grimly.

"He doesn't call you by her name or anything, does he?"

"No. It's nothing like that," Ellen replied, wondering what her sister would say if she knew that Seth was so consumed with memories of Laura that he hadn't wanted to make love with her.

"I still think you owe it to yourself to set the record straight. I mean, the guy must care for you, otherwise why would he get so bent out of shape over Kenneth?"

Ellen thought long and hard about what her sister had said. Maybe Seth really did love her. Was she making a mistake by not going to see him and explaining what had happened?

After a sleepless night, she decided that she would make the first move toward reconciliation. After all, she had been the one caught in what looked to be a compromising situation.

She knew it would be nearly impossible to work up the courage to phone him, and since she had never been to his house, the only place she could go with the hope of running into him was the health club.

After only a couple of visits she realized how futile that plan was. She had no idea what time he frequented the gym or if he even did on a regular basis.

With each passing day she became a little bit more worried that she'd never see him again. Each morning she would read his editorial cartoon, clip it out and add it to the scrapbook she had bought to display his work.

When the end of the week came and she had neither seen nor heard from him, she began to wonder if she had read more into their relationship than had actually been there. Once again, she decided the only way she would be able to get on with her life was to go see him. And once again, the question was where.

Of course! The answer came to her in a flash. The newspaper! It was perfect. They would be in a professional setting where there would be little chance of their discussion turning into the shouting match that had transpired last Sunday.

She hadn't expected that when she arrived she'd have to sign in at the reception desk and wait until Seth gave the okay for her to come up to his office. For a brief moment she wondered if he would give her permission, but soon the receptionist was handing her a visitor's badge and giving her directions to the third floor.

As Ellen rode the elevator she remembered Seth telling her that journalism was about fairness, objectivity and getting the facts straight. She only hoped he remembered that when she walked into his office.

The elevator stopped and the doors opened. She took a deep breath and walked over to his office. Because the top half of his walls were glass, she could see him sitting on a high swivel chair at a white drawing table, the board tilted, his shirtsleeves rolled up to his elbows. There was a look of concentration on his face, and never had he looked more attractive to Ellen than he did at that moment.

When he saw her, he slid off the chair and moved toward the door.

"Is this a bad time?" she asked when he motioned for her to enter.

"No. Come on in," he instructed, closing the door behind her.

"So this is where you create," she said as she looked around the square room. Her smile was shaky, her knees unsteady.

"This is it—at least while I'm at the paper." He shoved his hands into his pockets—a gesture she knew meant that he was a bit tense.

Ellen glanced around the room and saw a computer work station, a desk, copier, fax machine and even a sink. "It looks pretty much self-contained."

"Everything a cartoonist could want at his fingertips," he agreed, jingling the change in his pocket.

She noticed several bundles of mail sitting in a box on the floor and asked, "Is that all yours?"

He chuckled. "Fan mail. Or I guess I should say hate mail."

"Hate?"

"I ran a cartoon last week about one of our distinguished senators and a couple hundred of his loyal constituents didn't approve."

"You mean the one where he was sitting in the boiling pot of stew?"

"You saw it?"

She nodded. "It was perfect. The way he's been behaving he deserves to have his goose cooked."

"Well, not everyone agrees, as you can see." He gestured to the bundles of envelopes.

"Does it bother you to get hate mail?"

He shrugged. "Only if someone misses the point I'm trying to make. I don't draw a cartoon to be controversial. I simply want to express my point of view."

"And not everyone agrees with your point of view, right?"

"If people really like a cartoon, they put it up on their refrigerator. If they don't, they write hate mail."

There was an awkward silence and he said, "I'm sure you didn't come here to discuss my work."

She chewed on her lower lip. "No, I didn't. I think you know why I'm here."

"You don't like the way things ended any better than I do." Blue eyes searched hers for a confirmation.

She shook her head. "You didn't let me tell you why Kenneth was there," she said quietly, unable to tear her eyes away from his.

"That's because I thought I knew the answer."

"How could you?"

"Because I saw him there Saturday evening, his suitcase in hand. He was sitting on your front porch waiting for you."

"Why didn't you tell me you had seen him?"

"Why didn't you tell me he was at your house when I called Saturday night?" he countered.

They were like two opponents, testing the water before the fight began. She didn't like the tension in the air and tried to relax, but she could feel the stiffness in her muscles. "He didn't have anywhere else to go," she said quietly. "Dolores Townsend had already kicked him out of Rebecca's place."

"So out of the goodness of your heart, you took him in," he said with a wry grimace.

"No, I let him come inside and make a few phone calls. Then I took him to a hotel."

"Before or after the storm?" he asked, one eyebrow lifting suspiciously.

"Before. When I got home I tried calling you, but your line was busy. And of course after the storm I lost my phone service."

"I know. That's why I drove over to your place. We had a date, in case you'd forgotten."

"I didn't forget."

"No?"

"No. It was just that during the storm my mother lost her power and I had to go with Jeannie to make sure she was okay."

"So you weren't home after the storm?"

"No! I would have answered the door if I had been."

He didn't believe her. She could tell by the look on his face. "So you're telling me the Colorado Kid spent the night at a hotel and came the next morning to pick up his luggage?"

"Yes."

"I see."

Ellen wondered if he did. Before she could say another word, however, they were interrupted by a knock at the door.

"I'm sorry, Seth, but you asked me to remind you about the editorial meeting. It's in five minutes," a petite gray-haired woman said, poking her head into the office.

"Thanks, Rita." He raked a hand through his hair. "Why did you lie to me on the phone Saturday night?"

"I didn't lie. I just didn't tell you Kenneth was sitting in my kitchen."

"You made it sound as if you couldn't wait to get rid of me."

"It was Kenneth I couldn't wait to get rid of."

Again, the skepticism was on his face. "So has he gone back to Colorado?"

"No. He's decided to move back here," she said quietly.

"Alone?"

She nodded. "He's getting a divorce."

"Now why doesn't that come as any great surprise to me?" he murmured, slowly shaking his head from side to side. Someone walked by and rapped on the glass. Seth looked at the man and nodded, then turned back to Ellen and said, "Look, I have to go. I'd ask you to wait for me, but this is going to take a while."

"No, it's all right. I understand."

"Why don't I call you later this evening?" he suggested and hope ignited in Ellen's heart.

"Okay."

He grabbed his sport coat from the hook behind the door. "Can you find your way out?"

"Oh, sure." They stood staring at each other like two fighters who had just been told their match was a draw.

Finally, he gave her a polite smile and said, "See ya."

"Seth?" She couldn't let him go without letting him know how she was feeling. "I didn't want to be with Kenneth that night. I wanted to be with you."

He stood for a moment staring at her, a sadness in his eyes she had never seen before. Finally, he said, "I wish I could believe that, Ellen," and walked away.

As she watched his retreating figure the only thought going through her head was, *He'll never call*.

EVER SINCE HER DIVORCE, Ellen had worked hard to look at life in a positive way. Despite her fear that Seth wouldn't call her, she still thought there was a ghost of a chance that he might. She would have paid practically any price to get call waiting installed on her telephone line that evening. Every time the phone rang and it wasn't Seth, all she could think about was getting rid of whoever it was so that the line would be free for him.

One caller she couldn't easily get rid of was Rebecca. "Mom, thank goodness you're there."

Ellen sat down and braced herself for another round of newlywed trauma. However, it wasn't a problem with Roger that had her daughter upset. It was Kenneth.

"I had the weirdest phone call today," Rebecca told her.

"From who?"

"Tina. Mom, you're never going to guess what she told me." There was a pause before she cried out in a near whisper. "She's pregnant!"

"Is it your father's?"

"Well, of course it's Dad's."

"There's no of course about it, Becca. She ran off with some rodeo guy."

"She says he was just a friend and that Dad jumped to the wrong conclusions and she wants me to talk to him for her."

Ellen groaned. "Oh, Becca, don't get involved in their problems. It's best if you just stay out of it."

"But, Mom, if it is Dad's baby that means it's my half brother or half sister. Don't you see, Mom? I'm going to have a brother or sister!" There was an excitement in her voice that Ellen hadn't heard since she had first returned from her honeymoon. And all because of Kenneth and his child bride.

Ellen felt a rush of conflicting emotions. She was angry that Rebecca's stepmother had drawn her into her conflict with Kenneth. And as much as she hated to admit it, she was jealous that Tina was pregnant. For years she had wanted to have another child, but Kenneth had always been adamantly against it. Just hearing the excitement in Rebecca's voice was enough to think wistfully about what might have been if she had been the one to give her that brother or sister.

Unsettled, she said sharply, "I don't understand why Tina called you."

"She didn't know who else to turn to. Mom, she hasn't told Dad yet."

"Good grief!" Ellen exclaimed, her anger toward Tina mounting. She didn't like the position she had put her daughter in one bit.

"I told her she better tell him before he gets settled in here," Rebecca continued.

Ellen had a sick feeling in her stomach. Rebecca was acting as if it was a foregone conclusion that Tina's pregnancy would save her father's marriage. Yet only a short time ago Kenneth had told Ellen a child was the last thing he wanted or needed.

"Listen, Becca, your father and Tina have a lot of problems they need to work out. I don't think it's a good idea for you to get involved in this right now."

"Mom! We're talking about my brother or sister!"

"I realize that. All I'm saying is that you should be concentrating on your own marriage and leaving your father to handle his. Tina can't expect you to be her mediator."

"But, Mom, I don't want to see Dad get divorced again," she said with concern in her voice.

"Neither do I," Ellen admitted honestly. "But we can't solve their problems. Just promise me one thing. That you won't get caught in the middle, all right?"

"All right, but I don't know what you're so worried about."

Oh, if only you knew, Ellen thought as she hung up the phone. Why couldn't Kenneth have stayed in Colorado? If he hadn't come back, her relationship with

Seth wouldn't be in such a mess and Rebecca wouldn't now be dreaming of having a brother or sister. How many times had she wished him out of her life, yet he was still showing up and creating problems.

As the evening wore on and she didn't hear from Seth, Ellen began to worry that maybe he wasn't going to call. Then, just as she was about to get ready for bed, the phone rang.

"Hi. It's me, Seth."

Ellen closed her eyes and savored the sound of his voice. All week long she had heard it in her imagination and now that it was a reality, she realized just how much she had missed their late-night conversations.

"I'm sorry we were interrupted today," he said softly.

"No, it's all right. I shouldn't have come without calling first, but—"

"I know. You hate to call men."

She could hear the smile in his voice and it flowed over her like a warm summer breeze.

"I thought the newspaper would be a good place to talk since you were the one who told me journalism is about fairness, objectivity and getting the facts straight," she told him.

"That's true, but I should have mentioned that cartoons use unfairness, subjectivity and the distortion of facts to get at the truth," he said, a hint of amusement in his voice.

"You can uncover the truth without resorting to any of those means," she said bravely.

"And what do you think that truth is?"

"Maybe I'm the one who should be asking that question."

"I think..."

Ellen's breath caught in her throat as she waited for him to finish. When nothing but silence followed, she finally asked, "Are you there?"

"Yeah, I am. I'm sorry. I was just collecting my thoughts."

This is going to be bad, Ellen thought and braced herself for disappointment.

As a result, he took her completely by surprise when he said, "I think I misjudged the situation last weekend."

He did believe her! Ellen felt as if a huge weight had been lifted off her shoulders. However, part of it managed to slip back down when she heard his next words.

"But I also think that you still have feelings for your ex-husband."

"Yeah, anger and disgust." She didn't bother to hide the bitterness.

"Ellen, it's more than that."

"What are you talking about?"

"He has some sort of emotional hold on you and I don't think you even realize it's there. You tell me you're over him, yet I'm not sure that's true. As long as he's there between us, I don't see that we'll ever be able to have a future together."

For a moment Ellen was too stunned to speak. When she did find her voice, it was shaky. "You're wrong. He's not there between us. Kenneth is nothing to me except the father of my daughter, and unfortunately that's a fact I'll always have to live with."

"Then why are you always bailing him out? Why is it your doorstep he's always landing on?"

"I can't believe you're jealous of him," she said, offense her only defense. "You don't know me very well if you believe I still care about Kenneth. You're wrong, Seth."

"Am I?"

"Yes. You're so quick to put the blame on my feelings for Kenneth, but what about your feelings for Laura?"

"Laura has nothing to do with this."

"Doesn't she? Then why do you still wear your wedding ring?"

There was a silence as he contemplated what she had said.

"We both have pasts, Seth. We can't pretend they didn't happen."

There was another long silence and he said, "I want us to try again, Ellen."

"I want that, too." Her voice was so full of emotion that she could barely speak.

"Will you come to my house for dinner? Meet my kids?"

"I'd like that. When?"

"It's my mother's birthday on Thursday. It's the one day I can count on us all being together."

"I'll be there," Ellen told him. As she said good-night, she lifted her eyes heavenward and gave a silent prayer of thanks.

"Nothing will keep me away," she said aloud as she replaced the handset on the cradle. "Nothing."

CHAPTER SIXTEEN

ELLEN WONDERED if she had been wrong to introduce Laura Holloway's name into her relationship with Seth. Ever since Kelly had talked so intimately with her about her mother, Ellen hadn't been able to stifle the curiosity that nagged at her regarding the dead woman. She wanted to know who she was and what kind of life Seth had had with her, yet at the same time she had the feeling that it was a subject she should leave alone.

The opportunity to satisfy at least some of her curiosity came sooner than she expected when she ran into Bernice Benson at the grocery store. Ellen was surprised when the older woman led her by the arm to the coffee bar and insisted on buying her a cup of coffee.

"Isn't this a coincidence?" Bernice commented, a warm smile on her face. "You know, I normally don't shop here, but I had to go to the dentist and thought I'd stop as long as I was in the neighborhood."

Ellen accepted the cup of coffee with a thank-you and took a sip, listening as the older woman chatted on about the bargains she had seen advertised in the paper and the money-saving coupons she had clipped.

After remarking on how wonderful the melons were and asking whether she had tried the bakery's sourdough bread, Bernice slipped in a comment about Seth, catching Ellen off guard.

"He's not happy, Ellen. I know it's none of my business, but would it be prying if I asked if you're still seeing my son?"

"He's invited me to dinner on Thursday," Ellen told her, hoping the older woman wouldn't ask too many questions, for she really didn't want to be discussing her relationship with Seth with his mother—as dear as she was.

Bernice's eyes lit up. "For my birthday?"

"I take it you didn't know?"

"Oh, no, he didn't tell me, but I have to say I'm delighted. He was so grouchy all last week I thought something must have happened between the two of you."

Ellen would have preferred not to confide in Bernice, but there was such concern in her eyes that she found herself saying more than she intended.

"We did have a disagreement...or sort of a disagreement," she said awkwardly. "You know it isn't easy, Mrs. Benson, when people our age date. We have so much of the past in our present lives."

Bernice moved closer and gently placed a hand on her forearm. "It's not Laura, is it?"

Ellen shuddered. "Oh, no. Actually, it's my ex-husband who's creating the problems."

Bernice sighed. "I'm sorry about that but I'm glad to hear it's not Laura. Ex-husbands can be ignored but the memory of a loved one isn't so easy to forget."

Her words sent another chill down Ellen's spine.

"I wouldn't want Seth to forget about Laura," she told the older woman.

"Of course not, but he has a life without her. I have to confess that it's a comfort to know that he's not obsessed with her memory."

Ellen wasn't sure he wasn't.

Bernice downed the remainder of her coffee and gave Ellen's hand a squeeze. "I'm so glad I ran into you. And I'm very pleased you're going to be at my birthday party."

"I'm looking forward to it," Ellen said with a smile. "I forgot to ask Seth if I could bring anything. Can you think of something?"

"I talked to Kelly and she told me everything's taken care of. She's baking lasagna. It's a family tradition Laura started." She glanced at her watch. "Well, it's late and I must run. We'll see you on Thursday!" She gave a cheery little wave and scurried off, coupons in hand.

Lasagna, Laura's favorite. Ellen could only look distastefully at the coffee that had grown cold in her hands. With a grimace, she tossed it in the trash can.

SETH WAS in love with Ellen. There was no doubt in his mind about that. He was, however, having a hard time believing that she was in love with him.

Never in his relationship with Laura had he questioned her love for him. But then, unlike Ellen, Laura had been very demonstrative, very open with her feelings. She had never hesitated to throw her arms around him and kiss him, no matter where they were or what time of day it was. Right from the start she had chased him and made no bones about the fact that she wanted him and only him. He had been her first and only love and they had been happy together. He had never worried that she'd leave him for another man. In fact, he couldn't remember ever experiencing jealousy in their relationship.

That was why he was having so much trouble dealing with the feelings that now tore at his guts every time he thought about Ellen and Kenneth's being together.

He longed for the sense of comfort that he had had in his relationship with Laura, yet he knew what he had with Ellen would never be comfortable.

Their relationship was far too intense, too full of passion to ever be cozy. Suddenly he felt guilty. He was thinking about his marriage as comfortable and cozy and his relationship with Ellen as intense and passionate.

Why did he even need to compare the two? Could it be that Ellen was right? That Kenneth wasn't the only obstacle in their relationship? Were his feelings for Laura coming between them, as well?

He glanced down and saw the gold band on his finger. The only time he ever took off his wedding ring was when he was working for Two's Company and only because his mother had insisted it would make clients uncomfortable if he wore it.

He twisted it on his finger, then slipped it off. Had he been clinging to the past without even being aware of it? He did his best to make sure he wasn't on Thursday night. Before Ellen arrived he gathered his three children together and gave them specific instructions.

"I would appreciate it if each of you would remember that Ellen is a guest in our home and might feel uncomfortable if we talk about your mother."

"Why would that bother her?" Brian asked with the naiveté of a fourteen-year-old boy.

"Because she's Mother's competition," Kelly answered.

"She is not," Seth stated firmly, although deep in his heart he knew that in some ways it was true.

"Is that why you hid Mom's photographs in the drawers?" Kelly asked.

"I didn't put them all away." He ran a hand through his hair.

"Why would seeing pictures of Mom upset her?" Again it was Brian who asked the question.

Seth glanced at Kelly in admonition. "I didn't put them away because I thought she'd be upset." He shoved his hands into his pockets. "Look, it's not easy for any woman to come to dinner with a family who can't stop talking about how wonderful their mother was."

"But she was wonderful," Matt said quietly.

Seth looked at his son and sighed. "I know. We all know just how wonderful she was, Matt. But that doesn't mean we have to canonize her in front of Ellen."

"Relax, Dad. We're not going to pull out the home videos," Kelly reassured him. "And I won't tell her the lasagna I'm making is what Mom always made us on special occasions."

"Why are you worried about all this stuff if you're not going to marry her?" Brian demanded.

"Because I want her to have a good time. I don't want her to feel as if she's come to be inspected."

"I think we're the ones being inspected," Kelly commented, opening the oven door to peek at the lasagna. Then she turned to her brothers and said, "You notice, he didn't wait for Grandma to come before having this little talk with us."

Seth could feel his palms growing sweaty. "No one's inspecting anyone. Ellen's important to me and I wanted you to have a chance to get to know her better. Got it?"

Three mumbled sounds of agreement had to suffice for the doorbell rang, announcing Ellen's arrival.

Dinner went better than Seth had expected. There was virtually no awkwardness between Ellen and his children. Everyone was on best behavior, including his mother, which Seth interpreted as a sign that they liked Ellen.

The only touchy moment arose when one of Kelly's friends called to tell her their apartment plans had fallen through. Sullenly, she returned to the dinner table and tossed the information at her father with an accusing glare.

"I guess that means I'll be living at home again this quarter and fighting all that traffic just to get to class on time," she commented.

Thanks to a suggestion Ellen had made a while ago, Seth was prepared for her disappointment. "If you can get the other three young ladies to agree to leave the two gentlemen out of the living arrangement, I think I have a solution for you."

That brought Kelly's head up with a jerk. "You'd let me move out with Cara, Shannon and Amy?"

"Four women, no men," Seth confirmed with a nod.

"But where are we going to find a place now? School's going to start in less than a month. Everything is already taken."

"Since you've never lived on your own, I want you to start out in a dorm on campus."

"A dorm?" Kelly wrinkled her nose. "Dad, there's like twenty women to a bathroom in those places."

"Not all of the residence halls are like that," Ellen interjected. "Rebecca has a friend who lives on campus, and she's in a dorm that has suites. There's a bathroom, a living room and a bedroom in each one."

"But isn't it too late to get into something like that?"

"When Ellen told me about this I called the director of housing and put your name on a waiting list. I just spoke to the woman yesterday, and she said it looks as if you can get in. All you have to do is convince your friends.''

"You mean it'll be like having an apartment but still be in the dorm?''

Seth nodded. "You'll have to eat at the cafeteria, but at least you'll have more privacy and room than the regular dorms.''

"Kelly hates to cook, anyway,'' Matt pointed out with a grin.

"If this works out this year, next year maybe we'll consider the apartment idea,'' Seth told her.

"Thanks, Dad,'' Kelly said with a grateful grin.

"Don't thank me. Thank Ellen. She's the one who convinced me it was a good idea,'' he said, glancing appreciatively at Ellen.

"I've just had a little more experience as a parent of a college student than you have,'' she answered modestly.

When his mother whispered in his ear, "She's a winner. You'd better snap her up,'' Seth found himself in total agreement. He loved her, he wanted her and he'd find some way of dealing with the Colorado Kid.

He insisted on following her home to make sure she arrived safely. He also hoped that she would invite him in so he could spend some time alone with her. It had been nearly two weeks since he had held her in his arms, and the thought of touching her was creating a sweet ache inside him.

However, when he arrived at her house, she seemed a bit distracted. If anything, he felt as though she wished he would leave.

"I had a lovely time this evening, Seth. You have neat kids,'' she told him as they stood on her front porch.

"They were on their best behavior. I threatened to move their curfews up if they did anything to embarrass me," he said with a crooked grin.

"I hope you don't mind if I don't invite you in, but I promised to go into work early tomorrow and it's getting rather late."

Seth's hopes fizzled. "No, I understand," he told her, although he really didn't. "You've been awfully quiet. Is everything okay?"

"Uh-huh. I just have this big decision hanging over my head."

"Can I help?"

She smiled then, a grateful, yet sad smile. "No, it's something I have to resolve myself."

"Will I see you this weekend?"

She nodded. "I'd like that."

"Good. I promised Brian I'd take him to the Twins game tomorrow night, but I was thinking of going out to the Renaissance Festival on Sunday. Want to join me?"

"I'd like to, but I promised Becca I'd take her to the outlet mall in Redwing and I'm not sure which day she's planning on going. Why don't you call me tomorrow night when you get home from the game?"

Seth agreed, but all the way home he had a nagging fear that when he did try to get hold of her, she wouldn't be there. As much as she proclaimed to have had a good time with his family, he couldn't help but notice that she had been preoccupied all evening. The insecure, suspicious part of him could only hope that the reason didn't involve Kenneth Richards.

SETH WAS a die-hard baseball fan, but despite having seats behind home base and the Twins scoring more runs than their opponent, he found himself watching the scoreboard and wishing the game would end. He thought about giving Ellen a call during the seventh-inning stretch, but as he muscled his way through the concession stand crowd, he heard his name being called.

It was Roger Townsend. "Can I buy you a beer?" the younger man asked.

"No thanks. I think I've had my share for tonight."

They stood for several minutes discussing the highlights of the game before Roger said, "Say, I'm really sorry about you and Ellen. Becca told me things have been a little shaky."

Seth, figuring Roger wasn't up-to-date on the latest developments, answered amiably, "Hey, I haven't given up hope yet."

"Well, I wish you luck. I tell you, I can't begin to understand women, not with the way Becca's been acting the past few weeks...." He trailed off with a disgruntled shake of his head.

Seth grinned and landed a gentle punch on his arm. "So you're discovering the hard way that marriage has its up and downs, eh?"

"Yeah, for sure. I just wish her old man hadn't come back."

"Yeah, you and me both," Seth agreed.

"I think the guy ought to be strung up. I can't say too much because he's Becca's father and all, but when I found out what was going on—" he made a fist and raised it in the air "—I could have popped the guy."

Seth grunted in agreement and Roger continued on.

"I mean, here's Becca, almost twenty years old and an only child and she discovers she's going to have a baby brother or sister. And poor Ellen, I can't believe what he's put her through."

Seth couldn't speak. He was still trying to absorb what Roger had said about a baby. Ellen hadn't mentioned a thing about it to him.

"Now that he's told Becca he's going to stay in the Twin Cities I suppose he'll want to go back to Colorado so the baby can be born in the mountains or some damn thing." There was nothing but disgust in Roger's voice, but no way could it compare to the sick feeling roiling around inside Seth.

"Hey, enough talk about that, eh?" There was a roar from inside the stadium and Roger said, "Something good must be happening. We better get back inside."

"Yeah, right," Seth said numbly, shaking the hand Roger had thrust in his direction.

"It was good seeing you. Take care, you hear?" And with a friendly wave, Roger was gone.

Although Seth stayed until the end of the game, he couldn't have described the outcome to anyone. He had been too consumed with thoughts of Ellen and what Roger had said to pay attention to the action on the field. The Colorado Kid was going to be a father again. The question was, who was the mother?

Seth didn't want to think that it could possibly be Ellen. But the fact was Kenneth had been at her home the day after Rebecca's wedding two months ago. He had seen him there himself. And just last night Ellen had told him she had a big decision to make. Was she thinking about going with him to Colorado?

Then there was her obvious distraction when he had been with her. If she was pregnant, there was only one man who could be the father—Kenneth. The fact was, Seth had had a vasectomy ten years ago after he and Laura had decided three children were enough....

"ROGER SAYS he saw Seth at the ball game last night," Rebecca told her mother when she picked her up the following morning.

"That's nice," Ellen said absently, gazing out the window at the passing countryside.

"Well?"

"Well, what?"

"Are you seeing him again?"

"Sort of."

"What's sort of?"

Ellen sighed. "I'd really rather not talk about it. What I'd like to talk about is you. Has your father been creating any more havoc in your life?"

"Are you asking because you're worried about me or because you want to know if he knows about the baby yet?"

"Both," she said candidly.

"Tina's here. She came Thursday, but I didn't see any point in telling you."

"Then he knows about the baby?"

"Yes. He wants to stay here, but she's determined to go back to Colorado."

"With or without him?"

"I think it's going to be with. They stopped by last night when Roger was at the ball game and told me they're thinking about leaving tomorrow."

"You sound disappointed."

"Mom, he is my father."

Ellen reached across the seat and squeezed her hand. "I know, dear."

"And I wanted to know my little brother or sister."

"There'll still be plenty of time for that," Ellen assured her.

"I guess." She didn't say anything for several seconds, then said, "To be honest, Mom, it's a bit of a relief Dad's leaving. I was afraid he was going to ask Roger's father for a job and that would have been awkward.''

"Yes. I know what you mean."

They drove in silence for a while before Rebecca said, "I've been an only child for so many years I probably wouldn't be that great with a little kid around anyway."

"You'll just have to visit them often," Ellen said with a sigh, then leaned back and closed her eyes. "Gosh, I'm tired. I've been working so many hours and I can't seem to get caught up on my sleep."

"Wait. Before you go to sleep. You didn't tell me your news. You said you had something important to discuss with me."

With everything that had been happening with Kenneth, Ellen had avoided talking about the decision she was facing. "Oh, that. I was offered a promotion. They're opening a new clinic in Saint Cloud and they want me to manage it."

"Saint Cloud?" Becca repeated in horror. "Mom, that's so far away!"

"I know, but it's a big increase in salary and I thought now that you're married and there's really no reason for me to keep the house, maybe I should consider taking it."

"What about Seth?"

"What about him?"

"Don't you think he should figure in your decision?"

Ellen didn't want to admit that she had thought about him even before Rebecca. In fact, the more she thought about it that afternoon, the more she knew that she really couldn't make the decision until she had talked to him and discovered once and for all just where things stood between the two of them.

It was dark by the time Rebecca dropped her off. She figured Seth hadn't called her the previous night because the game had gone into extra innings.

That was why on Saturday morning she had bought an answering machine and connected it to her phone. At least this way she would know if he had tried calling.

However, other than messages from her mother and her sister, the tape was blank. Ellen made herself a cup of tea and sat down in front of the television, waiting for the phone to ring. Only it didn't.

Ten o'clock came and went. Then eleven. Eleven-thirty. Ellen grew more anxious by the minute. Finally, at a quarter to midnight, she could stand it no longer.

She picked up the phone and punched in his number.

"Hi, it's Ellen," she said when he answered the phone. "Did I wake you?"

"No. I was up." He sounded as if he had been sleeping, but Ellen decided not to challenge him.

"I know it's late, but I was gone all day and I was worried that I had missed your call so I thought I'd call and see if you wanted to come over for breakfast tomorrow."

"Breakfast?"

"Uh-huh. I have something I need to discuss with you."

"This wouldn't have anything to do with relocating, would it?" There was an edge to his voice.

"Yes, how did you know?"

"Roger told me."

Puzzled, Ellen asked, "Roger? How would he know about it?"

"Becca must have told him."

"But I only told her today."

When he said, "Look, are you sure this decision involves me?" Ellen knew she had made a mistake in calling him.

"I thought you'd want to be a part of it, but I guess I was wrong," she said, her voice cracking with emotion. "I'm sorry I bothered you." And with that she hung up.

As soon as she had hung up Seth felt horrible. Here she was trying to share something important with him and he had behaved like an idiot. He punched in her number but after only a couple of rings he heard, "You have reached 555-9177. Please leave a message at the tone."

He slammed the receiver down. "Damn." If there was one thing he couldn't stand it was having a woman hang up on him.

He jumped into a pair of jeans, pulled on a knit polo shirt and slid his bare feet into a pair of loafers. He was halfway to her house when he realized he was driving across town in the middle of the night probably just to hear her tell him she was going off with the Colorado Kid.

It didn't matter. He figured he'd never get back to sleep until he heard her decision, one way or the other.

There were no lights on when he reached her house. He stubbed his toe going up the porch steps and as a result, leaned against the doorbell a little longer than was necessary.

When she opened the front door, she was wearing a pair of white slacks and an orange top that emphasized her large bosom. Her feet were bare, and her hair hung loosely around her face.

"Seth?"

"Why did you hang up?"

"Why did you come?" she countered.

He stepped inside and closed the door behind him. He was all set to tell her that he understood why she had to leave when out of his mouth came, "I don't want you to go."

"Why?"

He pulled her into his arms and kissed her, long and hard. "Because I love you and I can't bear to think of you in another state."

"Another state? Saint Cloud is only an hour's drive north of here," she told him as he planted kisses all over her face.

He pulled back and looked at her. "Saint Cloud?"

"That's where the job offer is."

"Job offer?"

"From the clinic. I thought you knew."

"You have a job offer in Saint Cloud?"

"Yes. What did you think I was talking about?"

"Ellen, I have to ask you something," he said seriously. "Are you pregnant?"

"Pregnant?" A look of shock crossed her face. "Good grief, no!"

He threw back his head and laughed, then picked her up and twirled her around in the air. "You're going to Saint Cloud," he repeated gleefully.

"You want me to go?" She stared at him, a bewildered look on her face when he set her down.

"No. No. But if it means you're not going back to Colorado with Kenneth, I'll settle for that. I can always drive the sixty miles to see you." He stared into her eyes, the familiar warmth of her stirring his emotions.

"Why would I be going to Colorado?" Before he could answer she said, "You thought I was pregnant with Kenneth's baby?"

"Roger told me about Becca having a baby brother or sister and I guess in my jealous fit I jumped to all the wrong conclusions," he admitted candidly.

"You have nothing to be jealous about. I don't love Kenneth. I love you, Seth."

He buried his hand in the softness of her hair, tilting her head back so that he could kiss her eyelids, the curve of her mouth. "And I love you, Ellen." His breath came out on a ragged sigh. "I've never felt this way before. You thought I didn't trust you because I wasn't ready to let go of my past with Laura, but the truth is, I was afraid of my feelings. The mere sight of another man coming near you makes me want to act like a caveman."

"But you were devoted to Laura."

"Yes. I was. We had a great marriage and I'll always cherish those memories. But that was then. It's over and done with. I realized that the night I came for breakfast."

"Would you like to stay for breakfast tonight?" she asked coyly.

"On the condition that you'll share the rest of your life with me as well. Do you want to?"

"Oh, I do. Baby, I do."

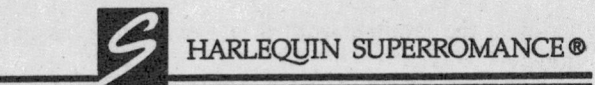

HARLEQUIN SUPERROMANCE ®

COMING NEXT MONTH

#606 SHADOWS IN THE MIST • Karen Young
Ryan O'Connor and Joanna Stanton had been divorced for
fifteen years. But when she showed up on his doorstep, running
for her life, he could hardly refuse her sanctuary. Then came his
grandmother, his editor, a fourteen-year-old boy and his dog—and
now that he thought about it, there was *something* about the boy....

#607 RIVALS AND LOVERS • Risa Kirk
(Women Who Dare)
Gene Logan was a champion rider who wanted to *win*.
Ross Malone wanted to keep her safe—a task that was much
harder than it sounded. If he withdrew his support, he'd lose her
trust, and if he encouraged her, he might lose Gene herself.

#608 BRINGING UP FATHER • Maggie Simpson
(Family Man)
Nick Lupton had always allowed his wife to make the decisions
concerning their son's upbringing. Now Vicki was dead, and Nick
was all Billy had. But Nick was too busy fighting demons of his
own. Until Betsy Johnson, Billy's principal, began breathing down
his neck about Billy's failing grades. Just as Nick thought life
couldn't get much worse...it suddenly got much better.

#609 TRUTHS AND ROSES • Inglath Caulder
Librarian Hannah Jacobs was happy with her life, just the way it
was. At least until Superbowl hero Will Kincaid came back to
town. After a knee injury put an end to his football career, Will
needed time to find a new future. For Hannah, however, Will's
arrival brought the past rushing back—a past she'd spent ten years
trying to forget.

AVAILABLE NOW:

Where do you find hot Texas nights, smooth Texas charm and dangerously sexy cowboys?

Crystal Creek reverberates with the exciting rhythm of Texas. Each story features the rugged individuals who live and love in the Lone Star state.

"...Crystal Creek wonderfully evokes the hot days and steamy nights of a small Texas community...impossible to put down until the last page is turned."
                                                    —*Romantic Times*

"...a series that should hook any romance reader. Outstanding."
                                                    —*Rendezvous*

"Altogether, it couldn't be better."   —*Rendezvous*

Don't miss the next book in this exciting series:
LET'S TURN BACK THE YEARS by BARBARA KAYE

Available in August wherever Harlequin books are sold.

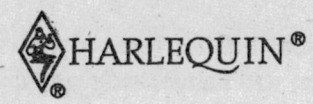

HARLEQUIN®

Weddings, Inc.

WEDDING SONG
Vicki Lewis Thompson

Kerry Muldoon has encountered more than her share of happy brides and grooms. She and her band—the Honeymooners—play at all the wedding receptions held in romantic Eternity, Massachusetts!

Kerry longs to walk down the aisle one day— with sexy recording executive Judd Roarke. But Kerry's dreams of singing stardom threaten to tear apart the fragile fabric of their union....

WEDDING SONG, available in August from Temptation, is the third book in Harlequin's new cross-line series, **WEDDINGS, INC.** Be sure to look for the fourth book, **THE WEDDING GAMBLE,** by Muriel Jensen (Harlequin American Romance #549), coming in September.

WED3

This summer, come cruising with Harlequin Books!

PORTS OF CALL

In July, August and September, excitement, danger and, of course, romance can be found in Lynn Leslie's exciting new miniseries PORTS OF CALL. Not only can you cruise the South Pacific, the Caribbean and the Nile, your journey will also take you to Harlequin Superromance®, Harlequin Intrigue® and Harlequin American Romance®.

- ◆ In July, cruise the South Pacific with SINGAPORE FLING, a Harlequin Superromance
- ◆ NIGHT OF THE NILE from Harlequin Intrigue will heat up your August
- ◆ September is the perfect month for CRUISIN' MR. DIAMOND from Harlequin American Romance

So, cruise through the summer with LYNN LESLIE and HARLEQUIN BOOKS!

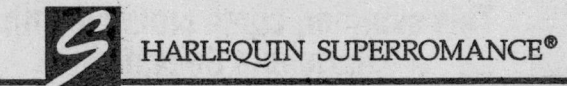

HARLEQUIN SUPERROMANCE®

The O'Connor Trilogy
by award-winning author KAREN YOUNG

Meet the hard-living, hard-loving O'Connors
in this unforgettable saga

Roses and Rain is the story of journalist Shannon O'Connor.
She has many astonishing gifts, but it takes a near-death
experience and the love of hard-bitten cop Nick Dalton to show
her all she can be. July 1994

Shadows in the Mist is Ryan's story. Wounded in his very soul,
he retreats to a secluded island to heal, only to be followed by
two women. One wants his death, the other his love.
August 1994

The Promise is the story that started it all, a story so powerful
and dramatic that it is our first featured Superromance
Showcase. Laugh and cry with Patrick and Kathleen as they
overcome seemingly insurmountable obstacles and forge their
own destiny in a new land. September 1994

Harlequin Superromance,
wherever Harlequin books are sold.